GREEN-EYED THIEVES

Imraan
Coovadia

GREEN-EYED
THIEVES

UMUZI

Published by Umuzi
P.O. Box 6810
Roggebaai 8012
an imprint of
Random House (Pty) Ltd
Isle of Houghton
Cnr Boundary Road
& Carse O'Gowrie
Houghton 2198
Johannesburg

www.umuzi-randomhouse.co.za

First edition, first printing 2006
ISBN-13: 978-1-4152-0009-4
ISBN-10: 1-4152-0009-2

Cover design by The Inkman
Cover illustration by Niki Daly
Title hand lettered by Sally Swart
Design and layout by William Dicey
Set in Minion

Printed and bound by Paarl Print
Oosterland Street, Paarl, South Africa

for Jerry, Zaheer
(+1, −1)

لب

Chapter One

Colours: the thousand and one shades of green, and the nickel sheen of a lady's Beretta.

Numbers: threes, lucky sevens, and the sixty grand we took on the Sun City job.

Places: Peshawar, melancholy Lourenço Marques, Brooklyn, New York.

Objects: keys to a blue Mercedes (an SL, not the old Roadster), a cigar box lined in green felt with small-bore ammunition scattered like change. Brioni waist-coat . . . Carrick electrical detonator . . . a rayon bra with big silver-white cups.

With these and many an additional circumstance I conjure my story into life, beginning with docket 3741 presented at the court for the Eastern District in Brooklyn. It arraigned Firoze Peer for impersonating a federal officer. I was also accused of selling passports to those notorious hijackers and violating the security of the United States. But that was the fault of my crackbrained brother Ashraf. We've nothing in common except the sulphurous glow in our green eyes.

Ashraf's not only a brother but a twin . . . an alibi . . . which is why I will never see the end of guilt heaped on me by this patron saint of revolvers, this adorer of Kahlil Gibran and Louis L'Amour, this skinless guy who models his looks on David Hasselhoff. Having the genes of a clod like Ashraf keeps me from having airs.

And keeps me behind bars. Like a caterpillar turning into a butterfly,

7

docket 3741 turned into a conviction over the course of a summer. I didn't retain counsel. The joke, in this country, is that a man who represents himself has a fool for a client. But with Ashraf as a brother I'd be crazy not to say a few words in my own defence.

The public likes its writers to be incarcerated. This condition indicates an author's authenticity, some knowledge of things beyond the confines of his skull. It symbolises the truth that a writer is trapped in the pages of his book surely as a bug in a drop of amber. So the world is prepared, I believe, to welcome a manuscript composed on an IBM Selectric on the lower bunk of a cell in Fort Dix penitentiary. (Theatrical inquiries to F. Peer, Master of Arts, #2663, Seven East, FCI Fort Dix – Federal, P.O. Box 38, Fort Dix, NJ 08640.)

Where was my brother? He was my only hope because the judge was unimpressed with my case. Thomas Lodge Cameron was a vinegary, red-bearded man in his sixties. Beneath his bifocals lurked eyes like carp. He spoke with mock respect, poking at me as if fighting a duel. I attributed his outlook to geography. In Brooklyn people need to show they've seen the worst in everything, and it doesn't change their mind about anything. By this July afternoon I expected Ashraf to improve Cameron's Brooklyn attitude, perhaps by the one-sided fisticuffs my brother relishes. But there was no sign of improvement.

"You won't condescend to tell us your real name, Mr Peer?"

"Your Honour," I returned, "You're jailing the wrong brother. I love this country. I'd never assist a man wishing to harm her. If I did encounter Atta, Mohammad el-Amir, it was only to notice he was a mixed up, very intense specimen. He attempted a seduction on me. I mean, the whole thing is a tragicomedy."

Cameron wasn't receptive. "For you more of a comedy, it seems. For us, a tragedy. Well, that's enough speechifying in my courtroom. Give me a moment, Mr Peer, if that is indeed your name, to finalise my decision."

I had time to think about love while Cameron did his calculations. The defendant stipulates that he falls in love at the drop of a hat. In four afternoons at court he surrendered his heart to Mrs Velasquez, a fifty-nine-year-old prosecution witness, and then to the court reporter, Irene, whose pea-green eyes flashed in his direction. Like her predecessors Irene was robust, built big around the hips, and small in her freckled shoulders. It's a rule of human nature that a fellow like myself, on the lesser side of scrawny, gravitates to a broad on the happier side of voluptuous, if he has any real confidence.

We make our own punishments. It's simultaneous heaven and hell, you know, to be inconstant in my way. I possessed a standard love letter done in the Persian style, intended for Fazila in Pakistan. I carry a torch for Fazila, yes, but there's room in me for womanly multitudes. I addressed a copy of the same letter to Irene on stationery pilfered from the gauleiter's desk at the Metropolitan Correctional Centre. It was typed on a battered Smith Corona in a booth allotted to defendants. At each stroke the golf ball subsided with a hiss. As a self-proclaimed writer I'm proud of the opening line. (Sweet Irene, Irene of the swallows and the sharks, let me bring you nightingales and such bales of roses, let me cover your humid mouth in parsimonious kisses . . .)

My love letter, I think, takes after my mother's purple prose. My life, my style, is my brother's fault. It's my mother's fault. It's the fault of my father . . . My mother Sameera Peer, an M.Phil. in philosophy, is a leading cultist of Valentine's Day. We're both scatterbrains; so my mother understands my tendency to fall head over heels. If Mom had bothered to attend my sentencing she might have appreciated Irene.

Working as a court reporter, I figured, Irene didn't meet interesting men. Few who appeared in the dock were defendants of any real calibre. The yardstick of a great nation, I believe, is the level of its defendants. In subsequent pages I explain how it is that American criminal talent, talent in the real sense of the term, is scarce. But my point is that the setting increased my chances with Irene. Intense situations favour love: bank vaults at half past midnight, the bucking back seat of a getaway car with Ashraf at the wheel, the second floor of a Peshawar mansion when, in the high ceiling, bullet holes appear like so many ears of corn. And, of course, this Brooklyn courtroom.

Not that Irene would be easy. The burly man in my future cell, I figured he'd be an easy catch. And Mr Atta, whose eyes were as dark as if lined with kohl, he – I promise – gazed at me with undisguised longing one Brooklyn evening. Whereas Irene required flowers, poetry, red wine and white, long walks under the stars. Look, I know I'm ridiculous. My brother forges passports whereas I'm a romantic counterfeiter, turning tragical everythings into trivialities. Then these trivial things worry me. The leg irons which escorted me to court worried me most. I was locked into them. A grand entrance is a suitor's great ally, but the chain's fifteen-inch radius prevented me sauntering into the courtroom. The bailiff released me when the hearing began.

Charlie Montague, the bailiff, was a chunk of a man who sat behind me and trained his stare between my shoulders. Montague had served in the Marines. His friend from the service was on the Pennsylvania flight, so the unfriendliness didn't surprise me. His military posture betokened his total identification with authority. The defendant instinctively wished to puncture such attitudes.

I tried to befriend the man while we were waiting. "You see your way to mailing this? It's to Fazila Parker, in Pakistan."

"Not a chance, Felix."

I whispered, "Then would you pass Irene this note?"

"Let me tell you something. You're proven guilty. It behooves you to behave with respect. The judge is about to read out your sentence."

"Could you at least tell her I care for her? Tell Irene, defendant 3741 is willing . . ."

"No. Even if I wanted to, I'd lose my job. Hire a professional."

"3741 is willing."

"Watch your step, Peer."

I had tried to do the reasonable thing recommended by bailiff Montague – that is, hire a private eye to find out about Fazila. We hadn't spoken in months. I didn't even know if she was in London or Pakistan. The detective should take photos, snoop around, and maybe drop my name in her ear in a favourable light. If more lovers turned to private eyes the course of true love would be smoother, and obviously less blind. The Yankee portion of my soul remarks that there'd be more work for detectives.

I had no money though. The arresting officer confiscated the bills in the Mercedes glove compartment ($3940 in dollars and roubles). My life, my love letters, were now deposited in a dead letter box. So, sure it's tough without a detective. It's tough to be an unrequited idealist when a country confuses me and Ashraf. It's tough loving a brother of tricks and turns who sold an expired licence to Atta. As they say every day in Brooklyn, those are the breaks. But I planned to fight back.

I describe my frame of mind listening to my sentence as identical to that of a prospective son-in-law meeting his bride's father . . .

"Mr Peer – you offered the names of Patel, Zacharia, and Goldberg, but let it be Peer – arresting people under false pretences is a serious offence. Your worst enemies, amongst whom I include yourself, will agree you possess your share of imagination. Posing as an animal control officer you apprehended Frieda Velasquez in the Athens deli and took her out to dinner with her chocolate lab. You arrested a short order cook in your role as investigator for the State University of New York Binghamton. You confiscated the bags of a Chubb executive under the auspices of the State Mental Health Commissioner. You opened an enquiry into suppressed medical research at Philip Morris head-quarters on Park Avenue. That's when you signed out a company Mercedes. And I haven't begun to consider the damage you did by selling documents to Mohammad Atta."

"I shouldn't have borrowed the car, Your Honour, but blame my brother. I only ask that the court recognise my standing as a prisoner of conscience."

"We do no such thing. I sentence you to a minimum of ninety-one months on the related counts. The Immigration Service will then pursue a deportation case. As a service to humanity, we should keep you here permanently under lock and key."

Among the spectators there was not one to mourn my misfortune. Fazila didn't show up. Neither did my mother in Australia. Neither did my father. Ashraf could hardly show his identical face . . . but why not show another face? My brother's victims were present and they certainly hadn't been selected on the basis of looks. Tony Costello, a bartender from whom Ashraf lifted a Citibank card, applauded the sentence, pink in the neck and red in the face, and smelling of Jaegermeister. Frieda Velasquez, resplendent in a plaid tent of a dress, steamed the Givenchy Eau Torride off her tented bosom.

In the back row I recognised Albert Satterfield, the Chubb honcho, hardly breathing in a double-breasted suit, his unmoving countenance topped by thin red eyebrows. In that English way Satterfield was careful not to smile, although a smiler, a joker, a prankster, as I will soon report, makes a terrifying enemy. Ashraf likes to say you get more with a smile and a gun than with just a smile. In my view the gun simply exaggerates the inherent terror of a smile, a fact Ashraf doesn't grasp although he possesses a softly menacing smile all his own. Seeing him and Atta grin as they trotted out political jokes, jokes about the mullahs, jokes about Israel, curdled my heart . . . but I'll get there. Here I was surrounded by my brother's enemies and where was my brother?

11

The jury's suffering, its evenings of television, was revealed in its twelve drawn faces. I felt responsible. It's an ungrateful defendant who doesn't take the fate of his jury to heart. I was in a forgiving mood even where the witnesses against me were concerned. I wished to greet Mrs Velasquez amidst her haze of Eau Torride, to shake no-hard-feelings hands with Satterfield and Costello. The testimony they gave was against a face. It was a mere comedian's face, with green eyes in its rafters, they condemned. I'm a hundredth as attached to that face as the next man, because the next man, with the same skullish face on his powerful shoulders, is my cockerel vain brother.

The jury watched me suspiciously as I was taken from the courtroom. As for Irene and Mrs Velasquez, I noted their wistful expressions as the defendant departed in irons, holding his letter on top of a pathetic pile of citations. I decided I had a better than even shot with either lady. Strange that I should harbour such a soft spot for people who helped send me to the calaboose, but this tenderness for a persecutor confirms my self-diagnosed case of Stockholm Syndrome. A hostage with this syndrome comes to love his captors. With a brother who's held me hostage for twenty-nine years, Stockholm is a basic survival mechanism. And it's not just me. It's the basis of a happy marriage.

The shuttle from court back to the Metropolitan Correctional Centre was a Chrysler van with seating for nineteen. It was a good portent. Chrysler is my favourite car company because it symbolises American energy, builds a solid truck. The metal benches were bolted to the floor. A screen separated the passengers from a thin, shotgun-toting guard in a neat blue uniform with epaulettes and all manner of insignia on his front pocket. The guard's slender face stayed in shadow.

The van's brontosauran engine was a six-cylinder diesel, I figured 330 horse-power. It's second nature to check. In a family dominated by the right-hand alley of the brain, the crucial facts are the calibre of a gun, the engine capacity of a car, truck, or motorcycle, the number of carats in an emerald (multiply the weight in grams by five). Putting a number to a revolver, a machine, a precious stone, consoles us.

I was alone in the van. My trial was the first to end that day. Cameron liked to do things rapidly. The guy was a pillar of the Republican Party. Republicans, so you know, recruited me in a New York minute to meet the president, but they were Indian givers. I have plenty to say about Republicans, that inexplicable group, but I don't hold grudges. Growing up around criminals has one positive effect: you can't be your own worst enemy since so many others willingly play the role. No, being one's own worst enemy is a thinking man's greatest luxury. Considering this fact, I struck up a song. It was a melancholy ghazal by Faiz, one of my mother's favourites. In the Lata Mangeshkar version I knew as a child on eight track, it's bittersweet as cooking chocolate.

"Don't sing that song in here, stupid."

"Why not? It's a free country, I've been told."

"Cabrón, I can't believe the gall," the guard responded in the screechy voice which is chalk to the blackboard of my soul. "A song your mother cherishes, and you besmirch it in the back of a prison van. Honestly, Firoze, or whatever you're calling yourself, you claim to be an intellectual. You just can't shake the disease of self-pity. Life is full of good things, my brother, not a series of traps and ambushes against you." He paused, only to resume his grievances. "But the airs you put on, because you set one foot in the White House and shook hands with the president, it scars my existence."

"You're the one who sold a Florida driver's licence to Mohammad Atta, of all people," I said. "Talk about poor judgement. Come to think of it, man, why did it have to be expired? Now people on both sides are against us. Both sides. Since when is your first language Spanish anyhow? What gives? I have to hand it to you, kid. Why in heaven's name did you get us mixed up with Atta? That was a creepy crowd."

"I had no idea what he was planning. You really can't trust anyone."

"Could we talk about getting out of here?" I asked.

"Let me speak my mind first. Then I have bad news to deliver."

The guard, of course, was Ashraf. I expected the cavalry during my trial and here it was, champing at the bit. My brother originated from the black hole of greater Johannesburg . . . a culture that should hang its head in shame. Ashraf had every encouragement from me to grow as a thinker. Yet he displays no interest in the meaning of the universe, no curiosity about stuff besides credit-card numbers and the sloping proportions of women's breasts underneath their shirts. This was my cavalry, my Calvary.

Whatever he did or didn't do with Atta, I must say that my brother is a sincere lover of the Stars and Stripes. Since we were teenagers he had a sweet tooth for the B-movie side, the flaky grandeur, of this country's culture. He was fixated from afar on a plebeian flavour of television star, starting with Telly Savalas in *Kojak*. In Standard Five, Ashraf walked like Kojak, pestered his Chappies bubblegum like Kojak, drawled like him, spat, cursed, and patted an imaginary holster. My brother does a splendid impersonation of Telly, raising both eyebrows and buttonholing me with his fist. The apparition is strange to behold in Jo'burg but in dog-eat-dog Brooklyn, in Crooklyn, where intimidation is the local specialty, the dude fits right in.

We are said to be identical twins by everyone besides our absent-minded mother. Ashraf plays up the resemblance. He harries me to wear my hair in the same bouffant fashion as Hasselhoff. There's no use being a flesh-and-blood alibi if you have different hair in the bank-camera photograph and in person. Since in this one instance he has logic on his side, and I don't want to see him behind bars where he belongs, I find myself on certain mornings gunning my hair with Ashraf's snailshell of a hair dryer.

We get to kill two birds with one stone describing my brother's appearance. It's often said a good story holds up a mirror to reality, and yet the storyteller who turns the mirror to his own face finds shards of glass in his hands instead. Ashraf is the mirror that cuts my hands. We share a small, shrewd boulder of a head and a frogged brown face which frequently strikes an onlooker as having sampled something untowards. Many women choose to love this face in its natural habitat upon my brother's shoulders. There's the Memon nose and radishy complexion, smoky-green eyes that seem as narrow and cobra-lidded as the mercury beads of the eyes on a snake, and straight, sparky-black hair which in my brother's case is rolled back and stiffed with a thick-as-molasses, black-as-Bovril teaspoon of Brahmi Alma hair oil.

Physically there are two differences between us – the narrow muttonchops and moustache my brother gardens with his Panasonic electric trimmer, that, and his muscular build displayed in the uniform that Ms or Mrs Lee must have sewn. (Ashraf claims there are three big differences and glances – really he leers – into his aerated underpants.) My brother compensates for his height by the small man's universal remedy: a top-gun attitude, and intensive weight training. By the time we dropped out of Standard Eight he had earned school colours for the pole vault and the discus. He comes off a sort of bantamweight rooster. It contrasts with my own paunchy frame.

I remark that we have resemblance without symmetry. I get mistaken for Ashraf all the time whereas no one, and I mean no one, mistakes him for me. Pairs of identical twins in the audience, bundled together as snugly as orbital electrons, will understand that the two of us went through the typical phases. We dressed the same, then we dressed in opposite colours. I helped him out by taking his chemistry and history tests. The only occasion anyone got wise to us that I remember was Tigerlily. I mention her on background before I return to a Chrysler van on its way to the Metropolitan Correctional Centre.

Tigerlily was one of my brother's entanglements, this time on a weekend stay with Mum in Hong Kong when the place belonged to the Free World. Ashraf likes exotics, ladies who are talented (as he puts it) at the sports of the Orient . . . which is to say sex, massage, acupuncture, would-be contortionists. He prefers women who happen to be exotic in a relativistic sense because of who he is, like tall Chinese girls, runaways, meter maids, and sassy Spanish-speaking girls from Corona and Roosevelt Avenue in Queens.

Tigerlily, a twenty-six-year-old masseuse, fell into more than one of his favoured categories. Ashraf was determined I should experience her. It was odd for my brother to care so much about me and my experience. I think the real reason is he wanted to have someone to discuss Tigerlily with. Ashraf went to a lot of trouble to disguise me as himself, brylcreeming my hair with his slurry of black hair oil beforehand and telling me in detail about their conversations. He got us out of dinner with my mother, who spent the afternoon shoplifting in Mongkok and Causeway Bay. He had a lot of advice about how to deal with Tigerlily. Ashraf may be as hardened a customer as you could wish but he has his own cargo of genuine good sense. He gave me a counterfeit traveller's cheque to pay for the evening and a forged Australian passport. Right before he pushed me into the elevator at Tigerlily's building out on Nathan Road, he gave me a jewel to put in her hands.

"Give this to her, Firoze, and she'll fulfil your wildest hopes," he said, holding the big gilt frame of the elevator door open. "In your case, okay, that's not so wild, but so what? As you say, Einstein, everything is relative."

"Space is relative. Time is relative. Junior Zaid and our aunt Nasreen are relatives. But gosh, everything is not relative, Ash." I knew I was being ridiculous but I had to explain. "There are moral absolutes and scientific absolutes.

There are many, many things that aren't relative. Otherwise there would be no yardstick to judge what's relative in the first place."

Ashraf closed the door. I gave the jewel to Tigerlily the moment I pushed past the curtain to her bedroom. She inspected the hexagonal white diamond with a curious brothel professionalism, pronouncing it to be costume jewellery as she rubbed it on a tooth and then underneath one ear. Whether it was I don't know. Tigerlily placed it in her shoe and didn't seem disturbed that I tried to pass it off as the genuine article. I got out her real presents. The Australian passport with its soldered burgundy covers seemed to satisfy her, as did the draft on Thomas Cook for forty of the old Hong Kong dollars. Tigerlily turned to the front of the passport and admired her black-and-white snapshot for a moment. She ran her fingernails along the edge of the photograph to check for glue.

"You do a nice job."

"I don't want to take credit," I said.

She put the documents in a drawer beside the bed. "One day you'll get in deep trouble for providing these services. Mark my words. You're at the intersection of every kind of underworld enterprise. I bet it's a strange crowd it brings you into contact with."

"I really don't see why people who need another passport, another driver's licence to get by in life, should be any worse than the average person," I replied.

It was true, at that moment, that I didn't see why they – people who needed a new identity – should be worse than people who were happy with their original names. Consider it a moral effect of Stockholm Syndrome, seeing right as the mirror image of wrong, good as the left hand of evil. It's a tendency amongst Muslims of a liberal bent, but my brother accuses me of liking generalisations over specifics (a trait that goes along with a flowery side), so I'll leave my philosophising at that.

With Tigerlily it didn't end well. Six minutes on her back proved to her dissatisfaction that the man above her and below her and then off the mattress wasn't who he claimed to be. Somehow she told us apart and, without hesitating, reported me to the Kowloon police department. She was offended. Then she replaced the heavy black telephone on its wall mount and rolled on her stockings, putting on a dressing gown decorated with red-and-gold dragons. The gown showed off her crossed legs, which were the same width all the way up, painfully thin in the thighs, and relatively thick in the calf. Her breasts, when I was briefly allowed to possess them, hardly filled my hands. There were tiny freckles on the inside of her neck, on her shoulders, and on the tops of her arms. And, of course, I was madly in love with every one of those pale brown freckles.

Tigerlily subsided after her telephone call. The situation was odd. She lit a Benson and Hedges, the universal brand of sex professionals, pulling out a chrome Zippo lighter. She offered me one and then lit it for me. I held her hand for a moment, admiring her nailboarded cuticles and the impasto strokes of nail polish. She eyed me coolly, drawing smoke into her lungs. She didn't seem to be at all displeased now the police had been summoned.

"How did you know? How did you even suspect?"

"Identical twins try to get away with these things." Tigerlily was formal in her speech, almost an English schoolgirl. "I know because I'm also a twin, although I have a brother. With my reputation and expertise, people try anything. They think if they can trick me, morality doesn't matter. Or they want to have two of us, like a sandwich." She thought of something else. "My dear, tell your brother if he wants to see me, apologise with a bouquet of flowers. I am grateful for the passport. I want the freedom to move to Sydney, Australia, in case the mainland Chinese get stroppy. Plus, it's purely pleasure with him. For such a young man your brother is amazingly well built. Sometimes" – she closed her black eyes so they were nearly shut and tidied my hair away from my forehead – "if I look at the right angle the resemblance to Sean Connery is right there."

"Sean Connery?"

Tigerlily shook her head. "Don't pretend. Ashraf told me about Connery's affair with your mother, the princess from Goa. Be proud of who you are, where you come from. Be proud to be a Connery boy."

"Hogwash, Tigerlily. I think Connery's a stage name." I tightened my striped school tie, which I wore to lend a measure of dignity to the situation. My watch, a Seiko self-winder and a gift from my mother on my sixteenth birthday, had not-so-mysteriously disappeared from beside the waterbed. I said, "I'm guessing maybe Ashraf sent me here as a kind of test. He wanted to see if a lady could distinguish us in the sack. It's typical of him. Frankly it's very painful for me. Are you very upset about the diamond?"

Tigerlily had a decidedly fierce glow in her face, as if she had been pinched.

17

Her eyelids burned with brandy. She put one of her small painted hands up to her earrings. "The police are on their way. Hadn't you better be getting out of here?"

Ashraf unlocked the back of the prison van and sat opposite me. It was reassuring to have my own flesh and blood close enough to touch. His green eyes looked almost black. But, while I was swooning over him, I could detect the sweet fellow winding up for round two. Ashraf doesn't get tired of dredging up a mistake and burying it and reburying it. The joke about the guy who – when he wants to bury the hatchet – buries it right in your forehead pretty much describes my brother. I wanted to distract him. I touched him on the arm.

"Where did you get the uniform? It suits you. You look good."

"Mrs Lee's handiwork." Ashraf put a hand through his hair, parted to the scalp on the right, and looked at me sideways. He has the strength of a horse rider in those hands, which mounted the shotgun casually as a trombone. "What, Firoze, are you saying it doesn't look right?"

"No, it looks absolutely great on you."

"Is that a fact?"

"Mrs Lee did you proud."

Since we're on the subject of Chinese dames, Ashraf's best friend in the universe since we arrived on these shores has been this very old, very gruff and generically surnamed lady who supplies him with outfits for every conceivable occasion. She created the uniform for a sergeant in the United States Fish and Wildlife Service ex nihilo. I consider Mrs Lee an artist in the true sense. She has an eye for the significant detail. She makes her garments look more authentic than the real thing.

It's appropriate, I feel, that Mrs Lee supports her household doing Broadway costumes, yet was formerly employed as a seamstress for the Peking Opera at the time of the Anti-Landlords campaign. Apart from her daughter and her mother, Mrs Lee spends her time with those flamingly gay theatrical men with whom she gets on like a house on fire. Isn't it odd that she gets on so well with my brother? Isn't that odd? With his love of outfits, his penchant for role playing, his bottomless sarcasm, handcuffs, false personalities, I believe my brother's overcompensating.

Ashraf's prison uniform showed the hallmarks of Mrs Lee's exact stitching. She lives with her daughter and her grumbling mother in a rent controlled apartment in one of those blocks on Riverside Drive. All three women have college degrees. They are wizards with needle and thread. They are also insular beyond all reason. Madam Lee hasn't set foot outside the building since Nixon's derecognition of Taiwan. Mother and grandmother rely on Miss Adelaide Lee to bring in provisions from the Safeway and the 99-cent store on Columbus – cotton, needles, noodles. And they live according to an unquestioned hierarchy. With greater age comes increasing maternal hauteur.

The Lees impress me because they are a self-sufficient society of women. None of them expect men to stick around. Doubtless, when Miss Lee gets knocked up, everyone will move a step up in the hierarchy as they've been doing, for all I know, for thirty centuries. They are well adapted to their niche. They have such small, precise fingers. Even in old age, even with Madam Lee's arthritis, the fineness never falters. I wished, for a minute, that I belonged to so perfectly adapted a tradition. Instead I have the mingy tradition of my brother and our peculiar histories.

"Ashraf, I took the Mercedes because I was angry with you," I explained. "Once the police surrounded the place I had to escape. That horrible fellow was in the back, which exacerbated my driving. What can I say? I'm a chump."

"Chump is the nicest word I could use. How about palooka? How about fathead? How about numbnuts?"

I said, "I accept it all without reservations. But I happen to be the one in prison. You happen to be the one who got me here thanks to your friendship with the hijackers." There was something else on my mind. "And Ashraf, by the way, you don't love this country for its ideals. You love it for what you can get out of it."

"It's only natural. Only a palooka from palookaville, Firoze, prefers the beauty of an ideal to the beauty of the real thing. You don't love this country. I love this country. You love the idea of it. That's why I call you a palooka."

I forgave his sarcasm. Defensiveness is our second nature – sarcasm, irony, cold jokes. Not to romanticise, but these thorns protect the rose of the soul. Ashraf typifies the hoodlums who, among the Johannesburg Dawoods and Peers, outnumber the philosophers by the fixed proportion of six to one, as if by some genetic slot-machinism.

But he wanted to set the record even straighter. "Let me tell you, I don't need your condescension. It was hard enough getting in here to see you. I had to swing by the guard's apartment, arrest him and his wife. Then I took his uncle into custody, and the uncle's three children who were on their way to school. The whole exercise ballooned out of control. I can't be certain of getting both of us out of here right now unless we want to shoot our way out." Ashraf rubbed the end of the shotgun as if it was Aladdin's lamp. "We can go out in a blaze of glory, you and I."

I said, "Let's not do that. You need to be a survivor to enjoy hindsight."

He changed direction. "Promise me not to be despondent, Firoze. I honour you as my brother. I will find a way to get you out safely. I'll organise something. You can imagine Dad's not happy with you being on the inside. If Atta hadn't played the lot of us, none of this would have happened. We'd be living in clover, on the Upper West Side."

Even before we arrived in Brooklyn my brother wanted to sound like a Chicago gangster, how he imagines stand-up guys like Dutch Schulz and Potatoes Kaufman conversed. It's fictional but anyone bewitched by the United States must be a sucker for the weird linguistic music of the place. When it comes to this verbal music, yes, there are tone-deaf people . . . sure there are tone-deaf people . . . which goes double when you consider whom this country's been warring against since Jefferson's attack on the Barbary pirates. I refer to America's beef with the Third World although we're not exactly Third Worlders as such.

Ashraf is a keen adapter, with his chameleon's tongue and kaleidoscope soul. In Jo'burg he sounds like the born-and-bred Johannesburger that he is. In Pakistan, in the desert, he swears, talks, and mounts a camel like a proper nomad. In Brooklyn he's Brooklyn to the bone. Ashraf is something of a Zelig figure. Nowadays (a reader asks) who isn't a Zelig figure? What isn't a Rorschach test? If every dot is Rorschachian and every yokel Zeligesque, then the terms have no meaning. To which I reply, we memoirists must be allowed the professional indulgence of our comparisons.

"You're better off on the inside, caballero," Ashraf observed. Seeing the driver he climbed out of the back and took his seat in the front before anyone was the wiser. He spoke to me through the grille. "Right now things are pretty uncomfortable, thanks to my big friend as you call him. They scrutinise men of Middle Eastern appearance, which means anybody from a skinny black Somali to a Syrian. I barely scrape by as Puerto Rican. We don't want to get you out only to end up in immigration detention for the rest of our lives. Look, Firoze, in front of the driver, call me César, okay? Also, do you have any last-minute requests?"

"Post these letters for me."

I slipped the two envelopes under the grating. Ashraf read the address.

"I'll do better than that, my brother. I will deliver it by hand to each lady. Only don't go sneaking around to Fazila behind my back. Remember, it's César." As the driver got in, treading heavily on the step, Ashraf opened the chamber of his shotgun. "Before I end my shift, man, I was giving this dude in the back a few words of advice. Where he's going I figure he can use it. This pata de puerco has an attitude on him."

The driver nodded. "Whatever you feel you have to do."

"He helped the hijackers."

"You don't say."

"I do. Some people, because of their own issues, hate this country beyond what's reasonable."

The driver was an enormous man, big as the both of us put together. He had brown overalls on, boots, and a cloth cap. He looked out of place in the middle of Cadman Plaza. But he carried his box of pastries with the sensitivity of a butterfly collector. He placed it on the seat. He seemed to ignore what my brother had said.

"Guy, can I offer you?"

"That's very gracious," I said. "Maybe a fruit Danish. Are those hot cross buns?"

"Pass it back to him, will you?"

Ashraf did so, using the opportunity to hand me a file containing my philosophical papers, a summary of our family tree in mirror writing, a money order drawn on the Cayman Islands post office, and my diary. Thanks to him I can assemble something like a coherent narrative (approximating a coherent narrative, I suspect, in the way that the soft roar inside a seashell resembles the voices on a cordless telephone).

I know I make my brother sound like a thug, but we don't fight. We look after each other. After his own fashion he has a feeling for music, love, poetry, and beauty. He worships Nusrat Fateh Ali Khan, adores dancing, paper lanterns, my mother's Barry Manilow records, and any aspect of gracefulness in a woman. God was a dark bride, an intoxicator, a prime number for the Sufi poets; the same comparisons apply to Ashraf. The worst you can accuse him of are the standard predilections of anyone in his milieu, which include a preference for instant gratification and a terrific zeal for violence.

The driver examined Ashraf as he was preparing to get out. With an odd look on his big face, almost a frown, he turned back towards me.

"You know, the two of you look remarkably alike."

"You're dreaming, muchacho," Ashraf replied, leaning through the window. "How's it possible? This pendejo is from Pakistan, whereas I am San Juan born and bred." He had indeed been practising his Spanish. "Five years ago mi padre, Benito, transferred the whole family, lock, stock, and barrel, plus two grandmothers, to Jerome Avenue in the Bronx. Jerome Avenue is where the finest monadas roam. If we meet again, you'll have to come and see for yourself, my brother."

لَبِ

Chapter Two

Our family business was a gingerbeer factory in the Fordsburg section of Johannesburg, behind the Caltex and around the corner from Shorty's Café. The building was filled with the smell of ginger and the stink of fish heads from buckets of glue. The boiler, sandwiched into the brick wall, radiated heat back and front. The beer was brewed in enormous copper-ribbed barrels. Piled in the corner were sacks of brown rice and cheesecloth bags of Huletts sugar. Rice, sugar, and ginger alike were ignored by my uncle Farouk. He was my father's older brother and an equal partner in the gingerbeer business, although his true interest in life was rubies, sapphires, and emeralds.

Around Jo'burg people called him Ten Percent Farouk. No compliment was intended, but with time it turned into one. In truth my uncle liked the idea that ten per cent of creation was rightfully his. To collect his percentage he was prepared to do anything within reason . . . as well as many things beyond reason, and several utterly without rational warrant. Farouk was the prince of the harebrained scheme. Some, I guess, ran at a profit. He collected pension checks on behalf of three long-deceased nonagenarians with the help of forged birth certificates and his contact in the Department of Inland Revenue. Some of Farouk's schemes made next to nothing, like the Datsun van and party of workers he organised to strip telephone lines for their copper. He was particularly proud of the Salvation Army uniform he donned each Christmas to dun shoppers out of their change. Yet my uncle spent more money dry-cleaning it every November than he made in twenty-cent coins placed in his upturned Stetson hat on Boxing Day.

Finally there were his harebrained schemes that were simply hair-raising. His latest plan had something to do with jewellery, but the details were unclear to me. Ashraf knew more than I did. He was more closely involved with Farouk and, to be fair, they were more on the same wavelength. Towards me Farouk was the archetypal South African uncle, by which I mean that he was sly, mocking, that he liked to shock me with his corrupt sense of humour. I feared him although I didn't care to show it. His baldness created a dome above his serpentine green eyes that confronted me when he bent down to look in my face.

"You have a minute? I have something to show you from my new business. It's under the microscope."

I asked, "What is it?"

He took me by the ear. "Just come along, you ragamuffin."

I knew that Farouk's diamonds were contraband. Truant diamonds from Sierra Leone, picked by light fingers at the Diagonal Street diamond exchange, and those from stolen rings and watches made their way to our factory on Sandra Boulevard. Amid the piles of rings and Rolex face plates was kept a Zeiss microscope. It stood beside a jeweller's lamp and a set of goldsmithing tools Mum shoplifted in a rare gesture of affection for her brother-in-law. And beside the Zeiss I was placed on a high stool.

"Have a peek through the eyepiece before your father comes to interrupt your education. That bloody fellow is sure to rock up the moment I try to teach you something valuable. Where is his much vaunted faith in learning?" A sleeve of wax paper opened beneath a pair of goatish hands. Bending over my shoulder Farouk wheeled down the arm on the Zeiss's conning tower. He adjusted the lens. "Fifty-times magnification. This is a Burmese ruby, Firoze. You can see that the redness comes from within the stone. Almost as if it's glowing. So how do you like it?"

"It's lovely."

"But what do you really think?"

"It's very beautiful," I said. "It's truly a beautiful ruby."

Ashraf came in.

I hadn't pleased my uncle. "Your brother, Ashraf, is a very arrogant character. Cagey as well," Farouk told the new arrival. "I don't like the way he's growing up. Move out, Firoze. Let Ashraf have a peek. It's something he will appreciate. Ashraf takes after me more and more each day for reasons you cannot possibly comprehend. Ask your mother why. Only don't let on that I put you up to it."

I was glad to give up my place but I took a last squint. The ruby was indeed beautiful. It shone with a witchy red light. On its miniature silver pedestal it was – like a musical chord, a prime number, a geometrical axiom – an instance of perfect being. Somehow it made me feel guilty. Ashraf had no such inhibition. He jammed his big green eye against the lens. I heard him sighing and grunting. The comparison with a perfect number wouldn't occur to my brother. In our crib, I swear, he preferred Rolexes, Bentleys, tinsel, and gilt, anything at all to my mother's bedtime stories. He had antibodies to her stories. Admittedly Mum read to us from Plutarch and the lives of the philosophers. It doesn't mean she deserved to be cuckooed by Ashraf.

After a while Farouk palmed the ruby and placed a ring in the slide compartment.

"You notice this one is dull in comparison. It doesn't radiate the light like the ruby. That's why in the shops the term for it is a fish eye. The jewel in this ring is as dull as a fish, as dull as your small brain, Ashraf." Just because the guy was tough on me didn't mean my brother got a free ride, but luckily much of what was said went over Ashraf's head. Farouk continued, "Well, I am afraid to admit that this is your mother's wedding ring. Your father never stoops to listen to my advice, and this is the inevitable result. You must speak to him, Ashraf, and you also, Firoze, my boy. Mirza should understand that he is still my junior by five years. Barring a miracle that's not going to change. The time has come to correct old mistakes. I can fix him up with something nice. It's not as if my brother is poor." Farouk must have read something in my expression. "What's the matter, shrimp? You don't want me to complain about your father?"

"If it makes you happy, Ten Percent," I answered, "complain until you're blue in the face. But you know how Dad hates to be rooked. If you tell him about the ring he's going to have a conversation with the guy who sold him the fish eye. It was so many years ago. Let sleeping dogs lie, I reckon."

"That's what you reckon."

"I do."

About my father Farouk liked to say that the two of them were as thick as thieves. In fact they were thieves. But their attitudes to their work could not have been more different. Nine-tenths of the variation in men's souls, I estimate, occurs between brother and brother. Like any older brother, Farouk wished to bend his sibling to his way of seeing things. A pleasure shared is a pleasure doubled. More than anyone else in the world it was Dad with whom my uncle wanted to share his peculiar joys.

I knew what these joys were because Ten Percent discussed them with Ashraf and me – the alchemical thrill of slotting a fat revolver into your hand, of placing a chain strung with solid red Burmese rubies around a woman's illicit neck and letting your hand fall on the half-open necklace of her collarbone, of listening to the tumblers of a lock suddenly fall open and have its wishbone part in your hands.

Dad was aloof the way he could be where his brother's stories were concerned, and so my uncle's Pygmalionist energies were redirected upon my brother. They had been close for years now and were getting closer. Farouk speculated that Ashraf was really his son, an argument that drove my mother to distraction. Mum got angry just thinking about her brother-in-law's suggestions. Mum wasn't a natural joker. With her philosophical bent she could seem dour, snippy, and almost Presbyterian. She was hardly able to stay in the same room as a funny fellow.

Dad, on the other hand, took his older brother in stride. He didn't object to the insinuations about Ashraf's true paternity. Logically, it was impossible for his brother to be the father of only one of a pair of identical twins, and he didn't see Farouk rushing to take credit for me. When he found us in the back room Dad was his equable self in a pin-striped suit, whistling Motown and tapping his cane on the shoeboxes filled with gems and Rolexes. Dad was twenty-nine years old and never to be seen out of pin-stripes in public unless he was roaming the house in his green silk dressing gown.

"So I see you have your first consignment of real jewels, Ten Percent. I hope this plan works out. You need a distraction from that woman of yours."

"Call her by her name."

"Elena then." Dad peered through the eyepiece of the Zeiss. "I assume you're going to pay a visit to your new friend Sol the Rabbi? With your new business I must wish you gevalt and brucha."

"Gevalt and brucha to you also." It was, I knew, the greeting used by the Jews in the Jo'burg diamond trade: health and happiness. Dad began saying it when diamonds started to interest my uncle. "To you, my brother," Farouk translated for us, "health and blessings."

26

"What are you doing with my boys?"

"Firoze, I am sorry to say, I have no use for. You've let his mother ruin him with books. Ashraf is helping me with the documents. When it comes to drawing, the boy really has a gift. Once we have a proper bill of sale Sol the Rabbi, as you call him, will place the ruby in the government registry and issue us an official certificate. So it's kosher. That way I can sell them direct to the retail jewellery guys on Moon Street. Cut out the middleman, you know. The only drawback is that old man Sol is keen to get out of the business altogether. We should be prepared to silkscreen the certificates ourselves. Ashraf is already learning the process. This way, hopefully, we save on Sol the Rabbi's commission. And I can work on my diaries."

Dad said, "If you want to win a popularity contest, you can make the diamonds halaal instead of kosher."

Sol the Rabbi was in fact Solomon Tarnofsky and not at all a rabbi. An orthodox Jew from Vilnius who lost his entire family during the war, he was conspicuous in Johannesburg for his unvarying black suit and waistcoat, worn without a tie, and also for his love of jokes. There was a community of the Orthodox in Yeoville but Tarnofsky was notable amongst them for the raffish cut of his suit and, above all, his sense of humour. I hadn't met him but my uncle marvelled at Solomon's store of funny stories and his method of luring his listeners onto a punch line as if reeling in a fish. People went over to the Gemological Institute where Solomon worked just to listen, including my uncle.

Farouk joked about Sol and his supposed religious customs with a curious light in his devilish brown countenance. For once I can defend my uncle and am happy to do so in saying there was no unnecessary malice in his attitude towards Tarnofsky. It's a revered South African custom to denigrate all traditions, including one's own. Farouk and my father often laughed at the Mussulmans as if they were an alien species. The Mussulmans did x, the Mussulmans were up to y, the Mussulmans won't take medicine because it contains alcohol. They found it uproarious to speak this way. They could have gone on forever dismissing the Moslems and the Christians, the Tamils and the Jews, the Sindhis and the Surthees, but Farouk had a piece of business on his mind.

"One more thing. You don't want to change Sameera's ring? I examined it under the microscope to check my suspicions. The facts are undeniable. It's a fish eye. Why not invest the money, Mirza, in something new? You'll never regret it. I have a lovely stone picked out for you already."

Dad smiled although he didn't agree or not agree to Farouk's proposition. "When all is said and done, Farouk, what are you making on the deal?"

"Cost price plus ten. Cost plus ten per cent. As far as my philosophy is concerned, there I cannot compromise." I had heard the same string of words a dozen times. "Ten per cent, my brother, keeps me in the game. All jokes aside, think about the fish eye seriously. Now that you know the truth, it will never be the same when you see it on Sammy's hand. Also, leave the boys with me this afternoon. Sameera asked me to organise a sheep for Bakri Eid. They can accompany me to the slaughterhouse. They might learn something about life and death, and how closely connected they are. I'll drop off Firoze at his maths lesson when I have the opportunity."

"Well, be sure to have both of them back at home by six o'clock or Sameera will have my head on a platter. Meanwhile, Farouk, do me a favour and don't mention the ring to her. For a philosopher and all, you know, she can be touchy about these matters. She's such a bloody romantic."

We accompanied Ten Percent to Essendene Road. On Bakri Eid Muslims were asked to buy an animal on behalf of charity. At the slaughterhouse the boys led us behind the building to a makeshift outdoor pen. Long before we got to the animals the inexpungible odour of zinc got to us. I didn't find it unpleasant, although it was a sensation that touched me deep inside and didn't let me forget its deathly touch.

Attendants were busy razoring the wool from the sides of a sheep lying on sordid carpet, revealing its bright pink flanks and rusted brown eyes. As we waited it was transformed into five-pound packages of mutton ready for charitable distribution. The supervisor hosed down another carpet, cleansing it of blood, wool, and short pyramids of spherical dung. He was a vigorous fellow. His forearm, I noticed, was hirsute in uneven portions, as if he would also benefit from a stropping.

The man asked, "You want us to do it for you, chief?"

Farouk was handed a thick old knife, much bigger than I expected. "I think I can handle it. One of my nephews here can help me out."

The man said, "He looks like an intelligent boy, chief."

"You're mixing him up with his brother."

An animal was brought up from the pen. The man said a short prayer over it from a leatherbound notebook. He stood next to me tying the loops of his plated butcher's apron. One of the workers steadied the sheep with a hand and a speckled strap while Farouk drew the blade along its neck, making sure to cross the thickened artery. He looked over to my brother. Then he gave the knife to Ashraf, who repeated the motion. Little pressure was required. It was as if my brother was unzipping a bag. The animal made no protest except, perhaps, to cough and then to buckle underneath the knife. There was a gush. I stepped back to avoid being splashed.

For several minutes afterwards the metallic blood drained through Ashraf's hands onto the mat. It flowed into the wooden gutter along the side of the building. The lifeless, sighing, nearly severed sheep's head leaned as tenderly into his arms as if it were a child. Its nose, I remember, was suede black. I looked at my twin brother and discovered a cruel green glow in Ashraf's eyes. I had never seen it before. My uncle noticed it too.

"You want to cut one also, Firoze? It's an experience you will never forget."

He was grinning at me. I went to wait in the car. Through the half-open Mercedes windows I listened to the dark music of the slaughterhouse. The saw, the voices of the boys at work, the slurring vowels of the prayers, made me dizzy. The place was a city block transported, like much of Johannesburg, from the moon. The red plaster walls of Mario's pawnshop stood on the far side of the street beside the warehouse for A1 Guns. I glared back into the sinister red eye of the traffic robot.

Before I knew it, my companions had returned with the brown paper parcels of meat. They were in a supernaturally good mood. Ashraf made me hold the sopping bags in my lap while he retied the string. To celebrate the big day, Farouk bought bunny chows for us from Shorty's Café. It was almost time for my first maths lesson. The author of these mixed-up, comico-tragical and sexological pages, these starred-and-striped pages, this star-crossed and star-striped author who remembers the red water which seeped out of the parcels onto his short pants, confesses that his first halting steps up the spiral stairway of love were taken with the assistance of a Cypriot maths tutor.

Private maths lessons were my mother's idea. Mum wanted a rocket scientist in the family. Like many people with a master's degree she harboured dangerous ideas about education. When Mum was told that something wasn't exactly rocket science she got disappointed. She didn't understand the narrowing effect of education upon the mind.

Mum was a big believer in numeracy. She wanted her sons to be good with figures, although Ashraf has only ever been on speaking terms with the hourglass kind. She had been anxious about our skills since we started playing hooky from school. When Ten Percent suggested he had found a maths tutor for me she agreed to pay the fees. She imagined that her brother-in-law wanted to redeem himself after his jokes about Ashraf's parentage. And, in his own way, I imagine that's what Farouk thought he was doing. He also wanted me to do his books for the business. There was no point paying an outsider, no sense in allowing an outsider's eyes to fall on our family's financial details.

Let's swoop in the back window of Millard's Fish and Chips, ignoring the motor-oil odour from the kitchen's heap of halved and beheaded sardines, their pewter complexions echoing the massive sink. Pay them as little heed as the papyrus sections of potato skin collecting behind the fryer, and concentrate on the discussion in the corner. I had been brought along to meet Farouk's mistress Elena.

Elena was a sight to behold. She was the most fascinating woman I had ever met. She was a big lady with cowish green eyes and white calfskin gloves. The old-fashioned whalebone girdle next to her skin had the effect of squaring off her trunk as she bent over the trestle and checked her addition on a pad of graph paper.

"Ten Percent, it's criminal what you're going to pull in on these diamonds," she explained in her smoky voice. "I mean, it's literally criminal. Firoze, your uncle is the worst man I ever met." She blew on Farouk's ear as if to cool it, settled a copper-tipped Woodbine on the ashtray, and left a train of ash queuing against the filter. Her strictly plucked eyebrows met. "Ace, why don't we ditch the boy and go upstairs?"

"You're not listening. This is my nephew I told you about. I want you to teach him everything you know about maths. His mother, Sameera the philosopher, is very keen on it. I mentioned your name to her and she had no objections. It will help my situation with Sameera as well. She'll send you the fees directly because she still doesn't trust me. So what do you say?"

"Anything you like, Ace."

With a grand gesture Farouk rose out of his chair and bowed to me. Then he sat back down, pulling Elena into his lap. "Firoze, my young Einstein, meet your new teacher Elena Lagadakapopolos. This lady is a real educator. She'll teach you the lot. Decimals, fractions, negative numbers. If you learn half as much from her as I have, you'll be a real Einstein . . . as opposed to a phoney Einstein. To top it off, Elena has a musical voice." Without waiting for an answer he put his arms around her waist. "Sit here, Elena, and speak Greek in my ear. I can imagine it's Italian. There's a language with a music of its own. There's a language of enchantment and mystery. You, Elena, you're such a hypocrite." He turned back to me. His eyes were dancing. "She promises to do anything to make me happy but when I ask her to speak a few Italian words at a choice moment she turns me down flat. Carmella, Elena, signora, do I have to bloody beg?"

Elena also spoke to me. "Your uncle is the limit. Gujarati is all he deserves, the cheeky bugger."

"Ah, Gujarati is the language of money-making. Don't forget it, Firoze. Greek, fine, it's the language of geometry. Speak to Elena in Greek if you want to know maths. Italian is the language of the bedroom. There we don't have an argument. But if you want to make a pile of money, okay, then stick to Gujarati." He pinched Elena. "Gujarati is the language of millionaires."

Elena looked at my uncle skew. "Ten Percent, till the day you die you'll be a cheeky bugger."

"But secretly, Elena, you like it. Say anything you want."

Millard's Fish and Chips was closing. Farouk went off to buy drawing supplies at CNA with Ashraf. For the first time I was alone with my tutor. Elena was, I thought, as vivacious as a Capetonian. She had adopted the Capetonian habit of holding hands with anyone and everyone. We went across the street hand in hand and up to her flat with its long oxblood lounge suite from Joshua Doore and the steel-framed mirror where she examined herself after a bath. This was the odd thing. As soon as we came in the door Elena retired to the bath. She spoke to me from there. She asked me to read my work out loud as I went down the page. I carried five, I carried four and put it in the next column, I averted my eyes from a satin brassière strung on the hat stand.

I was taught my very first lesson in long division through the steam of the bathroom door. I could see Elena scrubbing her back with a loofah although I concentrated on my sums. When I was finished dividing, she got me to bring her a towel from the linen cupboard. I had ascended the first rung of mathematical consciousness.

It was an afternoon of startling perceptions. Going past Millard's on the way back to the factory, I spied the owner through the open kitchen door scraping out the fryer while his assistant settled potatoes into a bucket of water to soften them overnight. The potatoes were startlingly white as they descended into the water. Their cleaned sides, I noticed, were cut in the staircase pattern of certain diamonds.

The municipal beerhall stood between Millard's and our factory. As I went around the oblong block of the building I saw the padlocked industrial tanks. They housed the alcohol which was available to Africans at the old-fashioned rate of a tickey per scale through the heavily taxed government beer halls. South Africa was a land of monopolies and the kingdom of rackets. Everyone had a racket. From his typically logical point of view the author also remarks that the Liquor Products Act of 1957 possessed a certain formal beauty as social policy, in that it taxed every drop available to the Africans and then it did its best to drive them to drink.

A brief explanation of my title is overdue. It's meant literally. The Dawoods, Peers, Dahlavis of Johannesburg possess green eyes, which remind people of those marbles with a swirl at the centre. If we believe the canons of poetry, our eyes are the cousins of jealousy, revenge, desire, and treachery. But colours, according to Wittgenstein, bewitch the mind. Green eyes made us unclassifiable under the old South African system of categories, where the search for racial precision extended to the cuticle and follicle. Perhaps these eyes are a Persian conqueror's insertion on the green-eyed coast from Port Natal to Calcutta. The point is that men in my family marry to preserve the distinction. Our mothers, green gems glinting in their broad faces, bring us boys up as worshippers at the altar of green-eyed women.

Johannesburg classics – "Sip and Fly", "Tomato Sauce", "Electricity", "Skokiaan", "Come Fly with Me". They were the mournful songs of the great labyrinth of illegal bars and music halls. They took hold of my brother's ears at the onset of puberty, and to this day they haven't relaxed their hold. Ashraf is a guy who's led by the ears. With one tubular exception it's his dominant organ. As a teenager he had the Bee Gees on an eight-track cassette, the Beatles, the Ramones, a pile of Louis Armstrong records. Of them all Dolly Dube from humble Johannesburg was his favourite singer because of her liquorish voice.

Ashraf claimed remarkable powers for Dolly's voice. With the sexual authority unique to a fourteen-year-old virgin, he asserted that no man could listen to Dolly doing "Sip and Fly" or "White Lightning" without developing a hard-on. I didn't find it to be necessarily so, but I was afraid to dissent. Ashraf lay on top of the covers, winked into his underpants with Mick Jagger eyebrows, and the effect was pretty distracting. He played his music so loud I couldn't hear myself think. My brother progressively deafened me to the point that I routinely ask things twice of a soft-spoken person. (When I ask someone "What are you saying? What on earth are you saying?" it's rarely a request for clarification. I just can't hear straight because of Ashraf.)

The only person who could get him to shut off the music at two in the morning was my uncle. Farouk lived above us in the big Fordsburg house, installed on the top floor of the house where he couldn't interfere with Mum's reading. He was noisy himself, spiritually noisy if that's a valid concept, a grumbler and a disturber. My mother's term for him was a stirrer. If the record player wasn't on I could hear him grumble in bed until late at night. He even grumbled at his dreams. But late one evening he was in a pretty good mood. He came downstairs and sat on the edge of my bed. We were tucked in. Farouk looked down at the stack of records on the floor.

"Sometimes I regret having exposed you fellows to this African boogie-woogie. I never hear the end of it from your mother. Sameera is a lady with serious inhibitions. At least there's good news on the diamond front. Ashraf, my boy, you've done stellar work today. Soon we'll be ready to take over from Sol the Rabbi altogether. You know, cut out the middleman. If you want to come with me to Tarnofsky's tomorrow, we can stop off at the record shop and I can display my appreciation." I watched the prominent knuckle of the Adam's apple in his overstretched neck vibrate. Since the slaughterhouse I had the impression, when my uncle spoke, when he retailed his jokes, that he wanted to reach over and cut my throat. "You can choose the Dolly Dube album of your liking. Only don't come home and play it loudly or they'll finally be forced to haul that mother of yours off to the nuthouse. Speaking of which, Mr Why and Wherefore, how are your sessions with Elena going? Do you like her?"

"I do like her. We're doing geometry," I said. "She's making me learn straight from Euclid. She says the ancient Greeks really understood shape and figure."

"Well, Elena is one ancient Greek who certainly understands her shapes."

Ten Percent grinned at me. "Don't try any funny stuff, by the way. I know you're not as advanced as your brother, but I don't want to be embarrassed in front of my lady friend because of your wayward hormones. Don't get the wrong idea about Elena. In her own way she's very proper, Mr Why. Listen, I've come to show you what your brother has been doing."

On the white sheet he laid out a series of documents next to each other as if he were a blackjack dealer distributing cards. There were British and South African passports, South African and Bophuthatswana driving licences, international driver's licences, international student cards, jewellery certificates, a Noah's ark in which the animals were laid out next to each other two by two. The two columns were identical. The photographs were all of Ten Percent, here grinning from the front page of a stiff red passport, here sombre on a homeland driver's licence. He was Vincentio Lazar on his student card, Dagmar Marienbad on his British passport, green-eyed Naren Vareswamy on the South African one.

"Look at the driver's licences particularly. You can't distinguish? The ones on the right are the originals. Well, at least I bought them from the proper authorities. The ones on the left are the copies your brother made. That's top-quality work. Your brother really has a gift."

Ashraf shrugged. He had, I noticed, the faraway look of an artist in his green sockets. An artist, a fraudster, a counterfeiter were much the same thing in my view. Nonetheless it was the first time my brother did anything he was proud of, besides chatting up matric girls at the Islamic Academy next door to our school and shoplifting records with Mum. Speaking as a prospective father, I argue that this was a milestone in my brother's development. He was starting to take an interest in something constructive.

I was also developing. My bookkeeping knowledge advanced to the point that I was entrusted with the factory's accounts at the advanced age of fourteen and a half. I didn't have so much time for cosmic questions, yet I had a good deal of freedom because once I was finished doing the numbers I had the run of the place. I worked at a desk beside the barrels of ginger beer. Stone-age gods, they towered over an ordinary man, attached at the base to hot water pipes. Into their sides were built narrow steps I liked to climb, but was soon shooshed off.

Most of the work was done by a dozen labourers, half of whom were Indians of schoolgoing age from Fordsburg and who must have been somebody's cousin or niece or nephew; not to be somebody's cousin, niece, or nephew was not to exist in the subcontinental scheme of things. Leaning dangerously over the side from the step, bare chested, the stirrers scraped the bottom every twenty minutes with their long wooden spatulas. I envied the glamour. I yearned to be a stirrer.

I put it to my uncle.

"Good heavens, you're earning real pocket money here by keeping my books, not chump change. There are not that many boys who can say as much for themselves at your age. Life is not supposed to be easy. Do you think that brother of yours comes by his talents the easy way? Not at all. Your brother is really putting his heart into his job. On top of it all your mother is paying Elena through the hat for your mathematics lessons. What more could you ask for in life?"

I said, "I'll take ten per cent."

Farouk turned to his audience. "You see, Sugarboy, I always tell you about this child, one day he is going to disgrace the lot of us by growing up to become a comedian."

Sugarboy, an African child, had acquired his nickname on the basis of his principal motive in life, as had my uncle. Maybe it was a South African thing. Sugarboy was in charge of tapping a barrel when the contents were declared ready and would steal a mouthful of sugary water from the hosepipe if he was unsupervised. He was the only person at the factory I identified with. Out of the corner of an eye I watched him filling the green glass bottles. He sealed each with a cork, smoothing on a striped label beneath the rim with the help of his jar of fishy white glue. The excess glue was scraped and returned to the pot.

Sugarboy did twelve bottles at a time, lining them up on the cement where he crouched. Finally he packed them, putting newspaper into the crate between the bottles to prevent any breakages, and trying to stay out of his employers' sight. No matter how much he scrounged, refuelling his fourteen-year-old metabolism, Sugarboy stayed as thin as the proverbial rake. His legs were long, very dull black poles, with a spider's quick and muscular dexterity. I felt, obscurely, that Sugarboy represented one of the basic states of man. My father, if he was in, shooed the boy away from the sacks of raw brown sugar in the back. My uncle, on the other hand, let him feast. Farouk came back out of the office after ten minutes, collected the envelopes from me, and, arms akimbo, watched Sugarboy in admiration for a moment.

"You don't put on an ounce of weight, Sugarboy," Farouk told him, shaking his head at the child. "No matter how much of my sugar you gobble up. My boy, I salute your appetite. Especially today when I am too nervous to touch a thing. You know when the call from Sol the Rabbi came in?"

Sugarboy put down the length of cork he was slicing. "It's difficult to say, boss. If you wait I am sure the other boss will be back and you can ask him."

"That defeats the purpose, Sugarboy. I don't want my brother to have his nose in all my business."

In my father's absence the workshop reverted to a slow-moving, quintessentially African concept of energy, as if sparing its powers for a future sprint. Dad was a perfectionist. He liked to have the details of something properly organised. Whereas Farouk didn't mind delaying the labourers, sending them on irrelevant errands, and bringing them into the back room to talk politics. It made him extremely popular with the staff. On this afternoon he climbed up to the barrels and checked the contents. From up there he could talk to everyone.

"Let's have a drink to celebrate my nephews' accomplishments," he said, smiling, and pouring the foaming brown liquor into an enamel mug. "Muslim beer, no alcohol. Sugarboy, you take a break also, my boy."

Teachers have spiritual effects, cosmical effects on their students, but, as with all forms of human action, the effects are never the intended ones. Elena indissolubly combined romance and the cold beauty of arithmetic in the author's chilly soul. I dreamed of Elena and the voluptuous curves of the numeral 5 in a single thought. I saw 7 as roller-skate skinny. The indivisibility of a prime number except by itself and one reminds me of the womanly mind. I stayed up late at night swotting in the bedroom I shared with my brother, a torch under my blankets or cottonwool in my ears, in order to please my maths teacher the next day. I was in love, and the geometry of love is always triangular.

Elena's place was my first experience of a woman's apartment. The pad was as overdone as its mistress, clotted and feminine. Having grown up in the Fordsburg house before being farmed out to a Catholic academy, I had never known a set of rooms so ornate and inviting. There was a bidet, the function of which I didn't consider, underwear soaking in a basin below the Truetone set, antimacassars, red drapes and mats, a glass rack of perfume bottles, sprays, and curl papers, all infused by the dry white wine smell of Pine-Sol. Water colours of Corfu were posted on the wall. A bookshelf was loaded with tarot cards, dictionaries, and European tomes my teacher took puzzlingly seriously – Nostradamus, Pearl S. Buck, and Anaïs Nin.

I was astonished to hear about Nostradamus, to have a passage from Pearl Buck read out loud in her limbo dancer's voice from a sud-soaked tub while I basked on the sofa, or to have Elena promise to lend me her volumes of Anaïs Nin when I was old enough to go with girls. She liked to talk to me about her books because she couldn't talk to my uncle. Elena was born in Cyprus, and shared the European idea of a general education. She had a shoebox of a mind. It was filled with cuttings from Nostradamus and Kierkegaard, from the *International Herald Tribune* and the pages of Kahlil Gibran. She opened the lid, rummaged among the envelopes, and produced a quotation. After twenty minutes of talk she ran the bathwater, shed her clothes into a tall rosewood laundry basket, and we got around to the lesson, conducted at our usual distance.

Elena's particular liking for numbers was something new to me. For the Dawoods numbers were the object of devotion. To take less than ten per cent would strike Farouk as violating his own identity. I remark that Islam is a religion of numbers, scales, and proportions . . . a calibrating and magistratical religion. Whereas for Elena numbers were cosmic and spiritual. She believed on Platonic grounds that numbers had an existence independent of human beings.

Elena taught me to add up the digits of a number to find out if it was divisible by three. We did long division, odd and even numbers, decimal points, primes, and irrational numbers. We did double bookkeeping and ways to keep money off the books and away from the thieving hands of the Department of Internal Revenue. Elena had memorised pi up to the twenty-first place and made me do so as well. She sank down low in the bath, so her big brown tits were submerged underneath the foam. I sat on the rim and recited the digits to the twenty-first place, only to be sent from the room as she emerged from the water like Venus out of the ocean.

Wrapped in her towel she pressed on the earrings Farouk gave her, touching her long ears like a merchant, and looking at herself sideways in the mirror. They were marquise diamonds, I noticed, with the pinkish stone phalanxed by white diamond studs.

37

She said, "Firoze, my dear, let's take a five-minute break. After my bath my mind is beginning to wander to the material plane. Can I get you some Turkish coffee?" Elena placed a fat hand on the plush bosom that I adored. She loaded the coffee pot with tablespoons of treacly black powder. "They call it Turkish in this country, but it's a Greek invention. Nescafé, please! How can anyone drink a drop of that rubbish? I tell Farouk, lay off the stuff before it proves lethal." She checked the time. "Speaking of the devil, where is your uncle?"

"He should be here. He and Ashraf are excited about their papers. They go in the back of the factory in the morning and send me out to get lunch for them. Elena, it's not like my brother to keep secrets from me. Keeping a secret takes half a brain and then what is there left for the guy to use?"

"Don't talk like that about someone in your family."

Elena brought over two cups on gold-rimmed saucers and we sat there drinking. Conversation with adults, rather than my fellow teenagers, was my forte. I knew that Elena liked to talk about my uncle, although I didn't always like to give her the satisfaction. Elena was a nice lady, I believed, nice in her methods of teaching, nice about numbers, but not all that nice, not super nice. I was – and am – able to study the human countenance out of the corner of my green eyes, a faculty that does nothing to deepen my faith in the species. A sly look passed over Elena's countenance when she thought I was concentrating on my exercises. That same sly look came over her as I stared into the tarry bottom of my cup. She sat closer to me and I sensed the steam on the inside of her towel.

She asked, "Dear, what does Farouk say about me?"

"Nothing."

"What does he tell you about women in general?"

"You know, he grumbles. Ashraf gets most of the advice on that subject from Farouk. By now, with the time he spent recently with Ten Percent, he knows every detail of the female anatomy plus the reasons for each part." I put down the cup because it was something I was serious about. "It's a big change. Since when did Ashraf know the name of anything? Since when did that merry fellow know the reason for anything? I beg him for a simple diagram."

Elena said, "It must make him pretty popular at school."

"For sure. He plays doctor with the matric girls."

Without seeming to listen she continued, "Ten minutes with a real lady is better than all the theory in the world."

"There's a lot to be said for theory."

"Do you know that you look a lot like your uncle?"

I swear there was a gleam in Elena's eyes. I swear that her eyes had stretched and changed colours. They were a kaleidoscope of shifting browns and greens. I swear that Elena was so close in her towel that I could hear her Cypriot heart beating in my ears. I swear that there was a wild rush in my head. I solemnly do swear that I was about to put my hand around Elena's rump when Farouk came in the door. He didn't offer any kind of a greeting. He was like that, a sudden appearer and disappearer. My brother was with him. Ashraf was cheerful. My brother felt that maths lessons were a punishment. He was grateful to avoid them, although he later said nice things about Elena in her towel.

Ten Percent didn't seem to notice me. He put his hands to Elena's ears. "Listen, do me a favour and let me borrow back those earrings from you for a few days. Please, to show a potential customer."

"You want them for some other woman."

"Nonsense, Elena. Why are you in that towel?"

"I just got out of the bath," she replied. "I was teaching Firoze from there. Why are you so irritated?"

Farouk, by the way, was not exactly irritable. Irritable is the wrong word. You could tell by his big-nostrilled nose and also by how he treated his neat hedge of rectangular beard, which was grey like the gut in an old tennis racket. He rubbed it when in need of luck. When my uncle had nervous energy he was rarely unhappy. He skimmed along for hours on the verge of irritability without getting angry, just to show that he could. He didn't want to get into a fight over the earrings because, I think, he hated having to apologise to Elena merely to enjoy her favours.

"Just give me the earrings, please." He unlatched first the one, then the other, from her ears. "And about that conversation we were having earlier, about marriage and weddings, I'd like to go back to that. Maybe I happen not to share certain superstitions with the other Mussulmans as far as three wives and four wives are concerned. And, by the way, superstitions and barbarous customs are there in every religion. It's not just the poor Muslims. Maybe the smart thing, the modern thing, is to have one wife, and then to keep women on the side. Not to bloody insult you." He seemed to notice my existence for the first time. "It looks like you two are getting along nicely, or am I mistaken?"

Before we went over to Tarnofsky's, we picked up the jewels from the factory. Farouk explained his scheme to me now that it was all in place. South Africa was a land of tariffs and taxes. To get articles into the country without paying duty, my uncle mailed empty envelopes to his connection in India. Across the ocean the connection, a Gujarati jeweller named Mr Das, crossed out his own name from the front and labelled them "return to sender" in red ink. Boys' small, tough hands could be rented in the province of Gujarat for a pittance and they were better with microscopic amounts. The guys in Surat, in Gujarat, used less than half the diamond dust required by the Antwerp and Haifa cutters.

Das steamed the envelopes open and salted them with a handful of minute diamonds. The return-to-sender letters were the perfect means of conveyance because neither the Indian nor the South African Post Office inspected returned mail. The certificates Tarnofsky provided were for these diamonds. Ashraf's licences and passports were a way to pay off Ten Percent's friends. Plus, Das's fees, his bribes, his reservations for the cutting saw, were anything but excessive. "That man Das ... That man Das is a real gem," Farouk told us. I'm sure my uncle didn't see the idea as unintentionally funny, although a villainous mind, in my experience, is usually on the alert for puns. There isn't an outlaw I've known who's averse to a pun, even if they tend to go over my brother's head.

Farouk took us down to Tarnofsky's office, a few blocks down from the Gemological Institute on a busy crossroads. Garment wholesalers wheelbarrowed bundles of second-hand clothing on the pavement. Traders picked through the merchandise. After negotiations they loaded the dresses, blouses, and pants into suitcases. It was a Jo'burg rule that the master of the house's handsome gold-button blazer would after a decent interval be observed on the gardener ... and after an equal time on the gardener's son ... who later sold it to a wholesaler. It happened with my dad's cherished safari suits and, once upon a time, with Farouk's beloved and battered Carnaby Street black leather jacket. Whether it was charity or an act of illicit liberation or fashion criticism, no one bothered to ask.

Solomon Tarnofsky waited for us behind a cloudy glass door, sitting on a high chair in front of a metal desk and jeweller's lamp. He didn't get up to greet us, yet he wasn't unfriendly. I had never met Tarnofsky before, but I knew a lot about him. The guy was famous around the diamond district for his creased and dusty black suit and stovepipe hat. Underneath his black clothes he was a corpulent man with corpulent hands. With his cool manner, his way of leaning back, and his comfortable place on the red leather barstool Tarnofsky reminded me rather of the caterpillar in *Alice in Wonderland*. All that he lacked was a hookah.

"So these are your nephews, Ten Percent?"

Farouk agreed.

"Well, they have your good looks. Take a seat. Take a seat." Tarnofsky waved although there weren't any chairs besides his own. Having satisfied the dictates of hospitality he asked, "What can I do for you, my friend?"

"Listen, Solomon, I need those certificates from you today. I brought you the Nedbank slip to show the money is already deposited in your personal account. This is my batch of stones. Nothing too big, in fact. Maybe you want to take one yourself. The idea struck me on the way over. Here." Farouk produced the pair of earrings I saw him get off Elena. "I've put the nicest pair in these earrings. Maybe Mrs Tarnofsky needs a setting."

"Mrs Tarnofsky, when she exists, won't be so frivolous."

I was embarrassed with my uncle for being such a small timer, a small thinker, but at least Farouk gave up and said, "I'll give you the measurements for the certificates."

"Let's take it one by one."

The jewels were weighed in a pan. Tarnofsky slid the beams around, added and subtracted decigrams, and noted the results.Then he typed out the certificates on a battered typewriter in a big black case. Finally he took a stamp from the drawer and franked each copy. Business was quickly accomplished. There was a mood of rejoicing in that dusty little office looking out on another set of municipal beer tanks. It's the most solemn custom of Johannesburg to celebrate when money is being born. Farouk took out a packet of beedis and tapped one onto his hand. Tarnofsky turned out to be an able host in that typical bachelor's style. He got up, and insisted on shaking hands with the three of us. Then he brewed a pot of Joko tea. He handed out Lucky Packets to my brother and me.

"So that business your father and your uncle own, what do you think Farouk takes off the top?" Tarnofsky asked me in front of the guy. "Sometimes I wonder, for what reason do they call your uncle Ten Percent? Forgive me, Farouk, if I don't understand this name. When they start to address you as Forty Percent, then I think they will be a little closer to the truth." He poured

41

us cups of tea. "Even from my worst enemy I won't take more than eight out of a hundred commission. Even from you Farouk, a Muslim, I won't take more than eight."

Farouk put his hand on my shoulder. "Please, for you Sol, a special dispensation. Don't feel that you have to be polite. Call us Mussulmans."

That evening Ashraf turned off the music for the first time and threw the blankets off his bed. On the white sheet he laid out one of the certificates Tarnofsky had provided, and alongside it a pad of butcher's paper, a protractor, gold leaf and silver leaf pens, scraps of linen, and some other tools of my brother's new trade. For once in his life Farouk was considerate, bringing around tea and a large lamp from upstairs so that my brother could see better. In defiance of my mother's orders they worked until the morning was blue in the windows. I took the opportunity to brush up my understanding of integrals, although I had an ominous feeling about what Ashraf's success at duplicating Tarnofsky's certificates might mean for Tarnofsky.

A man with a complement of Mum's romantic genes remembers his first love with affection for all her perfections and imperfections. The best thing about Elena, in my eyes, was her seal-like physique which, in its amplitude, suggested that, at her creation, someone didn't notice the mould was full, and kept pouring. Only a substantial lady like Elena, with so much to contribute to the fleshpots of life, moved me and my uncle as well. Elena's principal inconvenience for both of us was her desire to get married. She was three years older than Farouk. The gap worried her. She brought the issue up in front of me at Millard's. I think her aim was to embarrass him, which was a mistake because the man had no shame.

"Ace, I've been thinking. I can't get it out of my mind. According to your religion, you Mussulmans are permitted to have four wives, providing you treat them with equal respect."

"That's true, so far. You said the same thing last week. So what's your point?"

She picked at the sandy mussels on the table, a specialty of the house embalmed in squiddish Worcestershire sauce. The craggy shells clinked one against the other. She detached a mussel and tried, unsuccessfully, to feed it to me and then, with more luck, to Farouk. Mussels were my favourite dish because of their eternal pucker.

"Make an honest woman out of me. Later, if you want a woman from your own nation, maybe I won't raise a fuss. You know I can be extremely broad minded."

"You can keep dreaming, Elena. But it's not going to happen until pigs fly." Farouk's manner was too straightforward to be called sarcastic, part of why people liked the man, even if he was as spiritually porcine as an earthbound pig. "And anyway," he continued, "I cannot abide having this discussion repeatedly, in front of my nephew to boot. Who are you, you crazy Greek, to call us Mussulmans?"

"It's the term you use."

"It's different if I choose to speak that way. I can do anything I want. Your last name, Elena, how do you say it properly again?"

Interesting consequences followed on this disagreement. During my lesson that afternoon there was an odd expression on Elena's face as she undressed herself for the bath. It was the look an illegal Hillbrow boxer gets in the eighth round of an eight-round match, the lips stretched out and a thousand miles of distance in the eyes. Elena rose out of the bath and asked me to bring her the hair dryer. She let me comb out her brown hair as it dried. It was as smooth as the flax of a fairytale princess.

When we did calculus on the couch Elena sat so close to me that I could smell mussels. When we practised decimals she put a clammy hand on my neck and in my hair, a hand to whose fatness and juiciness every subsequent woman would be unfavourably contrasted. By the time we were on to squares and square roots I was sitting in her lap. She was blowing on my ear just as she did to Farouk. She rolled over me. I rolled over her. We rolled over each other. They rolled over she. She rolled over he. At a certain moment Elena sang Italian songs into my ears. In fact she spoke Italian from beginning to end, although I couldn't understand a word of it.

I am, I was, the kind of man who says anything in the course of true love but, of course, in English. I must have promised to marry her . . . I must have offered her my money and my dictionaries . . . I must have sworn to labour on sines and cosines. Decorum dictates that a veil be drawn over the oxblood lounge suite. As a gentleman manuscript writer I could never say anything that violates the privacy of a lady acquaintance. Let me add that for me prime numbers and squares and the square roots of negative numbers and the barely lingering effects of seafood on a sealish woman's lips are indissolubly linked to the joys of love.

As a gentleman the only person for whom I described the events on the Joshua Doore couch, which continued on the carpet amid a tangle of stockings and green eyes and talcum powder and Dr Zog's was, of course, my brother Ashraf. How, he wanted to know, did I spend my afternoon? How did he spend his afternoon? First he copied a British passport for an Indian from Uganda. Then he helped rig the traffic robot at the intersection of Canary Boulevard and Third Avenue so that his chums at Fordsburg's Caltex garage would have a supply of cars to repair on their very doorstep. He drank peach schnapps with the same mob of rude mechanicals as they waited for the first accident.

The Caltex guys cut my brother in on a percentage when a van collided with a bus on Third Avenue. He bought sixty-year-old Dolly Dube a drink in a White City shebeen on the strength of his earnings. Finally, on this glorious afternoon, Ashraf used an Etch-a-Sketch and a slide projector to produce a perfect copy of one of Sol the Rabbi's jewellery certificates. He had made the middleman obsolete, one of those fundamental morals South Africans go by.

I waited patiently until Ashraf finished his recitation. When, for form's sake, he asked me how I spent the afternoon, I told the sweet fellow every single detail. Reader, it was the happiest moment of my life.

The next act took place, appropriately, in a movie theatre. Balanski's Picture Palace stood on Jansen Street beside an Esso garage where the petrol pump, which bore a white clock gauge above its tank, was chained shut beneath a sheet of corrugated iron. Looking back, I believe that Ten Percent took us with him for the same reason he took us to the slaughterhouse – to teach us some obscure lesson about life and death. At home he took out a black shawl and placed it over his back. He made us also dress in shawls. Then he stretched a beard across his face and rubbed walnut oil into his skin so that his eyes stared greenly out of a very dark countenance.

It was my first chance to look at Hillbrow through the windows of Farouk's Mercedes. Hillbrow, at Jo'burg's heart, was a Petri dish of every kind of life and the first example of positive anarchy since the Paris Commune, with its children of a thousand streams of mingled blood, its churches and street philosophers, Anglican clergy and gang members in two-tone leather shoes, its *Drum* magazine poets, strivers, and weekend stabbings.

Balanski's itself was a two-storey building with a cubby-hole ticket office, tasselled velvet drapes over the posters, and reels of dark brown film mounted on spokes along the stairwell. We went in the entrance and familiarised ourselves with the layout. Instead of curtains there were grey army blankets tacked over the windows. People smoked, drank, quarrelled before the show. The posters were stolen, as were the films themselves. The movies were repeats and pilfered from the Ster de Luxe in town. The stolen canisters, gangster flicks, included twenty minutes of *Castle on the Hudson*, the middle reel of *Angels with Dirty Faces*, and a complete print of *Each Dawn I Die*.

We found our way to the camera room above the stairs. The projectionist, Charlie Mabilo, turned out to be an agreeable character. Like his clientele he drank a grape-and-petrol mixture of Commando brandy and Ribena while watching the machinery and reloading the spools. He was amenable, of course, to my uncle's goodwill money.

The afternoon show, when we went down, wasn't well attended. It was a modest eleven-foot screen that revealed the myriad imperfections in the celluloid, and there was white noise in the speaker, all of which appealed to my tastes. Ashraf and I sat right at the back and watched. Edward G. Robinson spoke to Jenny on screen as a man dressed as an Orthodox Jew, bearing a shovel from the building-supply store across Jansen Street, seated himself beside Tarnofsky. They were in the row in front of us. The two men spoke a few words. It was at that moment that my uncle, as he later said, saw in the dusk of the cinema that Sol Tarnofsky had the face of a child. I couldn't see myself because the two men sat in the shadow of the balcony.

Tarnofsky was a genial raconteur. Without raising his voice he explained the story so far. He was in the midst of doing so, his eyes like oysters, when the man beside him stood up and in a moment struck him on the back of the head with the shovel. It was so fast, so unexpected, so unbearably sharp and macabre, that the victim had no time to protest, only to smile. I don't wish to infuse the situation with unintentional comedy by observing that Tarnofsky was still alive to feel the sharp edge of the shovel in his mind. Ten Percent was good with his hands that way. Sudden, surprising violence, he felt, was the only logical kind. I didn't know what to think. Until then I had no idea of why we were going to the movies.

45

It was the right time to make a killing, Farouk had said, but to me it's typical of the villainous mind to solve a complex problem with a pun. Either it's a pun, I suppose, or a shovel. It's too painful for the writer of these pages to describe the expression in Tarnofsky's eyes when my uncle seized him from behind in the movie theatre and held him firmly to his chest, still stunned from the shovel. It's too painful to say that these two men stood with their heads as close as lovers as Farouk drew the edge of his Bowie knife across Tarnofsky's neck. Tarnofsky was soon heaved over the seat and laid out behind the last row of seats.

It's painful to remember that Ashraf helped with the body. And it's far too painful to remark that I was reminded of the strange tenderness of a cut sheep when Tarnofsky's sighing head sank onto Farouk's shoulder. The only positive result of the afternoon was that my uncle entrusted his diaries to me when he was shut up in the insane asylum and he never thought to get them back when he finally fled the country.

لـب

Chapter Three

The black beard and broken tooth of the Peshawar gunsmith who flashes me an enormous grin on receiving a crate of steel-pin punches and head-space gauges? The turrets of Sun City high above imaginary Bophuthatswana, or the bolted tin can of Jacques Cousteau's diving saucer in the Monte Carlo Oceanographic Museum overlooking Prince's Palace? Do I begin with an Indian waiter bearing a cockatoo's red crest or a raven-tressed woman in the Rosebank Woolworths pocketing a box of Salticrax? Do I mention the pigeonholes in the philosophy department office at Witwatersrand University, or do I page through an Interpol dossier concerning a man who has been like a father to me?

Armed with a drop of ink for a crystal ball, let me conjure a vision of a 1970s department store near Johannesburg, one of the leviathans that sell house-wares and shoes alongside electrical goods and groceries. It's the Ackermans in Rosebank, my mum's favourite on account of its fancy foreign goods – Swarovski crystal, Wedgwood dinner sets, Marks and Spencer biscuits, no local knock-offs. From the upper-storey windows where I stand, I spy the stamp batteries at the nearby mining compounds, and the headgear astride mine entrances with their immense tailings wheels turning like clocks. I turn my attention back to the corridors where my mother and brother are up to no good. The interior of the store is, as one expects from the ineradicably arriviste culture of wealthy South Africans, endless iron racks and rose-red carpet hallways pearled with chandeliers.

Ackermans has just allowed non-Europeans through its doors as part of South Africa's gradual movement forward into the eighteenth century. The goods are seductive. There's plated silver cutlery my brother weighs in his hands as if he can never put it down. There is Dutch blue-and-white porcelain I remove from the box and press cool against my cheek. We're shoplifting with my mother who, you would have thought, as a philosopher, would be above such things. But being above things and beyond things is not a trait of the Dawoods and the Peers. We're usually beneath things, below them, and, generally, in the middle of the muck. Ashraf wants a Bowie knife although, at his age, he should be beyond such things. I'm interested in the cool civilising radiance of a badminton set. We'll get both. Mum doesn't know how to say no to either of her sons.

"Do you have to grab all the knives in sight, Ashraf?" She takes them. "Can't you choose one?"

Ashraf insists. "Not just one."

"My doll, I'm afraid to walk out of Ackermans with a lorry full of forks and knives. They're difficult to conceal. And since when did we need steak knives, I ask you? Since when did I buy steak? I am concerned about you, my boy. You've never been the same since they put that crazy uncle of yours in the loony bin. What is it, you want to be a Boswell and Wilkie knife thrower?"

I say, "Ashraf is better suited to the clown section."

"Oh, hush. Both of you are pests. I fear that both of my children have gone wrong but you are the worst, Firoze. At least Ashraf is protected by his ignorance whereas you have no such excuse. Well, I will see what I can do about the knives. And give me the badminton box if you must. So if we're done on this floor let's stroll over to the changing rooms. On the way we can pick up some socks and underwear. Your father is in dire need."

This is the freewheeling way Mum talks. She insults us. She comments on everything and anyone under the sun. She deals out affection to all and sundry. She doles out advice and metaphysics. She treats my brother and I as if we're still teenagers, although we just celebrated a joint twenty-first birthday party. My mother Sameera, Sammy to her side of the family, is a compulsive shoplifter.

To fill you in about the rest: Mum, Mom, is a junior lecturer in the philosophy department at Witwatersrand University. She's virtually a child of the university. Since the age of seventeen she has been away from Wits only the year she spent getting a masters at Monash in Australia. On her return from Australia Mum began shoplifting, for whatever mysterious psychological reason. Sometimes it's all we can do, as her sons, to keep her out of jail where she – along with the rest of my family – belongs. I suspect it's because Mum was brought up a rich girl that she has so little respect for private property. It's the child of socialist and trade-union parents who never steals so much as a twig.

We walk to the staircase then to the changing rooms where numbers hang on a velvet board. We're given one and crowd into a red-curtained enclosure. The booths and drapery lining the corridor create the feeling of a playhouse. Inside Mum addresses the mirror on the wall with sidelong glances as she refreshes her eye shadow. Who is the fairest of us all? The mirror is as silent on this issue as any of its brethren. Within its sinuously cut green glass borders it shows a slender face dominated by nervous green eyes and unsteady, pencil-thin eyebrows which might have been drawn by a Faber-Castell marker. To follow them in their reflected state is to notice they are liable to shoot up and down without rhyme or reason. Mum's luxurious ebony hair is glossy, my brother says, as a Chinawoman's.

Mum sees I'm hovering and tells me, "Don't faff around here. Do something useful. Go into the corridor and make sure no one disturbs us. Tell me if you notice anyone suspicious. Ashraf will help me unwrap the things and pack them away. Remember, anyone suspicious."

Someone suspicious, in shoplifter's lexicon, is someone on the side of the angels. But Mum doesn't process irony. She's the only educated person I know who doesn't. It's wilful on her part. I think of her as a kind of department store Modigliani. When she comes out of the changing room with my brother I notice how oddly her head is articulated with the rest of her frame. You can't tell what she's looking at because her sea-green eyes dart here and there of their own accord. She's a born lightfingers, and it doesn't cause her a qualm. It's a matter of principle. Some people, like Mum, believe in principles. The greatest misbehavers, in my view, are free because of the emotional security of having principles.

We go over to the underwear section and Mum cruises the shelves behind the oval of her cavernous handbag. The handbag swings in a parabola behind her back and so do we. She has a shopping basket as well. Ashraf positions himself so as to screen her from any outsider's gaze. Mum adds first this, then that, to her basket, adds, subtracts, substitutes, and myopically pages through the price tags while her other hand, concealed from prying eyes by the column of my brother, pulls another article into the elastic depths of the handbag.

Today there's a guard around every corner in Ackermans. I worry. Only Ashraf is immune to anxiety. Mum and I get spooked, unlike true Dawoods. To a true Dawood danger is a sort of spiritual helium, making a flippant heart light as a feather and converting every sentence into a witticism. Yet there is an ounce of devil-may-care Dawood to each pint of quailing Peer, and a quaking smidgeon of Peer to every slice of brazen Dawood.

Anyone watching from behind observes a woman examining prices, cosseting her older children, and now and again patting down her long dark hair. It's sleight of hand. Like Ashraf, Mum is ambidextrous. One of my mother's hands hardly knows what the other is doing. The relationship between moral and physical ambidexterity scarcely needs to be spelled out in what is essentially a film treatment.

After she finishes with underwear Mum turns to me. "Have you found a shoplifter?" She's nice about it. "None of the usual suspects, Firoze, because we don't want to offend our colleagues. Who says there's no such thing as honour? Always remember that whatever we do in life, we belong to a community."

"It's hardly a community," I say.

"When you know someone's face they become part of your community. It's as simple as that."

I am aware of the faces belonging to our fellow practitioners of the dark arts. They range from an English lady in macramé gloves to a runaway with straw-coloured hair who can often be found trying on Bata shoes in the girl's section, to a Gujarati matron wearing a snaky, affronted look and a dollop of red sediment upon her forehead who robs bundles of fabric and the very batteries in the alarm system. Like the multitudinous ants lodged within an anthill Jo'burg's shoplifters are found at every turn in the endless commercial developments of Vrededorp, Germiston, Malvern, Brixton, Pimville, in Stuttafords, Checkers, OK Bazaars, and Game Discount World.

Mum's method depends on it. We trail another shoplifter, follow that person right to the door, and then denounce him or her to the management just as they go outside. Guards are summoned. The cashiers are in an uproar. In the commotion it's easy to make off with a packet. The main drawback is being summoned now and again to the magistrate's court on Jeppe Street as a state witness. I've testified twice already, so, by the way, the defendant is familiar with courtroom procedure.

I wander past the sock bins and up the staircase that leads to the men's section. Everyone looks innocent. The statuettes of the electric bulbs housed in dozens in each chandelier are shaped, I notice, like candles. The cosmetics counter is situated beneath such a chandelier. It's staffed by several severe older white women. Meanwhile Ashraf haunts the lingerie drawers and patrols the make-up desks. He's not having any luck. Finally I notice a red-haired woman, plaster-of-paris cast on her broken leg, loitering in the region of the dinner sets. Loitering is the wrong word; it's a two-legged word. The red-haired lady hobbles around an arrangement of striped Wedgwood porcelain cups and candycane saucers amid small crates filled with hay. I wait until I can see her right up close. Her complexion is chalky, decorated with many miniature moles. When she spots me her eyes are unsteady and over-easy beneath a pompadour of dyed orange curls.

The red-haired lady shoves me away, turning on her plaster leg to do so. After a minute she goes back to business. She harvests the cups and saucers, packs them with a handful of quickly gathered straw, and slides the next piece and then the piece after that down the inside of her prehensile arms. I motion to Ashraf who calls Mum. The three of us follow our redhead from room to room until she finishes. As she's on her way out of Ackermans, poling past the registers on her one good leg, my mother takes the lady guard at the door by her blue sleeves. It's the moment of the kill.

"That lady," Mum tells the guard, "who's hobbling out of the door, catch her before it's too late. We saw her pocketing a box full of crockery. Search her, for heaven's sake, and see what turns up. Poor Mr Ackerman. He'll be destitute if this nonsense is allowed to continue."

Instantly there's a phalanx of guards and clerks in the front of the store. The woman's handbag is turned out to the lining as she stands on her crutch. The guard pats down her pockets. There's nothing. They check the inside of her blouse and don't find anything there. It's a false alarm. I feel the irritation of the employees turning on us. My cheeks burn. I consider running for the street. Everyone's staring at us. At this moment a new and horrible idea dawns on our victim. Her thin grey lips tighten across the bottom of her face. She takes back her handbag and points at Mum.

"That Indian woman, oh my goodness, this is the second time she's denounced me to security. For shame, madam, you did exactly the same thing to me last time at the Ackermans on Commissioner Street. It wasn't six weeks ago last Friday. Don't you remember? Doesn't that strange-looking boy remember? Why is she picking on me? Why is she persecuting me? Ask her."

"Have a look inside her cast," Mum replies. She's never as magnificent as when we're in terrible peril. "There's nothing broken about that broken leg. She should have learned her lesson the first time."

I mentioned an Interpol dossier. The blue-and-white folder with its sword-and-globe logo sits on my narrow prison bed. It concerns a certain Suleiman, or Solly, Zacharia, well preserved for a man in his sixties, and a suspect in a multitude of offences. Zacharia is of uncertain provenance, given the number of his false identities and the geographical sweep of his crimes. The report speculates that he is the product of a Levantine upbringing from the counterfeiting centre of Lebanon's Bekaa valley. Perhaps he was born on the wrong side of the bed of mixed Arab parentage, with a Bedouin mother and a wealthy Saudi for a father. Zacharia was in Buenos Aires, perhaps, and perhaps in Mexico City, perhaps in Birmingham. Zacharia's last known address, a bedbuggy flophouse in Karachi, was checked out by officers from the French embassy and is considered a dead end. Perhaps.

The night porter at the Birmingham Comfort Inn is a principal source for the dossier. He loaned Zacharia electric clippers. There's an odd scene he conjures to do with these clippers. On a late evening run, balancing two servings of Cadbury's hot chocolate on a tray, the porter discovered a large hotel towel spread on the floor. One of two oldish looking boys reclined in a wicker chair, a smaller towel tucked around his neck, with one half of his head shaved. His sour green eyes didn't vary from the porter. Zacharia leaned over the boy almost tenderly, skimming off curls of mahogany hair with the clippers.

The porter, of course, being a porter, had to step in to prevent the further destruction of hotel property. He came downstairs with the towels in a laundry bag and the clippers bound in its four-foot cord, a turn of events Zacharia disputed because he'd only half shaved his son's head. Did the porter want the boy to go around Birmingham like an idiot? Was the porter some kind of idiot?

The Birmingham Comfort Inn gives us a snapshot of the troubled Zacharia family. The two boys were nervous, restless, and competitive, according to the night porter. They jockeyed around Zacharia, the one stalking the other.

That same boy, with the sour-as-crabapple eyes, was suspected of abstracting women's underwear from the drying rack in the hotel laundry. Coming up the stairs the porter thought he spotted a boy's half-shaven head buried in an armful of stolen lingerie, but he couldn't be sure. It was twilight in Birmingham, a time I remember brought out the place's aerodromical face – the conning towers of glass and cement on Hagley Road, the pervasive smell of aeroplane gasoline, and the yards of shuttered brown brick buildings which climb Hodge Hill. Birmingham is one of my favourite cities. It adds to my pleasure to remember Ashraf, half-shaven to the bone of his head, and with his snout in a basket of nylon underwear.

When the night porter complained to Zacharia about the missing laundry, he found that the trio had been joined by a woman in early middle age, possibly of Middle Eastern extraction. Plus they were four in a room with two double beds, against hotel policy. Nevertheless the newcomer was starchy. She didn't care what he had to say about hotel policy. The lady was fussily dressed in silk, a grande dame whose air was described by the manager as that of a wistful, gradually expiring beauty. She refused to believe that either of her sons would stoop to stealing laundry, even the bad one. She hustled the night porter out of the door and told him not to come back without a policeman.

Zacharia deferred to the lady, according to the manager, and even addressed her as Professor. The lady's title is not considered reliable. By the way, it's never clear to the Interpol reviewers whether Zacharia is or isn't joking. His every word is glazed with what may be sarcasm, or what might equally be good humour.

What is clear is the Interpol mimeograph of a counterfeit twenty-pound note, which was one of a hundred the Zacharia family spent in Birmingham. It's gorgeously engraved, a work of art no less impressive in its own right than the Claude Lorraine in the Birmingham Museum of Art or, to be sure, the forged Pakistani passports Zacharia presented for himself and his sons. In the corner of the note I see my brother's unmistakable credentials. The serial number of the twenty-pound note is my mother's birthday in palindrome form. It is, I suppose, Ashraf's circuitous way of expressing love.

I have no patience with Scotland Yard myth making. People allow their imaginations to run away with them . . . and if not their imaginations, then it's their professional definitions. The psychological consultant, for instance, argues in favour of a sociopathic designation in the Zacharia case. The personal charm, liking for expensive clothes, love of disguises, of riddles, of joke telling, of American music, the instinct for adventure demonstrated by Zacharia's willingness to embark on an impersonation, militate against an economic motivation. He offends, the consultant explains, because he lives, and loves, to offend.

Is Zacharia a type of Zelig or human chameleon? Does he really go by the name of Connery Goldstone and does the sheen of his eyes truly resemble mother of pearl? Is he a superhero? Is it fair to say, as does Father da Silva of Columbia Episcopal Seminary, that "every religion, every specific ethnic group, manifests its own brand of criminality?" Da Silva remarks that "the specifically Muslim dimension of Z—'s character, in my estimation, is the combination of an unlawful style of life plus his extreme levity and preference for a very cold manner of joking. Muslims, who are famously lovers of justice, are just as famously spiritually dislocated in today's world. They tend to extreme feelings of dislocation and self-pity, eventuating in unfriendly acts directed against the social order. So Zacharia openly laughs at his enemies. These jokes and riddles run so close to the truth that they expose him to capture and, hence, destruction." Can any of this be true of a man who loves nothing more than the warm texture of a Hermès necktie between his weaver's fingers?

At the back of Interpol's booklet stand four laminated sheets of photographs and fingerprints. The author of these pages is in a position to vouch for the authenticity of two of the black-and-white shots. They show a man with high shoulders, modest hips, and a sandpaper complexion, this last the result of childhood measles. Zacharia prides himself on his beaky nose and his square jaw. At his age he can also be proud of his full head of discoloured grey hair in which can be seen skull-white strands.

This is not the place to establish that the lining of a man's soul is shown in his smile, not his eyes, but let me observe that Zacharia's smile tends to be ironical, pert, explanatory in character. It's very different from the blank smile of the destroyer, the taunting smile of the arch villain, or the greenish smile of Uriah Heep.

M. Suleiman Zacharia dresses like the black men he admired in 1950s Johannesburg. If you said Zacharia was a man with a Sophiatown boxer's wardrobe, you wouldn't be mistaken. Like his acquaintances among the boxers he's overly formal, someone who loves garments in unusual sheens and colours. Since his brother's exile to India Zacharia has been emotionally liberated. He's taken over his brother's suits and Ten Percent's closet of shoes and ever more of his flamboyant personality, not to say his half share in the gingerbeer factory, which was finally sold to the municipality only last year in lieu of four decades of property taxes. There's more of the preener than I care to acknowledge in this man who, as I say, has been like a father to me. And I don't mean this last phrase as a witticism.

Interpol's second photograph deserves a thousand and one words. The footnote in the bottom corner dates the photograph to June of 1994. Zacharia sports a white turban and a colonial waiter's uniform – red shirt with gold buttons, red pantaloons, and long white gloves to go with the turban. The heavy layer of brown make-up around his eyes covers up crow's-feet. A touch of blue shadow has been applied along with drops of henna below the lashes. Zacharia's buggish, hen-brown eyes, corrected by colour-changing contact lenses, look as heavy as grapefruit. His long black hair is oiled and smoothly combed back to the lip of the turban.

Some degree of ill health is suggested by his waterlogged countenance. Not to read too much into the picture but this is a man who seems perpetually uncomfortable with himself. The impression of discomfort is heightened by a severe limp and my father's habit of twisting around the stiff pivot of one hip as he walks, as if trying to rise above an obstacle on that side. It is a style of locomotion he spent months practising with Sugarboy's help, hobbling dyspeptically on one crutch with one leg bandaged at the knee. There's no surer way to shake a pursuer, Dad discovers, than to change from a man going at full tilt to a man with a broken hip rattling in the opposite direction with his arm in the crook of Sugarboy's elbow.

Dad's withdrawn before the Sun City job, as he usually is before something big goes down. But he can only be quiet for so long. The desire to relate some anecdote strikes him and he leans towards me and Sugarboy, his overhung falconer's eyes following our slightest expression. I would argue that he isn't his usual self, but about my father the phrase has no meaning. He cups one of his hands as he talks, reeling us along as if telling a shaggy dog story. In this frame of mind he'll talk the ears off a wooden Indian, and he'll certainly talk them right off Sugarboy who's along for the ride.

"What do you say, my boys? Do we need a shot of Dutch courage?" In the van he's changing out of his favourite suit into the waiter's uniform. "You may not recall that this suit was one of an entire rack that we, ahem, appropriated from the Aga Khan? You know, the Ismailis' top guy. At the time you, Firoze, had your head constantly in a book while Ashraf was out developing useful skills." I can't tell if this is disapproving because he has his back turned for a moment as he oils his hair with the aid of a pocket mirror. "If you were nine, it must have been, what, 1976. Margaret Thatcher was already in office or was she? Sugarboy, you my dear were already working for my brother back at the fort. We were staying at the Sapphire in Monte Carlo. It was our very first European vacation, almost a second honeymoon for your mother and me and you boys. Remember, I ginned up a travel agent's diploma. With that certificate we could stay anywhere our hearts desired at sixty per cent off. Live like kings, for peanuts. And the best thing is your mother had no conception of how the trip was financed. Ah, Sameera was busy with her shopping. Every afternoon she came back with bags and bags." Dad pauses, starts to make up Ashraf now that he's finished with himself, and his voice softens as it does when he wishes to convey some poetic sentiment. "Your mother, back then, had a real quality of innocence."

I am the spy in my family, in my culture, and I watch my father with Interpol eyes as he briefly adjusts the waiter's cummerbund around my waist. There's a squatly corporeal being to the fellow that offends me in my capacity as his son. Tiny white hairs cover his ears, his neck, the top half of his fingers. There are tiny sanded pink polyps, like barnacles on a ship's keel, adhering to the underside of his eyelids. They make him look almost blind as my uncle did when in the grasp of some surpassing feeling. Otherwise there's not much resemblance between Dad and my memory of Uncle Farouk, presently exiled to Dubai.

Even in his undergarments, with his sherry-red shirt unbuttoned, Dad gains a solid three inches from his sandals. He has to bend inside the back of the van as he fusses around Sugarboy's outfit. The impression of bulk is hardly a function of fleshiness. It's psychological. Around Haji Dawood, the man whom Interpol identifies as Solly Zacharia, the father whom I have so often said has been like a father to me, the lines of space and time are morally curved. I am twenty-four years and I look to all comers like a schoolboy, I'm convinced, because I've lived all my life in Zacharia's moral shadow. It's stunted my physical growth as well as Ashraf's.

I look out of the back window of the Datsun van. The acreage of wire and scrap metal huts alongside the road make a bleak prospect for our afternoon. Those endless acres of homeland are parched for water, bearing power lines on their brown spines in the distance. We're meant to take a casino to the cleaners and I would rather be at home with Schopenhauer. You might think, by the way, that I disapprove of my father's shenanigans, but the way I see it is, when certain cultures have a head start in monopolising the good things of the earth, it's natural for certain other cultures to take short cuts.

Would the defendant name his co-conspirators? In the interests of providing the truth and the whole truth, so help me, I admit that Ashraf is central to the plan. He has been working in the Sun City complex for weeks, even if working is a charitable expression in my brother's case. But at least he's there when and where he's supposed to be. He lets us in at the back door of the hotel restaurant, leads us down the staircase into the pantry. Ashraf wears an apron over his waiter's Nehru-style jacket and turban, and he supports an enormous drill on his chest. From the pantry we go past a bank of refrigerators. We find ourselves climbing down a grille into the building foundations. Sugarboy stays behind on the pantry staircase to keep watch.

I close the grille behind us. It's dark underground. Dad sets out candles while Ashraf sets up the drill. He straps on aviator's goggles that must have been left in the cockpit of a Sopwith Camel. Soon he's holding the bit up against the wall, and straining while a cloud of mortarboard and vaporised concrete starts up about us. There's a terrific noise. I pray it's not noticeable in the hotel kitchen above our heads. Once I check and recheck my outfit, and tend to the candles, there's little to do until Ashraf makes it through the cavity. I encourage Dad to go on with his story meanwhile. He's amenable.

"I was on the way to the baccarat tables one evening when I noticed that the Aga, who was busy playing, was precisely my size and shape. You can judge by how perfectly this jacket fits after all these years. In the face of a coincidence you don't sit and scratch your head like a Zulu boy. So I came and got you from your mother. Under my careful supervision you made an appearance at the hotel desk.

"That's when I knew you were a genius, although it helped that you wore a sailor's outfit Zuleika, your cousin's aunt, made for you. You asked the hotel clerk not to notify your father the Aga. You were crying, so it was only natural that he led you straight up to the Aga Khan's penthouse. Once they'd left, you quickly opened the door for me, or was it Ashraf? I can't be sure. Maybe you recall piling all we could find into the dry-cleaning cart. I counted seventeen suits. Did he get any use from half his wardrobe? I suppose if you can't count on the Aga Khan to wear the best, what can you count on? There was this suit, then a navy Agnelli, a double-breasted Leporello, something more casual from Ponsonby and Sons, and the most exquisite three piece in houndstooth that your mother liked on me. She called it slimming. You know she says that about every article of clothing. But I will say that the wardrobe I acquired that evening has been indispensable. Far more so than the fuss about Omar Sharif and his Jaguar that exercised the Sunday newspapers. It still gives me rather a thrill to remember the Hotel Sapphire doormen helping us pack those suits into the Bentley's trunk. You don't think I'm telling you tall stories?"

"I remember every minute," I say. "I have to wonder though, wouldn't a normal father worry about exposing a child to these influences? Don't you regret what you might have done to me? To both of us?"

Sorry, as the expression goes, isn't in my father's vocabulary. "Ah, not in the least. It doesn't cause me a minute of worry. In Ashraf's case, I have to say, what could be a bad influence on that boy? I don't like to talk like this about my children whom I love, but consider that dunderhead with the drill and ask yourself if anything in his environment could have affected him negatively. Why, Ashraf is living proof of the importance of sullen nature over cosmic nurture. As for you, my child, how can I feel guilty about providing you with a little knowledge of the world? When you're in your thirties, which won't be long now, and I'm not around to teach you, you'll be the better for internalising such knowledge. You can theorise, and you can hop up and down on one foot until the cows come home, but when it comes to wisdom, my boy, you can't beat the value of experience."

It takes almost an hour, but Ashraf gets through the wall eventually. He unplugs the drill, puts it down. By this time I can hardly see in the dark space except for the pancakes of candlelight arranged in pairs down the cement hallway. I hear the tread of waiters' feet on the floors above us serving lunch. There's work to be done. I collect the debris in a bag while Ashraf goes after the safe. My brother has an acetylene torch which he keeps swivelling around and pointing at me. The hiss of the torch meets the resistant door of the safe. The edge of the safe glows orange although it doesn't yet give way.

After a while Ashraf replaces the tank on the torch and tries again. I'm frazzled. I expect the police to turn up at any moment. Dad, on the other hand, couldn't be more relaxed. He has an inverse spirit. The nuttier the situation, the calmer and cooler he becomes. He's a man of action. Put him in the midst of an ordinary Sunday afternoon and a family, though, in the round of family quarrels, and he develops the screaming heebie-jeebies. At Sun City, once the action gets going he's as cool as the much mentioned cucumber. He could be sitting at a seaside table at Biarritz looking out over the Mediterranean.

"There's a funny conclusion to the story," he announces, speaking so that Ashraf can also hear. "Three days later, by complete coincidence, who should I stroll past in the courtyard of the Savoy? Who but the Aga Khan? The three of you had gone back home. If I'm by myself in London, the Savoy is a personal favourite. As for the Aga, I will swear there was an instant of recognition in his eyes as his suit sauntered past. Then he must have decided he was imagining things. Shame, you mustn't forget that in the final analysis he is a fellow Muslim, even if he happens to be a bloody Ismaili and a playboy to boot. There's no real satisfaction in taking advantage of a fellow Muslim. We have to stick together."

Dad smiles broadly at his idea. His smile, which you have to see to believe, curls right over the gums. His terrific love of human beings, including himself, is why you forgive him, why you don't ask who he is to complain about the decline of modern values and who he is, exactly, to claim this world of hotels, casinos, and precious stones as his own. There's no stronger believer in heredity than this writer, but I wonder how a misanthrope like myself was born to such a father. We have zero in common. I am, nonetheless, romantic enough to believe that Dad's favourite audience is his sons. He has an intimate way of speaking to us, a soft-as-a-chamois manner Indian men use among themselves.

"In the entrance to the Savoy something hit me," he says. "About the Aga, what do you say, Aga or Khan? In any event the unlucky fellow was wearing nothing but a denim sports shirt and the most dreadful pair of slacks. In the context of the Savoy, which has really held its standards up over time, the poor fellow looked completely out of place. Now, Ashraf, it looks as if you've made it into that safe already. Congratulations. Stop blowing, my boy, or you'll turn the contents into ash. You're a real firebug."

Dad's most effective camouflage in Sun City can't be detected in a photograph. I mean an air of insignificance into which has been combed an ample dose of obsequiousness, the vice of colonial societies. This is someone who keeps his head down when answering questions, someone who avoids presuming on the questioner, someone who would scarcely think to look a European in the eye. A nicely waxed Fu Manchu moustache, visible in the snapshot, makes a lovely final touch.

Were you to meet this man, beloved script writers, everything in his sing-song voice and deferential manner would announce that here is a soul created to be a perfect minion. You'd struggle not to point him to your luggage. Were you a certain captain from Brixton Murder and Robbery and an assisting constable from the Flying Squad and you happened on this man and a team of junior waiters twenty minutes after the famous Sun City heist, you wouldn't give a second thought to his party of frightened employees. There are sirens everywhere, cops everywhere. International guests fly down the rural roads in their rented Jaguars. Gunshots resound in the nearby township and wood smoke hangs in the broken red hills above the shoulder of the highway. There are more important things to attend to than this broken-down man.

The four waiters, after all, come up to the assisting constable's shoulder. The trolley they trundle along the side of the hotel and into the kitchen is loaded with canteens, covered pots, and high stacks of blue and white porcelain dishes. Having spent some time working in restaurants myself, I can state that the principal drama of a waiter's existence is creating, balancing, and shepherding into the sink the tallest conceivable towers of crockery. I am careful not to upset it in the road. The trolley in question looks as innocent as the lamb in the left-over bowl of lamb-and-brinjals curry which Zacharia, that rare man who is willing to trust his instincts, offers to the captain.

"Please, sir, allow us to provide you with a modicum of lunch to propel you on the hunt. It's very mild, sir, an extremely mild dish suitable for a European palate. Can I say that it's lucky for us someone reliable is there to track down these fiends? Deal with them with an iron hand, pulverise them, when you apprehend the culprits. For the sake of the innocents." Zacharia studies the constable to see if he's laying it on too thick. He decides not, and goes on, "Amongst my own people there is a growing appreciation of the measures incumbent on the government, so as to forestall the chaos and banditry we observe in the rest of Africa."

"The rest of Africa", by the way, is a phrase that solves every intellectual problem of Europeans on the continent, an informal snatch of hymnody sung by choirs of the Rhodesians, the Portuguese in Mozambique, the Belgians in the Congo. In order to avoid our becoming like the rest of Africa, anything is permitted. Everything is encouraged to prevent us becoming a country where anything could happen. Those four simple words make the captain look with added warmth on the party of waiters.

"Nice boys you have. Your sons?"

"They're like sons to me. I feel I am wrestling with the entire moral atmosphere of this country to keep them on the straight and narrow. Please, shake hands. This is Vijay, my first son, then Billy, and finally Gideon whom I adopted, obviously. I tell them, whoever takes over the country, one of you will have the right name to prosper and lend a hand to your brothers. Sir, one second, one question, are you quite sure I can't interest you in a plate of this exceptional lamb?"

"We're in a hurry."

The captain, an inveterate fan of Holmes and Watson, finds it difficult to be irritable with the circuitous waiter. Seeing these humble Indians, as ridiculous as can be with their awkward smiles and neatly pressed turbans, renders him proud, once again, to be a Christian and a European. The nodulated green eyes of the young men, examining him in unison, I see, make him curious nonetheless.

"You fellows dead sure you didn't spot anything out of the ordinary? Rack your brains. It could be something that seemed insignificant. As a professional it's my job to make sense out of trivial details."

My father speaks for all of us, making sure we don't interrupt. "Come to think of it, there were two black chaps we passed. They were going full tilt in the direction of town. One must have been in his sixties. The other was busy wheeling a suitcase on the ground despite the thrills and spills. I assumed he was on his way to the Putco bus." Zacharia points his walking stick in the direction of the Pretoria to Rustenburg highway. Standing there are government buses with ramshackle roof racks. "They looked respectable, not like ruffians."

"Let me be the judge of that," the captain replies, speaking stiffly. "Now good luck with your boys. Set a good example, pull up your socks, and afterwards nothing will take them off the right path."

Unlike Ashraf, my father aspires to a certain innocence on the subject of women. The great object of his life, apart from his record collection, is, was, and will forever be my mother. It's an odd thing to have to say about one's parents, that they are obsessed in positive and negative ways with each other. They're idiotic about each other. Shouldn't they have cooled off in the past twenty-nine years? Do we have to hose them down, spiritually speaking? My mother's image of my father is his most precious possession.

It may be music that did it. I imagine all those Motown songs, Smokey Robinson, the Marvelettes, the Supremes, the Commodores, infected my father with a distinctly non-Muslim, non-Indian, form of sentimentality about his mate. He can't bear that she hears a whisper of how he makes his money besides the factory. His cover story, where Mum is concerned, is that he trades with his brother Farouk in India and garners his profits on a portfolio of overseas investments.

"Please, on your mother's life, don't breathe a word of this to her. It's for her sake alone I ask you," he tells me on the way home from Sun City in that rambling old Datsun. We're in the front seat. Sugarboy dozes on the bench behind us. "You and your mother are very much the same type of bird, Firoze, both thinkers and dreamers. Let me tell you again that Sameera is a real treasure. What an incredible hullabaloo she makes about Valentine's Day, Mother's Day, Father's Day, our birthdays!" He looks into the back seat where there are two small boxes of jewellery safe under a blanket. "Your mother is the glue that holds us together as a family. She's the tops, as the Americans say. The amazing thing, for me, is that Sameera is completely untouched and unaffected by all the negative forces in the universe. She could be living in a completely different universe and it wouldn't affect her a bit."

"She doesn't seem to notice anything."

"She merely screens it all out, in order to think," he replies. "When I met her, you understand, she couldn't set a foot out of the house without a chaper-one. The Peers were a wealthy family, but she travelled the world through the medium of her books. That was her favourite saying. Now, Firoze, my boy, if she knew one iota of how the business operates, one jot of what you now have the privilege of knowing, the knowledge would kill her on the spot."

"Maybe you're underestimating her, Dad."

"She's not a lady I can ever underestimate." He changes the topic. "I hope your brother is doing okay in the restaurant. The moment it's safe we must call him and remind him that he has all our best wishes. He put a lot of himself into this operation."

At the next red light my father unwinds his turban. He does the same for me, and then he leans into the back and does it for Sugarboy while he drives. Dad's exposed forehead, unstained by walnut oil, is many degrees lighter than the rest of his face. To clean us off takes half an hour of scrubbing. We wash under an outdoor tap. The turbans, tunics, dispenser of walnut oil, are returned to the trunk in the Fordsburg garage where they reside, along with the other paraphernalia of my father's art. It's not surprising, on a pre-emptive note, that Halloween has been Dad's favourite holiday since we emigrated. The logic struck him at once.

"Murder means one less witness, Firoze, one less witness to muck things up," he continues as we pack things into the trunk, interjecting one of his beloved lessons into the conversation, "but it's not my cup of tea. We could have dispatched those policemen at Sun City but what was the point in it? Two more bodies and no one is better off. However, to keep your mother in her cocoon, and I am not naming names . . . I am prepared to take the ultimate step."

He lets his eyes, which have never seemed so dark to me, wander in the direction of the grounds of our house.

"So now that I have taken you into my confidence where business is concerned, don't disappoint me. As for that brother of yours, now that I think about it, I pray he is not ruining the whole enterprise as we speak. A million years of evolution and we created a man in his twenties who thinks exactly like a donkey."

Those million years of evolution, a catchphrase of Dad's, were the backdrop against which he contrasted every inglorious act of humanity. He's a crank about Darwin. A million years of evolution . . . and we have dunces like his one son. We have the Nationalist Party cabinet. We have the tablighis, famine in Ethiopia, the ruin of the traditional family, and Disneyland. My father had no discernible politics, only a series of reflexes and prejudices, but, as with many Indian men of his generation, he called (and calls) himself as a socialist. Yes, he's a Robin Hood socialist, at least in theory, but as regards Darwin his faith is pure. Dad should have been living in the nineteenth century when it was a crusade to claim monkeys up and down your family tree. As someone who shared his adolescent bedroom with a monkey, as someone who really knows what it means to live with a throwback, I've never shared my father's abstract love of the evolutionary principle.

In a book modelled after *Goldfinger* there may be less space than one wishes to devote to the exploration of a good marriage as an act of mutual misunderstanding, but a short essay will perhaps be enjoyed.

My mother was born under Aries, the ram, which stands for energy, enterprise, elusiveness, and disruption. The Arian, prone to headaches and sunstroke, is a passionate but fastidious lover, liable to sudden reversals of affection but also a lifelong bonder in marriage. Mi madre is a real romantic. It's like having a spiritual sweet tooth. She's the principal adorer in the cult of her husband although she has no clear idea what he does for a living. (Mum has her suspicions but she's flat wrong.)

It bothers me that my mother is undiscriminating and sentimental. She falls for everything from syrupy movies to Bollywood and Hollywood gossip to Valentine's Day. None of it is traditionally Indian, or Muslim. It lacks the gloss of immemorial time. Plus it's stoked by a commercial machine that wants us to buy cards, candy, and fancy dinners, spiritual fast food. Yet it's addictive. Like my mother I believe in every word, story, red sheets and heart-shaped beds and chocolate boxes, and every snatch of sappy melody – Barry Manilow, Al Green, Bing Crosby, Lata Mangeshkar.

An Arian like my mother cannot occupy a middle ground between opinions or people. Loving straightforwardness, the Arian compartmentalises areas of her life that contradict each other, and therefore cultivates tremendous powers of denial. Where criminals are concerned, clusters of Arians are to be found amongst cat burglars, con men, and getaway drivers, anyone who benefits from one hand not knowing what the other hand is up to.

My father, on the other hand, is a Libran to his Vulcan ears. Libra I see as the green-eyed sign of the zodiac. Librans are confident and good looking, relaxed, charming, and worshippers of the fine arts, in particular music. The absence of moods gives a Libran a seasonless, Mediterranean quality. They hardly age, they hardly develop as time goes by, being fully formed by the age of eighteen. Librans don't see the subterranean dimensions of existence, resembling Arians in this but for the very different reason that their natures are located on the surface.

The Libran sentimentalist sees his profession from the point of view of the artist. A Libran makes a good safe cracker, an actor, a mimic. The negative traits of a Libran are frivolity, flirtatiousness, snakishness, and an unavoidable shallowness that comes with his remarkable receptivity to moment-by-moment impressions.

Nine-tenths of a Libran is on the surface while nine-tenths of an Arian is devoted to keeping a lid on things. It's no surprise that my parents are madly in love with each other almost two decades after getting hitched. They have almost no idea of how the other person's mind works. The unsigned Valentine's Day cards my mother insists on exchanging, the pink cushions and bed sheets, the crimson department store underwear she stores throughout the year underneath her stockings, all these things are treated by my father as witticisms and by mother as religion, yet they never discover each other's point of view. It's better that way. But accidents are the great enemy of useful ignorance. Accidents, I believe, serve the cosmic function of obliterating every form of human permanence; and marriage is the basic form of permanence.

One evening after the Sun City caper I go in to talk to my mother and find her weeping behind her pentagonal black spectacles. Her eyes are clouded like two panes of green bottle glass. As a fifteen-year-old boy I'm proud she cries in front of me. To my shame, on the other hand, Mum's very slightly whiskered at the corners of her mouth. I see that her long archer's mouth, bent by sorrow, is not unlike a Boswell and Wilkie clown. It's this awkward quality about her, her being in a state of pain and embarrassment, which humanises Mum for me and Ashraf and even for my father. It's a major reason, I believe, my father loves her so devoutly.

"I weep when I think of your brother slaving away in a restaurant in Sun City of all places," she says. "It's just not safe. Look at the recent spate of robberies up there, terrible crimes. And for another thing, what prospects does the boy have? He's absolutely unteachable except when it's tricks and turns. Does he know a thing about Aquinas? Does he have an inkling of Schopenhauer instead of those ludicrous American television programs they send over here to devastate our children's brains? I ask you, who's this Kojak? Whereas you're so easy, Firoze, it distresses me. You should ask for more, my darling. Ask for the earth. A book, a set of encyclopaedias, and you're satisfied. Last year, if you remember, I got you a subscription to *The Unexplained* and you were happy for months. Well, I have a surprise for you. Your father's big friend Bobby, at Mutual Imports, promises he can get you a Redstone computer from Taiwan. You know, the famous IBM clone. He says as soon as it becomes available. I want you to understand computers. I want you to be a programmer, if not an actual rocket scientist. It's a technological age, after all."

"Mum, I dream of owning a computer. Especially a Redstone."

She smiles. "Well, your father claims to have come into a pot of money. Not that he isn't a big talker like his brother, but this time I checked in the Nedbank account, and there's a small fortune in there. If some of it was spent on your education, it wouldn't be a total waste."

"We could shoplift the computer," I suggest.

She's offended. "Now who do you think you're talking to? Your mother. Please, Firoze, try to respect my dignity for once. None of the other men in the family do, to say nothing of religion as a whole. Be the exception."

Redstones belong to the realm of fabulous foreign commodities, like Maseratis and Dom Perignon. Assembled in Taiwan, counterfeits of the IBM originals, they are carted through Johannesburg customs by those many South Africans whose natural love of the phoney, in my experience, is equalled only by the men of the old Confederacy. Due to unforeseen circumstances the Redstone I am promised never does turn up, but I have more important fish to fry.

I want to say something about my mother's problems; and what man so dead to life that he doesn't want to discuss his mother? Mum's main problem, in my view, is she wants to reason her way out of her feelings of shame. She doesn't want to feel bad about stealing. This is the rare evening, with my brother two hundred kilometres away, when my philosophical mother prefers me. My mother loves me and me alone! For my leathery heart it's a precious moment. I hang upon her every word.

"Look at your father, so gentle with bird, beast, and bee," she goes on. "Where in heaven's name did Ashraf get his love of death and destruction from? Is television to blame?" She holds up a milk-crate radio from Ackermans which is missing the antenna. "Have a look at the quality of the merchandise, absolutely shoddy. The world is a wicked place, increasingly so, and even Ackermans is going to the dogs. Tomorrow I will try and exchange these things without a receipt." Often Mum simply brings items to the return desk without ever taking them out of the store and swaps them for something else, a transaction that seemed almost legal in spirit. The idea cheers her up. "Come help me tomorrow. Skip those unhealthy maths lessons with that lady. You can take the day off school and who knows? It may hasten the arrival of that Redstone." My mother, if I haven't pointed it out, possesses only the naive variety of cunning. "Ah, Firoze, do you ever think I'm setting you a bad example?"

I ask, "Wouldn't it be simpler to buy what we want?"

"We aren't millionaires. Besides, it's a sin to spend money on frivolous stuff. You must distinguish between essentials and frivolities. Furthermore," she recovers and smiles ever so sweetly, a philosopher's habit when she feels she's being unusually ingenious, "you think about it wrong. From a certain point of view I am only a bargain-basement shopper. It's just that my idea of a bargain is a price of zero. But for heaven's sake, don't quote me on the subject to your father. It will only confirm his ridiculous prejudices about women. Not that he'd believe you."

The distinction between essentials and frivolities is subject to Mum's manipulation. She alters her categories instead of her principles. Ribena, a penny polony, Eet-Sum-Mor shortbreads, Cobra white wax floor polish, Reader's Digest *Condensed Classics*, and hairdryers fall under the heading of essentials. They can be purchased with legitimate money from E.B. Moosa & Co. round the corner from the ranch.

On the other hand, Lucky Packets, Eid-time fireworks, Simba chips, *Boxing News* from London, and Ashraf's comic books, from *Jughead Jones* to *Justice League of America*, count as frivolities according to my mother. They need to be stolen. Or else we buy them with counterfeit ten- and twenty-rand notes, which Ashraf produces on Farouk's old engraving machine in the basement when he comes back from Sun City on the weekend. Ashraf's working on my father's authority, but Mum has no idea of where the money comes from. Life among the Dawoods and Peers has as many apartments and compartments, mental and otherwise, as an ocean liner.

For six months the great bulk of the takings from the Sun City casino are concealed in the cold compartment of a Delfield refrigerator in the room-service kitchen. It's difficult for my brother to safeguard it over such a long period. Ashraf is a typical thief in being so hedonistic and impulsive, qualities which militate against rational calculation. Whereas my father is patient, perhaps because the pleasures he takes in his craft are not of the wine, women, and song variety. Dad takes a sort of chess player's pleasure in contemplating a scheme. He's willing to let an age go by before he so much as examines the loot. So eleven nylon stockings, bulging with cash, watches, bangles, crosses, and necklaces, as if they were eleven Lucky Packets, lie among ice chips from June to December, inside cartons of Clifton orangeade, Velveeta, and bricks of Royal Brand instant jelly powder.

Whatever good you can say about a bird in the hand, it is the object of much anxiety, whereas two birds in the bush, paradoxically, are something you can continue to hope for. Ashraf keeps an eye on the haul while he is supposedly training upstairs in the main kitchen as an assistant pastry chef. For those who keep count of colour barriers, I note that my brother is the very first assistant pastry chef of Asian origins in South African history. He's kind of a Rosa Parks figure amongst mousses, milk tarts, chocolate custards, and flans. But he's nothing to be proud of. His flans are a big flop. In general he's a failure at hotel school and almost gets fired before we have the opportunity to move the loot.

One thing my brother doesn't understand at the age of twenty-four is that cooking a meal, like opening a safe or composing a memoir, is an art of details. Ninety-nine out of a hundred details have to be right. I grant that he's in a difficult position at Sun City, and that he improves later in life. It can't help that he's often having to rush downstairs to prevent a cook unbundling the wrong tube of Velveeta.

I'm lonely in Fordsburg and take the Indian bus up to Sun City to see my brother in the middle of the week. It's the strangest and most thrilling twenty-four hours of my life to date. Ashraf takes me into the kitchen and shows off his leather butcher's apron that has to be tied across the shoulder. Working as a cook, Ashraf has bulked up. There's no danger of people spotting we're twins. My brother doesn't look as if he's from the same ethnic group as me, with his trough-green eyes and dimpled chin. He pats his enormous hands on the apron in front of the oven, a Sweeney Todd under the thick brown leather. We go down to the pantry late at night, and run our hands through the coins and necklaces in the freezer compartment. Then Ashraf escorts me to the roulette wheel where in twenty minutes he blows his month's earnings. It doesn't seem to trouble him at all. All the staff lose their wages at the tables. It's a reverse perk of the gaming industry.

My brother, being a Dawood and half a Peer, has some classiness rattling around like a pebble in his tin-can soul. He shows it, strangely enough, with ladies of the night who form a large proportion of the female population at Sun City. Sun City is where South Africans, in particular white Johannesburgers, come to relax from Calvinism.

After roulette we find ourselves in a hotel room with Ashraf's new best friends in the world. Around them, Rukaya and Simone, he's a model of decorum. They're fish-brained courtesans, and sit there rolled over on the bed watching recorded soap operas as Ashraf rubs lotion into their backs, first Rukaya and then the younger one, Simone. They drink sparkling white wine without conviction, alternating with Sprite. Now and again the hotel telephone rings, and one of them goes off on a job. First Simone goes, and then they're both gone. Rukaya returns after twenty or thirty minutes.

"Honey, can I get you anything?"

"I'm fine," I say.

She persists. "Can I rub your back? I'm good at it. I know all the pressure points."

I agree, and lie there on the bed with my shirt off as Rukaya and Simone take turns sitting on my back and chatting. They rub lotion into my shoulders and pound my lower back. I twist my head around to look, and I can't say they're beautiful although my brother treats them as if they're society ladies. Rukaya is a drained redhead, cushiony and dyed to the roots of her horsey hair, a coloured woman and a Capetonian to go by the up and down pitches in her voice. When it comes to money she's a grasper, hoarding five-, ten-, and twenty-cent coins in a drawer. She checks under both of the beds in case money has fallen there, and she removes all a client's change when she has a chance.

Rukaya is the first woman I know who truly sashays. She's brought motion to an art form. To watch Rukaya lazily pass down a hotel staircase, her double-barrelled hindquarters trailing behind and from side to side in pendulous syncopation, is, as my brother remarks, to see something akin to human sculpture.

Ashraf says that Rukaya is always together with Simone. Simone is young enough to be her friend's daughter, bronze-skinned, a slender teenager, a manic swearer in four or five different languages, also from the Cape originally, but with a distinctly sinister twist to her small bud of a mouth. Simone flavours this last organ with the sharpest ingredients available, sucking lemons between her puckered lips as if in need of vitamins, as well as menthol cigarettes, Chappies bubblegum that carry questions inside the wrappers, yellow tabs of Chiclets chewing gum, Sparletta, and twenty-cent cigars from which a confetti of friable brown leaves descends onto her tongue.

The closets and bins are full of Simone's wrappers. Cigars, cigarettes, chewing gum, cold drinks, and her other necessities arrive in a box at the hotel door, every second or third afternoon, with my brother as their blushing bearer. It's room service as Ashraf understands it. In the afternoons, as I gather from Rukaya, my brother sheds his clothes at the door and stalks into bed with whichever is willing to have him. He doesn't demand her favours. He doesn't try to enter her. He just likes the contact, or so Rukaya informs me.

"Firoze, give me a chance with the girls."

They roll onto him. Ashraf's their benefactor. He collects their debts from other members of the staff, remembers their birthdays, brings them his failed pastries, escorts them downstairs to Milky Lane, Skyline 55 in the Skyline Hotel, and Café Zurich as far away as Jo'burg, tapes his records for them on aluminium cassettes, drives them in the hotel bus to the outpatients' clinic of Baragwanath Hospital for fortnightly penicillin shots . . . listens to their myriad complaints . . . inspects them for lice . . . and for what exactly? What's he getting out of it? From what I can tell Ashraf isn't romancing either of these women, although once in a bluish moon he allows wild horses to drag him into a heavily perfumed bed.

What's he really getting out of it? I think basically their big advantage over other people is that they don't despise him. For a change he's the cleverest fellow in the room. Our family, Mum and Dad at least, can be rough on my brother, I know, because of his lack of brains, whereas there's something tolerant about Rukaya and Simone, and even about the staff in the hotel kitchen, that he hasn't found before. Liking to look down on one's friends is a modern – specifically an American – vice. Contempt is something Ashraf excessively fears, not seeing as I do that to hold someone in contempt is also to free him from your influence.

It's six in the morning. Out of the eighth floor window the fleets operated by Sun City become active under a night-blue sky. Buses, trucks, vans, Mercedes taxis, scooters burst into life in that enormous palace of phoney fortune and misfortune. Ashraf waits until we're alone for a minute. Rukaya is fiddling with her electric toothbrush in the bathroom and Simone is off on a job. Which one, he wants to know, is more my type? There's a salacious expression on his enlarged lips that brings Mick Jagger to mind. He has an important question. Which one reminds me more of Elena?

I say the obvious, of course. By the time Simone returns in lingerie and slippers to the arms of my disrobed brother Rukaya and I lie in a heap in the bed by the wall. Rukaya's as quiet as I am in bed, quiet as a church mouse although strain shows on her orange-shaded face, and soon we hear Simone's screams in the next bed. She's louder than Elena. If I could see the four of us from above, we'd look like two long iron frame beds each topped with a tortoise shell that bends and heaves and stretches. It's worthy of Botticelli. There's a long minute when Rukaya is finished with me and I lie contented in her arms listening to the doleful music of my brother in the adjoining bed. Later on he turns on a cop show while the ladies doze off, and we watch together in happy silence. We smoke red-tipped Benson and Hedges and swig Johnny Walker Red from a graduated medicine cup. It's a moment when this Hasselhoff brother and I could almost be friends.

For all his machismo, or perhaps because of it, Ashraf is terrified of winding up in prison for the Sun City job all the time he's pretending to be a cook. People call No. 4 prison in Johannesburg the Fort. We know the names of the procedures the Security Branch uses behind its pentagonal walls against reluctant inmates – the telephone, the switchboard, the diving bell, the bicycle chain. Yet Ashraf is far more frightened by the rumours about men and boys. In my experience fear is the straightest path between you and the fearful thing. In accordance with this principle Brixton Murder and Robbery Squad pick Ashraf up for questioning and sequester him in the Fort.

There's no real reason for Brixton to take my brother into custody beyond the enduring South African belief that you have got to squeeze oranges to make orange juice. The family is traumatised, particularly my mother, who never seriously contemplates the possibility of being sent to jail for her own misdemeanours. Dad's overseas in India, consulting Ten Percent on the mechanics of some deal, so Mum and I go alone to the Fort the moment we get the news. I follow my mother through the visitors' entrance and I'm more worried about her than about Ashraf. Mum's in bad shape in her white weeds, with white, peeling and perpetually murmuring lips. For the duration of my brother's imprisonment in the Fort grief makes her face a tombstone. I've never seen her so bad.

71

As for me, I'm rather engaged by the experience. The long, low hallways, the African men who loom up behind each new set of bars, the stink of the wood-handled buckets, are of considerable interest to me, perhaps because I am subconsciously studying to be a political prisoner in the United States. We don't even have a family lawyer to go with us, O.R. Tambo having long since departed the country for London. My uncles, especially on my mother's side, believe that non-movement lawyers can't be trusted. Dad disagrees, arguing that it's better to be at the mercy of one lawyer than at the mercy of all lawyers.

It's a shock to see my brother. Ashraf's big, donkey-brown face is puffed up from the beating. He has trouble seeing out of his clouded green eyes because, as we later discover, the one cornea is detached. There are starchy welts on his shoulders and back which he lets me finger. There's an older Indian man in there with my brother who lies on his bed without stirring. Is it a good sign that he's a fellow Indian or is it a bad sign? Is it an act of respect on the part of Brixton Murder and Robbery? When the other inmate does sit up later I scan his dark brown face for any sign of possessiveness where Ashraf is concerned but I can't say that I find it. Mum's weeping. Ashraf makes fun of his mother for her tears. It's a good sign, I suppose, that my brother has a sense of humour. He never had much of a sense of humour before. Then I too burst into tears as if something has been broken that can never be repaired.

Ashraf is released after spending the week on the inside. He's a hero after his cornea is restitched by the prison surgeon. The day he comes out is a Monday and, coincidentally, Mother's Day. Of course, every day, in our culture, is Mother's Day. It's a double celebration. My mother, with her usual energy for ceremonials, has our house festooned with streamers and silver balloons, a glazed fruit cake in the refrigerator, and a strung chicken in the roaster, packed with cumin, sage, rosemary, and breadcrumbs, which Ashraf devours to the very joint. Putting more fat on his bones is regarded as essential to recovery.

Somehow my mother's angry at me throughout the afternoon. She sulks, I think, because I didn't go to prison instead of my brother but, in her defence, she would have been mad at Ashraf if the situation were reversed. She's angry at the university, which made her take a day of unpaid leave. I don't know what to tell her to cheer her up. Ashraf, on the other hand, possesses exactly the right sentimental touch. He brings her a selection of Swarovski crystal from Ackermans that she's known to admire – a miniature heart on a cut-glass pedestal, a lean-legged greyhound, an hourglass. I'm back where I started with my mother. I'll never be certain of her affections. How can anyone have a philosopher as a mother?

To my mother's relief Brixton Murder and Robbery soon finds a gang of eleven black men from Gillits, one per stocking, to charge with the Sun City job. The Brixton squad is notorious for their efficiency, which in South African terms means their ability to find an African suspect to pay for any particular crime. There are times when they apprehend more suspects than they have dockets open. Then they hold people until an appropriate charge comes up. In a triumph of justice the Gillits mob are tried, framed by the barristers, convicted, and imprisoned in Pretoria Central. It would be fair to ask, does their punishment trouble my conscience? In the absence of true justice, in my book, you do justice to you and yours. There's no cause to feel guilt about the Gillits gang because obviously there's no such thing as a completely innocent South African.

No, the saddest fact about the Sun City job is the aftermath. Ashraf doesn't get his cool back for a while. He finds being in the hotel unnerving. He goes back to his position as an assistant pastry chef, but he sneaks off to the casino after hours with Simone and Rukaya. Moody as he is, he's doubly susceptible to the lure of lucky numbers. In his cook's uniform he plays baccarat, five-card stud, and the slots, barters one of a pair of diamond earrings . . . then a platinum cigarette case . . . here a silver bracelet . . . there a parcel of tiny rubies. He's meant to be bringing this stuff out to Fordsburg, little by little. Instead, with a nice feeling for poetic outcomes, he takes it right back on to the gaming floor. Around Sun City, there are any number of informal pawnbrokers who dissolve gold and precious stones into a stream of gambling chips.

It's not until one of them who happens to know the family whispers something in the ear of my father that we have an inkling of what's happening in the freezer compartments of Bophuthatswana. By then the debt Ashraf's run up is equal in value to anything remaining in the storage room. He's squandered hundreds of thousands of rands at the gambling tables and perhaps ten times as much in the worth of the items of jewellery traded away. He's a thick-headed donkey. Ashraf's behaviour is a blow to my father more than anyone, not only because the effects of a beautiful plan had been erased.

Like any other family in this line of work we believe that wiping out an errant blood relation is the sincerest proof of familial devotion, but we don't get around to it with the frequency of *The Godfather*. That's just in the movies. Instead, to calm down after he finds out about Ashraf, Dad locks himself in his room for an entire weekend with only his piles of Marvin Gaye, Al Green, and Commodore records for company. He calls his brother Farouk, now in Bombay, and complains to him at length. He doesn't even come out on Saturday evening. Mum hardly notices his behaviour because her rose-tinted glasses cover her ears as well as her eyes. Ashraf needs the left-over stitches taken out of his eye so I escort my brother to the outpatients' clinic at Baragwanath and stay with him as a big-boned nurse fishes them out with needle and thread. I wince at every motion but my brother, who doesn't know the meaning of shame, couldn't be happier. His large inflamed green eye scarcely blinks as he tries to gross me out.

ـل

Chapter Four

By this time, as I remember, our entire existences were pursued behind
walls. Libraries, trains, dams, municipal buildings, shops and restaurants
were all segregated in South Africa. Europeans, Lebanese, certain Indians did
what foreigners of means always do in uncertain times in Africa – shield their
lives from birth to death behind walls. To be poor in Africa was unthinkable
because it meant to be without walls.

Within the walls, life was sweet. Property was cheap and we maintained
vast lands. I dream about our Fordsburg house from my prison bedroom. It
was palatial, from the paved yard surrounded by a gate and brown brick walls
to the disused stables, servants' quarters at the back which smelled curiously of
mint leaves after rain, the avocado tree in its untidy condition, the mermaid's
fountain, the row of truck tyres which served as the swings, the chalked and
rechalked outline of a badminton court, and, just outside the gate, a cricket
pitch redolent of creosote.

The government had been trying for years to evict all the Indian families
from Fordsburg in order to turn it into a white suburb, but some of the owners, including our own family, had tied up the evictions in court for years
and years. We saw the cost of defeat from our bedroom window. Whenever
someone lost a case against the municipality, another home was demolished
by wrecking ball. On either side of our place were these destroyed properties.
Here and there, alternating with the barren lots, were still vibrant houses like
our own. With its multiple gaps the street looked like a boxer's mouth. The
cricket pitch had been drawn on the foundations of a demolition job. It was

75

my brother's haunt. Behind the wicket Ashraf wrestled with our cousins after jumaa namaaz and refused to accept a surrender.

Long into his twenties my brother spent much of his time tinkering. He was a long-time lover of gadgets, pinball machines, potions, crosswords, puzzles, transistors. In the Fordsburg house Ashraf whiled away many a Michaelmas break repairing the mechanism of a Wurlitzer 1015, an American-made jukebox that was his prize possession. During school holidays he was often to be found lying on his back in the servants' quarters, smoking a vertical Benson & Hedges as he peered up into the nests of blue and red cords that sagged beneath the motor.

He kept going at the jukebox until it was fixed or reduced to a heap of components. Ashraf adjusted, soldered, rewired, polished, and replaced items until the thing got going and a long-ago melody of Dolly Dube or Louis Armstrong floated out of its raised hood. My brother is a natural tinkerer. He narrows the world down to something tiny and can't see beyond it. Even today Ashraf can't cup an object in his hand without thinking about its insides. It's the one time he uses his imagination.

The Fordsburg house was the fruit of many forgotten hands. Who nailed up the swing? By whom was the bougainvillea planted? And who was responsible for the Valiant mounted on bricks behind the garage with its rusted engine block seated amid a snakepit of rubber hose? Who lodged in the avocado tree the shoebox in which generations of Class One silkworms nested?

Parked inside the gate, on a red-sand section of the yard, were four family vans and Farouk's disused 1950s blue Mercedes 190 SL (the first model year when muscular fins and Detroit-style radiator grilles captivated the honest Düsseldorfers). Elsewhere the acre of ground was soft and grassy. It was dappled by the bending tops of the avocado and other trees, displaying shifting bands of light and dark that impressed my senses.

A doctor uncle with microbiological leanings showed me how to use my uncle's old Zeiss microscope as well as how to mount and fix a slide. A supply of toothpicks, a tube of Canada balsam, and a bottle of distilled water let me play at being a natural historian. Ashraf, in this one instance, was content to be his brother's shadow, as we sloshed through the yard in raincoats and black rubber wellingtons, carting tadpoles in a milk bottle. We were already too old to be doing this, in our twenties, too old to be natural historians, but it was a respite. It was, in fact, the last sweet summer of our lives and the last summer in which we were a real family.

Rain drove me and my brother outdoors, and the white afternoon light that prevailed over Johannesburg in its wake. Rainstorms encouraged the fauna and flora to flourish under an unending iron sky. There were rambling summer flies, mynah birds, army ants, lizards, millipedes to investigate. So great a quantity of life was preserved within the compound.

The place housed an indeterminate number of cousins, aunts, grandmothers, and assorted children. The diversity of their origins testified to a stone age method of dividing up human beings. About particular youngsters, no one could say whether or not they were staying at the main house. A house is the molecule of a civilisation, so let me hazard a theory. The cousinly vibe is a clue to the redirection of these colossal Muslim energies into underworld endeavours. It's not acceptable among Muslims to compete with someone to whom a sense of familial familiarity attaches. We like to keep our adversaries at a distance.

The dinner table was a precise rectangular map of our small seventeenth-century society – my father and mother, their surviving parents, other uncles and aunts, nieces and nephews, some of Farouk's illegitimate children, Ashraf and myself, lesser sons and daughters. My brother, who'd recovered his half a wit, was in a swinish mood, which wasn't helped by his being in the doghouse over Sun City. At the far end of the table, with a mixture of sheepishness and cow-eyed good humour, sat the African retinue of the Dawoods and Peers, among them a miraculously preserved Sugarboy in his mortician's coat. The only time Mum went anywhere without Sugarboy at her side was when she went shopping.

Platters of scallion omelettes, hot milk running with almonds, a selection of pickles in a palette dish, copious quantities of Fanta and Sparletta, and naan from Moosa's bread shop were distributed along the table. I remember the tableau with pearl-handled clarity. A bowl of kowseh, regarded as a delicacy of the house, was brought through the serving window from the kitchen, a raft of steaming yellow Burmese noodles afloat in the soup. It was passed from the head of the table gradually downwards until, still slowly steaming and giving off the chalky yellow odour of saffron, it arrived at the far end where the Africans waited.

Throughout this operation Mum watched the moving bowl and the diners.

She stood arms akimbo. Whatever her virtues, and they are many, my mother is the same sort of cook as me – humourless, devoid of joy, and anxious until people start in on their plates.

She declared, "Mirza, since you're here on time for a change, say bismillah and tell everyone to begin."

Dad nodded, raised his sparse, bone-sprung eyebrows in my direction, and recited a word of blessing. "Let's eat. Sameera demands it. We have a lot to celebrate. Not only am I on time for a change but, even if my wife has forgotten, today is the date of our twenty-ninth anniversary. You forgot, didn't you, Sameera?"

"Nonsense."

Dad shook his head. Mum changed her story.

"Okay, I did. I can't believe myself. It's never happened before. What did you bring me? Where are my presents?"

"They're still coming," Dad returned cheerfully. "It's not your fault, Sameera. It's been a long time. As far as Ashraf and Firoze are concerned, it's been their entire lives and for me, it certainly feels like a lifetime. More than a lifetime, as our Hindu brothers and sisters say. Look, Sameera, I can see by your look of disappointment that you only want to hear about your presents. They're in the post, I promise. Firoze helped to pick them out. Can you guess?"

"Books."

"A pair of shoes, Sammy," he said.

Shoes were better than books. My mother had an uncommonly brilliant expression in the jade of her eyes and Dad, with his short arms thrown over the back of the chair, displayed a sense of happy proprietorship in his wife and table. Everything was perfect except my brother which means, logically speaking, that everything stood on a tragic brink. Ashraf began talking about a Mercedes franchise. It was his dream to run one along with a McDonalds and a Nike shoe store. The only institution of higher learning he wanted to attend was Hamburger University run by McDonalds in Oak Brook, Illinois.

"Are they going to sell one to an Indian? Or do they assume we lack the sophistication? What's the situation, Dad?" Ashraf talked business because it gave him the feeling he was involved in the family's affairs. "Let's press on with it. As for McDonalds, people say it's like having a licence to print money. It's better than printing our own money. Maybe there's some character in the head office we can pay off. Business is business."

"I am keeping my eyes open. But this is South Africa. It may not be feasible," my father replied. Taking a Johannesburger's natural pleasure in moral nakedness, he continued, "In an ordinary country you might be able to pay off someone at Mercedes and acquire the franchise. Here, in South Africa, you have to pay them double what the previous fellow already paid to pay them off."

Mum said, "Mirza, please, don't joke like that in front of the children and all. You'll distract them from their studies." She still believed we were keeping up with our baccalaureate-by-mail courses. "Take into account that they're not accustomed to cynicism. They don't comprehend when you're pulling my leg."

"No, I am really not joking."

"Yes, he is."

Mum wasn't the first woman who, in a fit of reasonableness, chose to address her sons rather than her husband. "Your father, Firoze and Ashraf, is a real kidder, a typical comedian. Don't listen to a word he says. Ashraf, my dear, this applies to you particularly because your mind is susceptible to immoral suggestions."

"But I am still not joking."

Aries is the sign of those who approach life with the simplest of tools – for philosophy, a pencil; for protection, a knife; for love, a lively imagination; for thieving, a staple gun and staple remover. With the staple-remover you can open any shopping bag and with the stapler you can make it seem as if it had never been opened. The staple remover should be the sign of Aries.

On the other hand Arians are not noted for their close engagement with reality. They see things through rose-tinted spectacles and their hearing is not so grand either. My mother, a classic Arian, is deaf to the rapid knocking of fate on the changing-room door on this afternoon at Ackermans department store. She says, "Firoze, my darling, go and reason with these buffoons. See if we can pay a fine."

"They're not going to reason, Mum."

"Go see what you can do. Before your father gets here. Otherwise I'm going to die of shame. See if you can find Ashraf."

I finish stapling our Woolworths bags before I go out. There's nothing too valuable. An electric kettle, a set of ornamental teaspoons, and a small lace curtain for a bathroom window quartered in a linen box . . . these comprise our meagre takings. Maureen, the red-headed lady whom we had twice followed on her broken-legged way to denounce her, lingers there in the corridor. She's brought a guard who's knocking vigorously on the partition of the changing room. It's Maureen's revenge. I curse myself for ignoring the figure straightening and bending a crook leg as it shadowed us from department to department. I curse Maureen and her long-anticipated revenge. I curse my mother under my breath. She's taught me philosophy and my profit on it is I know how to curse. The curse words, though, all come from my brother, who prides himself on the Capetonian completeness of his descriptive powers.

The moment I open the door we're seized and transported to the manager's office. Some of the guards line the stairway and jeer and clap. The shoppers watch us morosely. They're Jo'burgers and not particularly moralistic. Maureen follows and looks on in satisfaction as a kettle, teaspoons, and curtain are heaped on a corner of the manager's desk. Her red hair shows a patch of oddly reddened scalp.

The owner of the mahogany desk, a Mr Ferreira, writes out a description of each item and gives it to us to initial. Ferreira is portly and official, with a brisk manner about him, a headmaster's manner, and the habit of sharpening his waxy nails against each other. His heavy gold cufflinks, moving with his hands, ring like a cash register. He unfurls the curtain in his hands. He slaps Ashraf when he refuses to let his pockets be searched and holds my brother's arm behind his back until Mum agrees to his terms. Then he lands one more slap on Ashraf's cheek for good measure.

"I used to be worried about schoolgirls," Ferreira announces after we sign. "Now the goods fly off my shelves into the handbags of Indian women. Madam, aren't you grateful for the special dispensation we give you to enter the store? Or are you so oppressed, so low, that you have to compound the problem by exposing your sons – whom I assume are your sons – to a devastating lesson in morality?"

"Between the two of us, Mr Ferreira, can't we work something out? Blackmail me, if you want."

"Blackmail is an ugly word. I wouldn't use it, Mrs Peer." Ferreira articulates each of his sentences at the front of his mouth. "Shall we suggest a certain sum of money? Shall we call that sum two hundred rands? We'll categorise it as a contribution to the general kitty. Oh, and Maureen here, who reported you to me, also needs a reward. Your husband, incidentally, is on the way. I took the liberty of telephoning him. He's promised to pay whatever's reasonable under the circumstances."

I don't hold the two hundred rand against Ferreira. Blackmail, in the opinion of one sympathetic to the dreary science, is the quintessential economist's crime, because it maximises utility for both customers. What I do hold against the man is contacting my father. Dad, who's entertaining a new interest in the Formula One races at Kyalami, pitches up at Ackermans in forty-five minutes. He's clad in a pinstriped green-and-white suit and wearing an ascot for a collar. So, Dad might be a crook but he knows how to behave with a modicum of dignity. Two hundred rands are duly paid to Ferreira from a wad of brown notes. Maureen is paid off. Then Dad escorts my mother arm-in-arm across the length of the store and into the doors of our Ford Cortina, as if promenading her along a ballroom floor. We follow behind them as if we belong to the retinue.

Ferreira and Maureen: 1. Dawoods and Peers: 0. We don't like being at a disadvantage. Three months pass and then a Mossberg Model 500 with ghost-ring sights pokes out of a blue Mercedes in front of Ferreira's home in Stanleyville and levels the score. I'm not sure whether it's Dad or Ashraf who dispatches Ferreira but in the grand scheme of things it doesn't make a whole lot of difference. As far as my parents are concerned the best part of their married lives is over. Indeed our family life is over. Mum knows too much about Ferreira and my father knows too much about her to believe entirely in her halo of innocence. They don't glow in each other's presence anymore. My mother used to tell Dad about her seminars and students the moment she came home but nowadays she goes straight up to the bedroom.

A good marriage, in my view, is a happy harmony of misunderstandings. Without the lubricant of misunderstanding things start to break down in our household. Mum's not a temperamental shouter. Neither of my parents are, but now she shouts at everyone up to and including my father. Dad has his head permanently in his hands.

"Where's your mother, Firoze? She was right here."

"She just went upstairs," I say. "You want me to call her?"

"No. Leave her be." He looks at me through his hands. "Maybe you and I can go out for a round of golf."

"I don't play golf," I tell him. "And frankly, neither do you. Look, if you want to talk to Mum, let me call her on the intercom."

"Please don't. If you could fetch me a blanket. I'm going to sleep on the couch. It's better for my back."

That's as much as I want to say on that topic. After the death of Ferreira my parents scarcely look one another in the eye. Their marriage has been shattered like an eggshell. I take the liberty of drawing a veil over the dissolution of their marriage. Do I have to talk about it? Does a first-person narrator forfeit his right to privacy? Can a jailhouse narrator show no inhibition, no energising capacity for reticence on a topic too painful for consideration? Does literature not come at things at an angle rather than head on? Among the many things in this narrative that may distress the reading public, then, is the fact that the author is a child of divorce . . . and I leave the whole sorry tangle there.

Events provide a way out. Mum is offered a junior lectureship at Melbourne's Monash University. Australia, of course, is the continent to which the yearnings of those South Africans with absolutely no spiritual leanings are attracted. It's seen by nervous Johannesburgers as the safest bet in the world.

Mum asks, "Would you like to come with me, bubble?"

"I can't imagine living in Australia. It seems so bland. Surely you, Mum, know that philosophy, real thinking, grows in an interesting climate?"

"I need peace and quiet to read," she says. "But maybe it's better this way. Your father needs someone to look after him. When we went to Hong Kong that once I remember he was quite bereft without you two boys."

My parents don't quite acknowledge that they're separated. By the terms of her contract Mum's at Monash eight months out of the year. When back home from Melbourne she lives out of a suitcase in the bedroom above the garage, as far removed from us, or me, as the planet Neptune. Ashraf is usually in Hillbrow with his rented women. Dad is setting up his Pakistan connections because Farouk wants him to start doing business there, arguing that the subcontinent will be the future headquarters of global crime. The four of us in our post-atomic family hardly run into each other on three occasions from one Monday to the next, not to say one January to the next.

At least I'm educating myself. I'm taking correspondence courses in metaphysics and Zen Buddhism through the University of South Africa. I try to involve my mother in conversation about Sartre, Schopenhauer, Schrödinger, or, when I'm reading through the K shelf in Johannesburg Public Library, Kant, Kleist, and Kotzenbue, but she really doesn't let herself be interested. My relationship with her deteriorates. She's hardhearted over the telephone as well as in person, living ridiculously in the cement room over the garage, and she's extremely irritable. It's painful to deal with her for any prolonged period. There's a spiteful aspect to her relations with me, I believe. Normally I'm a filial sort of person. It's the first time in my twenty-five years I recall being truly furious at one of my parents.

On reviewing these pages I see what an implausible and anachronistic character I have made of my mother. Maybe it's because of the spiritual distance between us. We're interested in the same subjects and yet Mom's perpetually aggrieved with me. She's not soft towards me. There have been times when I was clearly her favourite son, when she revealed her preference, and, being Mom, she's always going to punish me for that. Plus she's intellectually intolerant. When we discuss philosophy she criticises me for poor logic and insufficient rigour.

Imagination, according to Mom, has no part in constructing a scheme of the world. It's clear she thinks, in defiance of all her maternal instincts, that my mind is as sloppy as a pail. She doesn't to this day believe in the creative power of analogy and when I call her in Australia to try out a new comparison she doesn't give an ounce of intellectual generosity. Whereas, in my view, in my one poor joke, rigour is a form of rigor mortis. It's only on Mother's Day that my mother and I have anything like a decent conversation and that's because we're both smothered in sentiment. Then we try to talk about Dad and my brother but Mum gets angry and our conversation peters out.

My mother's not an unselfish person. She never relaxes her hold on her own point of view, intellectual or otherwise. A selfish person, I think, is as much attached to each one of her viewpoints as to any possessions. But enough whingeing. Whingeing is antithetical to stoic philosophy. I talk about my mother in the main to bring out a contrast with my tenderhearted father.

After the episode at Ackermans Dad lies low. There are rumours of a docket being issued for his arrest in Ferreira's killing. One can only intimidate so many witnesses before it's easier to intimidate a panel of judges. And Dad's intimidated by the idea of divorce. To my surprise the divorce, finalised in magistrate's court, is something he talks about constantly. Then I'm angry with Dad. He's obsessed with Mum's faults, her sins, her injustices, her kleptomaniacal streak, her influence on the children, her dyed-in-the-wool ingratitude, her potential infidelities, as if it's a wound he has perpetually to touch.

Their every argument, letter, long-distance phone call to Melbourne and East Finchley, across which my veil has been drawn, provokes a relapse. Borrowing from my mother's beloved Simone de Beauvoir I see the drama of my parents in a cosmic perspective, believing that we're painfully living out the twilight of patriarchy. Being a traditionalist I side with patriarchy in the shape of my father. And let me also say that only a crazy person puts his happiness and his monetary future at the mercy of another human being. This late in the history of misanthropy, I feel, we should know better than to rely on the humanity of others.

Dad, I, and Ashraf go to Pakistan and end up one morning looking out the sixth-floor window of the Pearl-Continental hotel. It's meant to be a family reunion in honour of which I slip into the present tense as slinkily as Tigerlily moved her limbs inside her robe. My uncle, believe it or not, is behind the trip. Ten Percent, who's been battening off his Bombay gangster pal Dawood Ibrahim, wants us to go in with him on some deal with a Pakistani brigadier but there's no word from the guy. He's meant to be in town and we have no further instructions. So we wait around for a telephone call from Farouk or from the Pakistanis.

It's my first time on the subcontinent and I'm bewildered; is this our homeland? Did our black loins spring from this patch of ground? In monsoon season the Pakistan sky is filled with transcendental cloud. I'm filled with wonder, and unsorted suspicions about my uncle. Whereas Dad's in a conversational frame of mind. You know, he still treats me like an adolescent instead of an adult in my dangerous twenties. Instead of gazing out at the endless low brown and red houses of Peshawar, its tea shops, bazaars, fort, and officers' clubs, I am supposed to appreciate the needlework of the suit my father dons for the occasion. He rubs the material of the suit between his fingers, savouring its density to the touch, a mercantile gesture he repeats often enough for me to wonder if, in some other life, he wouldn't have made a good shopkeeper.

Standing there in his underclothes he peers nearsightedly into the mirror on the door of the immense cabinet. He folds the cream cloth of his jacket in one hand while tweezing an eyebrow. Dad's so finicky about appearance, particularly after the divorce, that I see him as rather a peacock. Mirza Dawood, Suleiman Zacharia, Leo Connery Goldstone and innumerable trousers, jackets, coats, and ties are a form of spiritual plumage. I go so far as to say that my father possesses a completely superficial and yet infinitely various soul. This superficial creature sends me a various and superficial look – a geisha's look delivered across the shoulder – while Ashraf is out of the room.

"So what do you think?"

"What do I think about what? What are you asking about? What I think is that there's something fishy about Ten Percent's invitation. That's what I think." For once I am determined to unburden my mind. "For crooks, for criminal masterminds, you and Ashraf are far too trusting." I arrive at my most incendiary charge. "I'm afraid Mum's right. When it comes to Ten Percent you don't use your brains. That chap has no interest in helping out his flesh and blood. He can't imagine what it means to be an uncle, in a civilised culture."

"Firoze, you're a loaded gun today," Dad says admiringly. "I wasn't asking about my brother. I was asking what you thought about this suit."

"Okay, I misunderstood. Let me see it from the back." He turns to the side. I know what I'm supposed to say. "It seems fine. It flatters your figure."

"A good suit is never something you regret possessing. Of that I can assure you," the owner of this wonderful garment tells me. "And please, Firoze, remember this," he continues, smiling again, reverting to the middle-class Indian habit of interpolating object lessons into casual conversation, "whatever it is, even if you didn't work for it, whomever you took it from worked jolly hard, so treat your possessions with respect. I see every day that you don't respect material objects and it pains me. Unlike your brother, poor Ashraf, you're not too stubborn to learn. The ability to learn is what differentiates us from the savages." He adjusts his cuff links. "Hang up a suit in the evenings and it will take care of itself. Clothes make the man, in my opinion, is not an idle remark. This suit, incidentally, is from the Aga Khan." He sees something in my face. "Am I boring you?"

"Is that the telephone?"

I'm relieved to hear it ring. My brother may be a reduced incarnation of my father, the Hong Kong imitation, but when it comes to stating the obvious, these are two peas in the pod. They talk down, hector, preach, and babble to me. What they say makes no sense . . . who exactly were those savages? Who were we to wear suits? Who were we to take this high-handed tone? All the same, father and brother mesmerise the defendant. They take my existence hostage and my ears, and meanwhile my Stockholmed heart admires them for their strength.

The brigadier's secretary is on the line. The secretary is also a military man, and therefore peremptory. I hear him barking down the receiver at my father. The Pakistanis want to see us at once. They've noticed that Farouk hasn't arrived yet and they don't want to be scammed again. We're to meet them at Grindlay's Bank downtown in fifteen minutes but Ashraf is nowhere in the hotel. Later I find out that my brother's gone off with the bellhop to buy a set of blank passports. So I accompany Dad to his meeting with the brigadier's men. We take a rickshaw and shelter in the back from the brave roar of its motorcycle engine. The suspension is hard so that every jolt, pothole, and corner is communicated to my back. Dad stops talking about clothes and concentrates on the view. I am too terrified by the drive to be terrified by the Pakistanis.

In Peshawar there's no distinction between main streets and side streets. Canvas awnings border the roads, their ragged majesty sheltering bullocks, bicyclists, side-car riders, three-wheeled Vespas and Yamahas, pack horses, and vans. All these passers-by are swept into our wake. Even as a native Jo'burger I have never been driven so fast through such masses of humanity. The stench and its attending scents, cinnamon and wood smoke and cow-pat fires, belong to central Asia. It's ravishing on this border with Afghanistan.

My father isn't interested in the city so much. It's not that he's unimaginative. For him the Third World is a place of business. There's no mystery, no enchantment. He wouldn't dream of going backpacking in Thailand or leaving to see Angkor Wat. Harrods, the Lake District, and Orlando, Florida, are where you go to relax. In New York Filene's Basement will be a place of mystery and enchantment as will be Tiffany's and Century 21 in Bayridge, Brooklyn. Whereas Angola, Bangladesh, Colombia you visit to make money. That's why we're in Pakistan after all, not to return to our ancestral homeland, not to admire a thousand pieces of architecture. In tune with this sentiment he ever so elegantly brushes the orange dust off his suit as we thunder past Islamia College. He makes a feeble attempt to talk about Mum again but I forbid it.

"Now I have some advice for you, Dad. Talk about something else. Keep your mind on a different topic. Tell me why Ten Percent wants us to be here. You've been unnecessarily secretive."

"Please, call him Farouk. Even better, Uncle Farouk. Show respect. You know that I object to that other name. As to why he wants us here I'm not exactly sure. Let's find out. Here we are at the meeting place."

Grindlay's Bank is an orderly arrangement of imposing gilt and marble counters, potted plants, stern cashiers, and strict air-conditioning that gives the air a charged-up feeling. It seems to have been created in another universe before being winched into place in downtown Peshawar. We bring dust in from the streets and feel like invaders. The gilt and marble, the staff's attitude, even the Arctic depth of the air-conditioning are a trench that's been dug against external chaos. I notice it's the same with all the banks and travel bureaus and international hotels wherever we go in Pakistan – islands of low entropy defended against a South Sea of disorder. There's hardly time for this thought to pass through my mind before a short and officious man approaches us in front of the cashier.

"Solly, I reckon? Ten Percent's brother?"

Dad agrees.

They shake hands. "I'm the brigadier's driver and secretary. Shuaib Binnowalla, at your service." The man asks, "This is your son?"

"I believe so."

"He looks like a nice boy."

"Ah, you just don't know him well enough."

The Pakistanis may be good humoured but they're not ones for jokes. They smile, yes, but they won't make the effort to understand a joke. Shuaib is no exception. He ushers us out of the bank and then, elaborately polite, into the back seat of a long black Mercedes idling on the pavement. There's a guard on the passenger side wearing shades. Shuaib puts on a similar pair of tinted spectacles to match the car's smoked glass and we're off. The Mercedes is an E-class diesel. I imagine it's a nice touch on someone's part, to make us Johannesburgers feel at home. Later I discover that a diesel Mercedes, with a walnut interior, is the choice of strongmen everywhere on the planet.

"Make yourself comfortable." Schuaib opens his arms as if he's giving us something big. "It's some distance."

Dad settles in and closes his eyes. I watch the landscape. There are slums, a plateau dominated by government buildings and an electricity substation, soldiers at the gates of an encampment, and then a landscape of small farms. Cottages, black ditches, black oxen in harness, and towers bearing electrical lines pass on either side of the road. On the horizon, which must be towards Afghanistan, the sky edges the stairway of broken-backed hills with deep blue ink. We head into the high ground.

Eventually an enormous compound hoves into view. It consists of numerous two-storey mud buildings situated at the very top of a hill. As we roll to a stop inside the gate the proprietor opens the car door himself. The brigadier has never met us before but he's emotional. He embraces my father as we step out of the Mercedes, weeps for warmth, and immediately takes us on a tour of the estate. He's been waiting most of the day for us and for Farouk. Another Mercedes had been sent to the Peshawar airport to meet the afternoon flight but Farouk never materialised.

"No, Solly, I must tell you, I'm exceptionally disappointed with your brother," the brigadier tells my father. "I like him. I'm very fond of him. He's a man after my own heart. He charmed my daughter's heart when we first met him in Dubai with that big Indian gangster fellow. But what a character your brother is! We have big plans together. And where is the sweet fellow? Well, we have to cut our losses. I'll show you everything we have established here and your brother will suffer by losing out on the experience."

"That's his loss."

But my uncle's absence is really our loss, and the brigadier's. We gather from what our host tells us that Farouk is in hock to the brigadier for seventy thousand dollars, which works out to about a billion billion rupees . . . a king's ransom. I wonder if we're the ransom note. Whether we're voluntary or involuntary guests isn't evident but Khan's enthusiasm for our presence seems genuine. We're shown the works. There's a generator on site, a movie projector, squash court, chicken coop, even a rifle range where two young men are disassembling a Kalashnikov.

Brigadier Zafirullah Khan lives in the high-on-the-hog style of the Pakistan elite. His house is built on ancient ground. From this vantage point local rulers have long governed the region in Mongol style. It's the nucleus of a comprehensive feudal organisation that stretches over the rocky land, including Pashtun herders with wild brown eyes, sheep shearers, wool carders, teachers, toll collectors, mechanics at the Shell garage on the trunk road. The renovations on the house, down to the hallway portraits of the family, are of more recent provenance, paid for from the coffers of Inter Services Intelligence and indirectly by the Langleyites of Virginia who were most generous during the Afghanistan war.

The brigadier tells us more about his daughter Fazila as he takes us around in the jeep. Brigadier Khan lost his wife many years ago and has mutated into a supremely proud father. He cherishes Fazila's piano playing, he tells me in the jeep, her love of French films and Angeleno hiphop, her way of dressing, without understanding any of it. This mention of Fazila doesn't interest me. I can't imagine she's much of a looker based on her father. He's a stooper, even inside the vehicle. When he looks back at me his beady brown eyes, close together across a longish beagle's nose, make him look stupid. The one on the right, looking in, is a lazy eye. It trails in the footsteps of its companion, never closing the arc to within half a right angle. I have the uncanny feeling that what there exists of the brigadier's intelligence scurries now into his good eye . . . now back into the lazy eye.

Dad is painfully bored by Khan's conversation but, as with my mother and brother, I don't object to meaningless chatter. I sense, from his beagle eyes, that the brigadier is starting to like me on our drive around his miniature kingdom. He entrusts me with the job of collecting his rent, or what he calls rent.

"My son," Khan tells me, "do me one favour, eh, while your father and I talk shop. Go in there and get the money from the guy inside. You can see. He's waiting with the envelope for the rent."

The guy inside – at the Shell, at the toll booth, and at the police station – keeps the dough ready for his lordship. In all honesty, I ask, what sort of rent do you pay on a police station? It's weird that the brigadier personally collects his share of baksheesh, the daily bread of the Muslim world. I suppose it gives him a purpose in life beneath and beyond the adoration of his daughter Fazila. I try to be useful. I count the contents of his envelopes while he drives and converses with my father.

The pink five-rupee notes display Jinnah's head and shoulders but in my imagination they are silver dirhams from the time of Harun al-Rashid. The Sanskrit sages claim the cosmos is made of one gigantic turtle standing on the shell of another turtle even more gigantic; I believe the links in the great subcontinental chain of being are not turtles but fleas. One flea sucks on another flea which in turn has its tiny teeth locked in the dark meat of a third of its fellows. To leach, bum, milk, sponge, and scavenge are activities as basic to our underlying nature as language.

I consider my half-hostile feelings towards the brigadier when we get back to camp and I have the chance to spend an hour in the bath. Perhaps I feel envy towards Khan's antecedents . . . envy, the green-eyed sin. On his mother's side, the Zafirullahs of Punjab, the brigadier's family claim descent from a companion of the Prophet (peace be upon him). The Zafirullah men wear a black ribbon in commemoration. So they have the rigorous side of the faith down cold.

Then there's a wholly different aspect of the family's religion. The Khans are dependent on itinerant holy rollers, pirs, magic healers, astrologers, numerologists, memorisers of a thousand sacred verses, Sufi dancers, fire eaters, for their authority. These holy rollers and Sufis work at the Shell garage and inside the Quonset hut as Khan's toll collectors. So the fire eaters labour at the stoves and the astrologers tend the vegetable garden behind his great kitchen, so what? I'll stop complaining. Negative energy, my brother says, is a boomerang. Use it but don't be in the same place when it comes back.

Quoting my brother leads me to thinking about him and then recounting his flaws. Soon enough I call up the kitchen at the Pearl-Continental and hear his familiar scratchy voice on the other end of the line.

"They think I'm you, over here," I tell him. "They think there's only one of us. How absurd. But it's going well although we seem to be hostages. You're okay?"

"I'm okay. Just mopping. Any news?"

"There's a beautiful girl, apparently, although I haven't laid eyes on her," I say. "But she's the brigadier's daughter, so it's strictly hands off. I never understood how strange these Pakistani men were before I got here. They make us, from Johannesburg, look positively Western."

"We are Western."

The oddest thing about Brigadier Khan, by the way, is this theatrical tendency so common among upper-crust men from parts of Pakistan and Afghanistan. Dad doesn't notice but I do. You see that overheated, soupish quality in every gesture he makes. He's one of those Pakistanis who carry their sense of aristocracy into and out of London and New York, coming and going as they please and utterly unaffected by democracy and its correlates. Khan wears a red scarf over his military tunic in the warmest weather. With his scarf, Valentino moustache and those big purple lips of his, camel lips curiously padded about his teeth, he sets one's radar singing. Not, I hasten to add, that anything of that kind should be held against him.

Khan's not merely a parasite. He doesn't keep everything to himself. He donates substantial amounts to a foundation, a waqf based in Karachi that publishes and distributes stapled pamphlets, cassette tapes, and posters on such utilitarian subjects as hygiene, religious pride, schooling for girls, tropical diseases, proper methods of circumcision, and Western stereotypes. He talks to me about it at length on the road home. It's a matter of spiritual self-help, meant to help simple-minded people find their way in a complex world. One of his most interesting advisors in the field is coming up for the week. I look forward to making a friend of Mohammad the Egyptian who's rumoured to be something of an intellectual, and better still, a graduate student. We're sure to have a lot in common.

When evening comes there is still no sign of my uncle whom I have mixed feelings about meeting again. At first it doesn't hurt our standing with our host. At dinner, surrounded by cousins and henchmen, he seats my father on his right-hand side and myself next to Fazila who's on his left at the head of the enormous table. The table groans with bowls and pots. Dishes are arranged in single file down the centre.

The meal itself is a free for all. People reach in, load their plates, pull black-ened, parsleyed kebabs off heavy wooden stakes and soften them with sluices of lemon juice and yoghurt. A vast copper pot filled with halim travels the length of the room, its black contents hot off the fire. It occurs to me, tragically, that the scene is a barbaric rendering of our dinner table in Fordsburg. Who would have supposed that was the peak of our civilisation? As if he's reading my thoughts the brigadier sets off on a new line of argument.

"You mustn't get the impression we're backwards here, compared to India," Khan explains, adjusting the collar on his olive tunic, and eating with the other, puckered hand. He's changed into ceremonial dress. A Sandhurst graduate, he speaks in phrases, discrete pellets every one, which emit a soiled, manhandled odour when you listen to them. "Our religion is an aspect of how modern we are, in fact. We are very forward-thinking in Pakistan, Professor."

He goes on in this vein. Meanwhile I am falling in love with his daughter. You sense about Fazila that she's a sulker even if there's no outward sign of it. Her moods, I think, must be as thick as molasses. I am too terrified to utter a word in her direction. But I listen intently to what she tells my father. The brigadier's daughter is recently returned from boarding school in London at the age of eighteen and a half. She's unselfconscious, motherless like me, and has the run of the place. She's a tomboy. She rides horses around the estate and the brigadier keeps a stable on her account.

Fazila loves cinema as well as horses. She lectures Dad on the subject, sounding as if she's quoting from her Knightsbridge teachers. She's evangelical about Jean-Paul Belmondo, Jean-Luc Godard, Anaïs Nin, amongst other Frankish influences. She speaks confidently on every conceivable topic although there's a brittleness in her manner that appeals to me. I don't say a word about her appearance because I can scarcely look her way. But ridiculous as she may be, I've found the girl of my dreams. I know so because it's in Fazila's voice that the people in my dreams speak to me during the night. Only she, I believe, can cure my sadness, for a time . . . she's the one I want to be sad around . . . which is the highest compliment a melancholic can pay.

The conclusion to dinner makes it appear, again, that we're the brigadier's hostages.

Khan strikes the table. "We must come to an understanding, Suleiman, because things have come to a pretty pass. With interest your brother's debt to me stands at seventy thousand dollars. That's in hard currency. Farouk promised me that when it comes to passports you, and your son here, do the finest work. Can we come to an arrangement then? Can we have something definite between us? I have to put my trust in you and vice versa. After all, up to this day, I don't even know what country you fellows are from although I've heard a lot of talk about your stay in Johannesburg."

Dad takes an odd tack with our host, I feel; he's whimsical where he should be serious. "Ah, brigadier, the one lesson of my life is, never let anyone pin you down. South Africans, you know, live to pin people down and put them into boxes and categories. Who am I? A divorced, middle-aged man. Am I Lebanese, a Parsee from Bombay, an Iranian or a whatnot, an Indian from India or from Bangladesh . . . or perhaps from Pakistan? All jokes aside, we are prepared to help out as my brother promised. I understand Farouk recommended us to make the passports and other documents for your guys. But to get started in a place like New York it will take capital. We have to agree on the right price."

"Well, we can discuss the matter further in private." Khan's sharp little green eyes swarm out of his sulking countenance. "Considering the amount of my capital that went missing in your brother's custody in Bombay, please, Zacharia, if you don't mind, let's not bargain like two swinging merchants. It's beneath my dignity, man."

"Well, whatever you say. Maybe we can work something out. But I'm not making any promises."

"Until that day arrives," the brigadier promises, "please, accept my hospitality." He puts his hand in my hand. "You too, my son. I've heard very good things about your abilities from your uncle. He says you're an absolute wizard with pen and paper."

Whether I'm a wizard with a pen you be the judge; whereas my tongue is tied behind my back around Fazila. It's a long, slow, hot afternoon and the compound at the top of the hill is as hushed as if it were the night before Christmas. The brigadier has taken my father into town to pick up silk-screening ink. I talk to Ashraf who's been working in the kitchen of the Pearl-Continental in the hope of turning up something interesting.

It's futile to express feelings to my brother. He has too much to say in his own right. He's full of ideas and wicked commentary about Punjabi hotel maids and the veiled girls behind the hotel's reception desk. The conversation, if you can call it that, leaves me dissatisfied, yearning to share the secret of my admiration for Fazila with someone. But I'm not about to whisper into the wind. The plight of King Midas reminds me even the wild ash has ears.

I think I'm alone in the house but then I spy Fazila heaped up inside a towel on a deck chair, secretly cupping a Rothman's inside unexpectedly pink hands, her knees drawn into her hipless body. She's been swimming in the dechlorinated water, an otter with long legs seen against the green tiles of the pool basin. Without noticing my presence she changes into a bra underneath her towel. The hot afternoon dries the towel around her at a visible pace. She's a thing of nature. Her dark-gold toenails, which she irreligiously clips now as if punching holes in her feet with a stapler, are the only artificial colours. I go up to her.

"Have a nice swim?"

"The water's great." She smiles, and it's Hiroshima. "Why don't you jump in? I'm going in the house to shower. We could watch a movie later. Or play Monopoly, if you prefer."

"Either would be great. Both, I suppose. I'm a big fan of Careers."

"Terrific. If you want company, that's Mohammad el-Amir over there, changing. He works for my dad, doing something in Karachi. I think I mentioned him. You two might get along."

Fazila goes into the house. The visitor and I get to talking by the swimming

93

pool. Mohammad el-Amir Atta is ill at ease in his own skin. He's a big brown man, a scowler, and from his corner of the tarmac there arrives at my nose the distinct smell of sulphur. I know at once about Mohammad Atta that he will never amount to anything. At the same time I find him interesting. He's an Arab, an industrious Egyptian and an engineer, not a Pakistani and a loafer, and he doesn't do a lot to fit in. Like everyone else, it seems, in this part of Asia, Atta's moving to the United States. I ask him about this as he changes into his swimming costume underneath a towel.

"What are you planning to do in America? Where are you planning to go? Do you know people there? I have to be honest," I say. "Something bugs me about people who are going to America. Going to America, okay – what does that mean? Something bugs me about the whole idea of the place in people's minds. I feel like it's just a blank space people project their craziest ideas on to. So do you have some career in mind or do you want to go there merely as a way of getting out of your ordinary life? Which is it?"

"I'm learning how to fly." Atta grins but he isn't smiling. He has long lips, I notice, like a pipe-cleaner. They curl down across his face as he puts his bare feet into the water. He rolls off his T-shirt and settles backwards into the pool. "I want to know how to handle a plane. Through his foundation Khan gave us some money. Ziad, my friend, and I just enrolled in a flight school down in Florida but we want to spend time in all the major centres." He stands up and spits into the pool. "New York interests me. Actually I'm up here to talk to Khan about our mission. He can do a lot for us. One of the reasons you're here is that Khan believes you can assist us on the technical side. And you owe it to us. Considering how your uncle took Zafirullah Khan to the cleaners, you're lucky to be given a chance to redeem yourselves. You know, after all he did to set our operation back, I quite like old Ten Percent. He's a man after my heart."

I ask, "What's your mission?"

"Top secret. Do you have any feelings about America?"

I say, "I hear it's a dreadful country. My mother, at any rate, believes so, and I have no reason to question her judgement. How do you know Ten Percent?"

Atta keeps talking as he does backstroke up and down the length of the pool. "I know your uncle from Jiddah days. He told me, and then I told Khan, that you make the most beautiful passports and driver's licences. In fact Ten Percent showed me one of your creations. He says it's an art the way you fellows do it. Passports, brother, are the new form of weapons. To begin with I need a few good British passports and a Florida driver's licence wouldn't hurt. When do you think you can do it by?"

"Look, I'll tell you a secret. You're thinking of my brother Ashraf. It's not me who's the expert at forgery," I tell Atta. "I can understand the confusion but Ashraf is the one you want. I can't help you. But put your mind at ease. My brother will help you in any crooked enterprise you desire."

"Let me tell you what I'm planning."

I block my ears. "Please, not a word."

Later that evening, speaking of the devil, my brother shows up on the estate. I've told him what we need to help the brigadier. Ashraf has brought his equipment from the hotel and unloads it on my bed: compass, protractor, a pair of iron arms that allowed him to duplicate a line or a curve, bottles of ink, calligraphic pens, a pad of blue graph paper, and a supply of different density papers from W.H. Smith in London. He's also brought his tape recorder and installs it under my bed. My brother, like my father, is a big believer in Motown and plays Ray Charles, the Temptations, the Supremes, Bing Crosby, while he meticulously reproduces a passport, Bophuthatswana homeland driver's licence, and other documents in general demand. He gets cracking. He needs specimens of his work to show Atta. I tell him to keep well out of sight.

I arrange to meet Fazila in the brigadier's private cinema. She plans to spend the evening showing me her favourite movies – *Nostalgia*, *The Lady Eve*, *Pather Panchali*. Fazila's been waiting for the chance to watch movies with somebody, anybody, in Pakistan since she returned from London. I feel lucky. For the first time since Tigerlily I get out my striped school tie and fumigate my arms with cologne. Dad's in the makeshift wedding hall putting away a fifth of scotch with our host and assessing cigars. Otherwise the camp is quiet beneath a distant Chinese behemoth of a moon which sits in the sky like a circle of yellow silk.

In the clean, cold, dry air of the hills, like detergent in my face, the bejewelled railroads of the constellations wind through the easternmost heavens. The buildings, I notice, are wrapped in endless vines headed with white melons that look silver in starlight. I steal into the theatre where the projector's already on and discover my brother in the back row with his arm thrown around the

95

back of Fazila's seat. Her head nods onto his shoulder. I skulk around in the doorway, trying to attract Ashraf's attention, but he waves me away. He looks as comfortable as a husband.

Ladies and gentlemen of the jury, what can I do? What can I tell her? I'm sure that Fazila thinks my brother's right out of the movies whereas, as I know, as you know, he's a shoddy television rip-off. In Ashraf, of all people, Fazila sees Belmondo, Jean-Pierre Leaud, and Paul Newman floating by turns in his marble green eyes. I slink around, waiting to catch Ashraf's attention again without alerting Fazila to the fact that there are two of us brothers. But it's no use. I retire to bed. At two in the morning, as I'm steaming in my covers, my brother climbs in the window to report that Fazila has surrendered the treasure guarded by the brigadier as closely as a dragon. This stinking guy has filched her virginity. He could have robbed me of anything, my good name, my notebooks, with less pain. I have tears in my eyes that I don't want him to see.

I ask him, "Don't you think Dad's going to be furious when he finds you're fooling around with Khan's daughter? You could jeopardise his whole deal. There's something very delicate going on. It involves Ten Percent Farouk and some loan he took from the brigadier. You don't want to fool around with this guy's one beloved daughter."

He goes out on the balcony and I follow him.

"What do you mean, fool around, mess around? That's the wrong language to use. I'm serious about this one. You shouldn't be a cynic when it comes to a blood relation." Ashraf loads a rifle on our second floor veranda and then sits on the swinging bench so he's out of sight. He rolls the red-and-gold cartridges around in his hands. "Fazila is a really funny girl. She has a real sense of humour though she doesn't reveal it until you get to know her. In fact she's hilarious. She reminds me of our mother."

"You said the same thing about Tigerlily. There's no way either of them has a sense of humour. It's just a halo created by your hormones. That's what I think, anyway, whenever you say a girl has a sense of humour. You and your imaginary senses of humour! Let me remind you that our mother has no sense of humour whatsoever. Plus I have dibs." Then my curiosity gets the better of me. "Does Fazila really tell jokes?"

"Yes, she really does. And that's not the important thing. Even if you don't have a heart, Firoze, imagine that others do. Imagine that other people are capable of falling in love." Ashraf stands up and points the rifle idly at the security box at the gate. "Believe me when I say that this thing with Fazila is for real. I want her to be the mother of my children."

The next few days are agony for me. Ashraf courts Fazila in his madcap style although only one of us can be seen in public at a time. He buys a banjo in the village and serenades this future mother while I read Schopenhauer in the bath. I sit beside her at dinner and try getting her to laugh. She's reluctant although, when Fazila does eventually laugh, she brays in the most attractive way, her long teeth standing out over her lips. Ashraf borrows my tie and sneaks into Fazila's bedroom while I keep Atta company by the swimming pool. Ashraf browses through her underwear drawer while she tells me about her plan to go to NYU film school and become a famous director. I offer to write her a screenplay while Ashraf offers to relieve her of her virtue once again.

In a skirmish like this, inevitably, my brother has the advantage. I put my hands in my pockets around Fazila while Ashraf puts his hands up her skirt. Am I Ashraf? Is he suddenly Firoze? Does Fazila know that she's being wooed by an Ashraf-Firoze? I have a hundred questions to put to her about this double-headed and half-hearted but single-minded beast yet, like any philosopher, I store up my questions. After all they're my only real capital in this world.

Meanwhile my father is in the doldrums. Negotiating with Brigadier Khan and having the run of the Peshawar estate, the benefit of Peshawarese luxury, does little to lift Dad's long-term mood. As the responsible son, the devoted son, I worry about him. It's not only Mom's fault. It's been ages since the divorce. Dad's been looking forward to seeing his brother. He isn't pleased to realise that Farouk might have been setting us up all along.

So what my father needs is a crisis. I do my best to arrange one. At dinner I say things to the brigadier about his daughter that he can't acknowledge hearing. I stay close to her side in Khan's presence and once I overcome my inhibitions, pinch Fazila's bottom, and make her jump. The brigadier's boiling with suspicion. His cheeks are bright red and his small piggy eyes swollen. He shadows Fazila while I shadow him and soon enough he finds Ashraf in her bedroom.

A fight ensues. Shots are exchanged although only the chauffeur Schuaib is wounded in the calf. Dad jumps off the balcony with our suitcases while Ashraf packs his rucksack with silverware and the brigadier's photographic equipment. Fazila locks her father in the bathroom and sweet-talks her way past the sentry. The camp is in alarm. It brings out the best in everyone, even Atta who helps to hold off an entire Paki battalion with a cutlass until we can find a car to escape in. We take Fazila with us. She sits next to Ashraf in the stolen Mercedes and I get in the other door. It's the first time she sees the two of us together.

"There are two of you. You're exactly alike."

"No, my dear." Dad leans into the back seat for a moment. "There are subtle differences between my sons, at least on the outside. On the inside they're equally rotten, however."

Fazila's practical about the situation. "Well, look, I need to get to the airport. I'll catch the next flight to Karachi and then to London. If you could take me there I'd be incredibly grateful."

Dad's receptive to his potential daughter-in-law. "No problemo. Maybe it's a blessing in disguise that my wastrel brother Farouk never turned up. So let's get out of here. Hold on."

My father guns the engine as we crash through the gate at the front of the compound. He watches the brigadier in the mirror as the sand road comes up to meet us. This is the best medicine. Dad's immediately cheerful. Having a principal adversary is a pick-me-up for anyone's soul (unless that principal adversary happens to be one's wife). It's especially good for his spirits to know that Khan's blue Mercedes is in our possession, its brown leather steering wheel, hard as luggage, ensconced in his hands.

We turn onto a dirt road about ten miles down to outwait any pursuers before we head to the airport. As the child of a single and occasionally sad-sack father I am delighted to see his new joy in finding the Mercedes trunk providentially filled with 5.67 mm ammunition stored in nylon belts. It is wonderful to see him running his calloused hands along the nylon just as he once caressed those beloved suits we left in Khan's compound in our hurry to escape. It's even charming to see Dad comfort Ashraf at the boarding gate where my brother, for almost the first time in his life, is heartsore at Fazila's departure. He finally forgives Ashraf for Sun City. My brother is still claiming to be in love with the girl when it's clear that he doesn't know the meaning of either word.

And then there's our new friend who reeks of the pit. However sulphurous Mohammad Atta might be, he's a good friend to my father during this week. Atta's a mother's boy, I can tell, so he knows how to talk softly to a wounded man. In our makeshift camp at the side of the road outside Peshawar the two of them stay up late talking beside the fire. Atta listens to Dad's rants about Mum and says little to discourage him. It's clear the guy doesn't like women. Well, that's a typical understatement on my part. But as I say, Atta's good for my father and not a bad swordsman to boot.

The Mercedes grinds to a halt twenty miles outside the city. The diesel blast of the engine, exposed by an open hood, permeates the car's inside. It whirs, buzzes, and retrenches to a lower gear but it isn't about to move us in any direction on the sand road. Ashraf gets out to push. Atta keeps a lookout, with his curved sword in hand. We haven't seen the canvas-top army jeep which has been pursuing us in well over an hour. And what are they going to do if they catch us, I ask myself, kill us? And after that?

On the run from Khan, while trying to fix the car, we spend a few nights in the Cholistan desert outside Bawahalpur where I come, oddly enough, to appreciate my uncle for the first time. I have his diaries in my possession and nothing else to read and a feeling of heartbreak after Fazila's departure. We're amongst nomads so there's no other form of entertainment except shooting stray cats.

My uncle's diaries are astonishing. Almost above stealing was Farouk's love for writing which he indulged twelve hours a day from the sinecure of the Roodepoort mental hospital before escaping first to Dubai and then to India. The government psychologists even classified my uncle, amongst other things, as a graphomaniac. Farouk's existing journals, a baker's dozen, are bound in thin brown calfskin, so soft to the touch you run your hands up and down the covers as you read. I brought the diaries to give back to my uncle and so I'm at least as disappointed as my father when Farouk doesn't turn up in Peshawar. We can't seem to reach my uncle on his Bombay telephone but I do have these journals.

The many-coloured stars, the tall tribal women bundled up in yellow-and-red striped blankets, the slumbering camels anchored in a line outside the camp and over whose muscular yellow shoulders are slung bandoliers filled with long cartridges in the Mexican style, all these form the backdrop to the endless pages of my uncle's diaries, letters, and remarks of a philosophical and cosmological nature. In his loping Catholic school cursive and numerous crabbed brown-ink diagrams, Ten Percent Farouk sets down a chronicle of events. Even more valuable are his nuthouse observations on such matters as the role of questions in life, the concealed traps of Chubb safes, putting a Primus stove to work as a blowtorch, train robbery, death as a night bridge over a dark river. It's from my uncle, by the way, that I learn the details about the curse of green eyes that runs like a serpent-green sash through generations of Dawoods and Peers.

My literary debt to Farouk is immense. It strikes me that if there's something relentlessly negative, merciless, nihilistic, unlikeable about the man then it's a spiritual disposition I inherited. But what I most remember contemplating in the desert, on the sanded table of that rolling plain in supreme Pakistan, is my own lunar religion. The nearby moon, which loves all the world's tribal peoples and their sacred places, is astonishingly low, broad, and orange. I imagine that among its favourites the moon watches the Dawoods and Peers.

The next morning Ashraf and my father go back to work on the engine while Mohammad Atta scolds the peasant women in a nearby house. I sit inside working the accelerator pedal like an old-school weaver. Dad leans in through the window. He isn't having any luck with the motor. "I've been thinking, Firoze. Who am I to impose this kind of life on the two of you?" he asks, fond as he is of using any occasion for a lesson. I am reminded again of the neutral and scrubbed quality of his way of speaking, no evidence of a scratchy, singsong, Indian Johannesburg accent. He opens the water bottle, walking alongside the driver's door as the vehicle gradually begins to roll. "Your mother is totally correct. If you choose such a life for yourself as I have chosen for myself, well and good. The vital thing is to be your own man." His green eyes move up like the icons in a slot machine. "But I want you and your brother to fit in somewhere, not always to be a so-called square peg in a round hole."

"We fit in here, in Pakistan. We look like everyone else here. That's a great advantage. We can have a life in this part of the world without sticking out."

The diesel barks gloriously into life. Dad jogs around the other side and gets in, pushing Ashraf into the back with Atta. "We can fit in anywhere, Firoze. So let's try the big time for a change. Let's try New York. I've been talking to

Mohammad here about the matter. It's astonishingly easy to change identities in the United States. Americans don't pin you down. Americans don't need to put people in boxes. Plus it's the global capital for fraud, the perfect place to set up the business with Fabergé eggs." He points. "Head straight down the way you're going and try to drive properly for once. If it wasn't for your mother's irrational hatred we would have moved to America ages ago. Now, for me, her horror about the place is a positive virtue. Besides, Mohammad here has been talking to me about it and that's where he's headed. The guy has real plans and a real future in America. He has all the contacts we could want when we need to set up shop. Have I failed to mention that it's a friendly country to people like us, to ordinary Muslims?"

"You must be joking," I say.

"No, I am really not joking."

لــب

Chapter Five

The boat ride from New Brunswick to Rockland, and from there to the north shore of Long Island, avoids Coast Guard patrols. The route was Atta's suggestion although he left Pakistan by a different course, promising to meet us in New York City. Allow me to blur the details in order not to land a certain French-Canadian sea dog in hot water. As a micro-Tocqueville and a miniaturist in the line of Captain Cook, I will get to everything in turn but first let me say a few words about the eternal topic of New York life, which is, of course, real estate.

Our apartment building stood between a panel beater and a Mexican hole in the wall run by a mob of Chinese. The rooms were the size of South African closets. It was odd to see my father and brother, so much larger than mere life, coexisting in our new pad's tiny red-brick confines. But then everything was different in the New World. I have never been more surprised than to see Dad humming and balancing a load of laundry against his hips, then taking it down to the washing machines in the basement.

Our building was part of the great wishbone in downtown Brooklyn formed by Atlantic Avenue and Flatbush. Across Atlantic was a nail salon in the window of which we saw bow-tied Korean maidens sanding the hands of their clients beneath pipes of purple light. Ashraf started to hang around the nail salon. I didn't see him make any headway with the employees though. I guess they weren't impressed by his Johannesburg act.

My brother's first order of business, apart from seducing the nail polishers, was to perfect his driver's licences. He got right down to work. Monsignor

Atta had arranged to fetch a batch in a month's time. Ashraf expected a lot of subsequent business from that quarter. His methods were typically weird and Ashrafian. My brother introduced himself to students at adjoining tables in Dunkin' Donuts. He sold to students at the Pratt Institute who wanted to go drinking. If they wanted to splurge on two of his documents they could go drinking and driving. He soon had a whole bunch of friends at Pratt. With his licences and his new connections, my brother was doggishly making this part of Brooklyn his territory.

He kept multiple irons in the fire. Perhaps because of our childhood he was very interested in the mail. Ashraf borrowed a truck from the Brownsville, New York, post office parking lot and used it as the perfect cover to break into suburban mailboxes. I'll say this for the guy. His scheme was ingenious. Someone without extensive experience of fools would call it foolproof. Who would ever suspect a postman of removing the post? It's not logical. Who would think to look inside a postal truck for stolen letters? What cop would pull over a mail van? In fact it was the safest way to travel.

Bank statements, car registration renewals, driver's licence replacements, gun permits were harvested in enormous quantities and then lost utterly when Ashraf backed the van into the concrete wall of his storage locker in Red Hook and had to run for his life. He blamed the accident on cultural difference. He wasn't used to driving on the right-hand side of the road. He wasn't going to admit to being a terrible driver. Like all male twins we were extremely competitive when it came to cars.

Meanwhile I made an American friend. Felix Corvalho Villaverde worked at the 7-11 down on Bergen Street but really he was the super's nephew and a skinny-as-a-rake lounger who lived in the basement apartment of our building with his widowed uncle, the super. It was Felix who got me a job as a cashier at 7-11. He was always looking to do a friend a good turn. Felix, I believed, was our point of entry into American life. He was going to introduce Ashraf and me to girls, to new circles and levels in New York, to buyers and sellers of everything. I imagined that he would replace everything we had lost in leaving Johannesburg.

We soon struck up the very best kind of masculine friendship, one in which each of us was perpetually trying to reduce the other to the level of a sidekick. Felix wanted me at his elbow and I didn't mind if he trailed along with me to Dunkin' Donuts to consult with my brother on his various difficulties.

Felix's name was the most conventional thing about him except for his mind. Part Jewish and part Japanese, with slightly tightened eyelids, as if the screws holding everything in place were given an extra turn, he was not unhandsome. His eyes were plum black. Sure he was ridiculous. His way of striking an expression was to smooth it across his cheeks. Sure he had a ridiculous method of barrelling into a room and greeting each person with a touch, a smile, a raised and lowered eyebrow, and some telegrammatic words. He quoted phrases rather than talking. But he was my friend and to see him slouching at the apartment door lifted my heart.

"What's up, Firoze? What's happening? Say, what's going on, brother?"

We shook hands. "Nothing much, Felix. How are you, my main man?"

"Can't complain. I mean, I won't complain. If I tried, I could complain, no problem. Five O tried to arrest me last night when I showed one of your brother's driver's licences. I have to tell Ashraf. You know, Firoze, about skimming as much as we do, I was thinking . . . it's not our fault. It's the fault of 7-11 for paying us minimum wage." It was one of my friend's misdemeanours. "It's the system that's broken, amigo. I just hope it's so broken they never clue into the fact I've been robbing the register blind. Anyway, what are they going to do? Lock up everyone in this country? Say, is there anything in the icebox?"

Felix was the nervous sort. He was perpetually anxious, a power plant generating nervous energy, fingering the scuzz on his neck until he scraped it into our sink. Chicken-necked and possessed of a tubular Adam's apple, he gardened his hair in our bathroom mirror with Dad's blue-and-white biplaned Shick. Felix was the carrier of so many worries that like fleas they had spread into the bedding of his mind and would never be dislodged. Little did I know my new friend was standard Brooklyn fare. In the five-petal metropolis Brooklyn breeds the nuts. With all this craziness on his side of the ledger, though, Felix thought of me as the oddity, if a likeable oddity.

Felix was fond of people to whom he could provide a service. His self-esteem came from being a fixer and a go-to man. "I can hook you up" was, therefore, his favourite expression. Even I started saying it.

Felix made all manner of promises. "What do you want, Firoze? What do you want, man? You're a mystery, muchacho. Do you want girls? Is it girls?

Is it cars that you desire? Is it entertainment? How about a really big Apex television set? Say the word and it will fall off a truck. Remember," he frowned without being angry, "you live in my uncle's building on the greatest street in the greatest city on earth. I consider you, and your brother and your father, my responsibility. We're all immigrants to New York at some stage. Someone has to show some hospitality. So, how can I hook you up?"

"Isn't it, sorry, what can I hook you up to?"

Felix was appalled. It was our first argument. "Can I believe my ears? You're correcting my grammar." Stung by the idea, he turned to my brother who had materialised with a towel around his short body. "Ash, tell me, does your brother know what it means to show respect to a member of the Latin Kings?" He shook his hand at me. "He's lucky to be testing me before he wanders out onto Atlantic Avenue and some maricón busts a cap. For his own good, lay some science on the guy." But Felix's problems were with both us brothers. "By the way, Ash, that licence you sold me is garbage. It almost got me arrested last night. I had to scramble through the subway turnstile at Borough Hall to get away. Five O was feeling frisky."

"No fears, Felix. Let me get you a cup of jungle juice meantime," Ashraf responded. He was adept at handling people's nerves when he wanted to be. He went over to get the Bacardi bottle from under the pull-out bed. "Look at your hands, caballero. They're trembling with anger. Relax. You'll feel better when we get something cold inside of you. About Firoze, look, as his brother I can tell you, he's not the easiest guy in the world to be friends with. He has an odd way of asking questions. It comes from thinking too much, from being locked up in his head with his spooky concepts. But look, the guy has a heart of gold. A heart of gold. He'll give you his last penny. My advice is to have a spot of lunch before you guys go down to the 7-11. I'll do the honours."

Felix considered these words for a moment. "Maybe you're right, gerente." He was as quick to subside as to rise, like a pan, I thought, maintained at a rolling boil. "You stay here, and I'll get yesterday's chicken from downstairs. I still want a refund on that licence though."

"You'll get more than a refund," Ashraf promised. "You'll get a replacement, and a firearm licence too. Now how do you stay so skinny with all that chicken inside you?"

Felix's nerves burnt the kilojoules but he wasn't thin for lack of trying to get fat. For a supposed thug he had finicky ideas about the necessary elements of an afternoon feast. There must be a sliced pineapple, a rewarmed bucket of Popeye's chicken and biscuits, liquid refreshment in the form of Bacardi 151, which he religiously referred to as jungle juice, perhaps a blue-and-gold cigar box containing six Philly's Blunts sold at the Korean delicatessen for two dollars, and then perhaps a round of fifty-five-cent White Castle hamburgers (hold the onions per his instructions, add a glob of ketchup, and place a porous slice of manufactured American cheese on the side of the tray).

These indoor picnics were an indispensable element in our new friendship. My brother was great at putting them together. Ashraf, to look at him, doesn't manifest a chef's delicacy even after his days labouring at the ovens of Sun City, but he actually has tremendous organising ability. With his locomotive stamina, he assembles and beautifully lays out a feast in no time. He used to do it for my Mom often, while she doled out presents. And it's just what he did for Felix, arranging the pineapple slices on the decorated rim of a black lacquer saucer. I think the ceremony was almost directed at me, as if my brother felt fondness burning in his heart like a phosphor. The saucer, depicting wrestlers, by the way, was one of a set I bought at the 99-cent store in a fit of Japanoiserie, if that's the right word for a mood of yearning for the mysteries of the Orient.

When Felix returned Ashraf ushered the left-over chicken into the microwave, teasing apart the blackened bones with a plastic knife to cook better. Coming out of the oven the drumsticks, with their rubber tips, left a damp impression on the paper plate. There was a sediment of bread crumbs beneath them, as if to attract birds, which Felix scooped into his mouth. Then Felix sat back on our long leather rented couch, a piece of furniture inert and unlovely as a hippopotamus, running his hands along the arm rest. I saw that he was mollified by all the activity, as Ashraf intended.

Felix rescrewed the top of the Bacardi bottle and picked up a thought left hanging in the air until then like a musical chord. "Because to me, caballeros, I can do without water and air, yes, if it's necessary. But without the proper dimension of respect life is not worth living. If you and you and you are not going to give me respect then you can chupar es mi pinga" – he whistled as he said this – "if you know what I'm saying . . . but okay, I am not going to belabour the point. Say, Ashraf, when am I going to get the new licence you promised?"

It seems too obvious to put on the page but crooks love money. My brother's a connoisseur of the Gibraltar pound and the Kenyan shilling, of dinars and pesetas and escudos. He loves holding money and he, like my father, loves its physical properties. Ashraf takes a sort of predator's joy in handling money, even his fake money, rubbing a billfold between thumb and forefinger, memorising the lucky numbers on twenty-dollar notes to bet on Powerball tickets, and testing the freshly milled edge of a pound coin on his tongue.

My brother will do anything to make money . . . and I mean make money. Yet Ashraf wasn't having any success at making twenty-dollar notes. They weren't easy to duplicate. The colour was off when he produced his counterfeits. The right paper wasn't readily available. And the design was difficult. He made me hold up his rectangles of green linen to an infrared lamp only to discover that the geometry was misaligned. I thought it might be possible to slip them to a bartender, or perhaps to a teller at Foxwoods Casino, or to put them on the horses at Belmont out on the island. But then Felix got arrested in Washington Heights trying to spend forty dollars my brother had given him in change. So that line of business was going nowhere fast. We spent two hundred and forty real dollars bailing Felix out. Ashraf turned up with a false licence so that no one would have to show up at trial.

Amid all these confusions Mohammad Atta was the one constant point in my brother's endeavours. We thought he was really going to help us out. Atta was our Godot. We knew he had rich friends in the Middle East. He was our hope for economic self-sufficiency. We didn't want to sponge off Dad who had financial troubles of his own.

I hadn't actually heard Atta's falsetto voice since Pakistan, until one afternoon I picked up the cordless telephone in my father's bedroom and followed a conversation between him and my brother. Atta interested me. Plus my brother and I have no real secrets from each other. So I listened in. They were having a logistical conversation. Atta was matter of fact and exacting with Ashraf. He was, I knew, an engineer, a man of action and therefore of few words. Certain documents had to be produced. Certain air tickets had to be booked and copied. Certain people had to meet certain other people . . . and a certain Cessna had to be landed on a mere strip of a runway that afternoon. A certain hotel room had to be booked in Portland, Maine, ahead of time for two men travelling together. In return a certain sum of money was winging its way by Western Union towards Manhattan.

There were numerous sounds in the background that suggested Atta was calling from the hangar of his flight school in Gainesville, Florida – a forklift going onto the apron, the decreasing whine of a turbine engine, and the calls of a mechanic from underneath one of the aircraft. Against the din Ashraf had to shout to be heard on the other end.

As he hung up the phone my brother leaned his head in through the bedroom door and found me eavesdropping. He sat down next to me on the bed and put his arm around my shoulders.

"Your boyfriend's busy?"

I said, "If you mean Felix, yes. But I wouldn't call him my boyfriend."

"Since you were listening in on the conversation, you know I have to set something up for Mohammad with some moulana. You want to come with? It'll give you something new to think about. Besides, I know you're weirdly fascinated by Mohammad and his crew."

"I think it's the other way around, Ashraf. But in answer to your question, yes, I'd be delighted to accompany you."

Ashraf smiled. There were still moments I and the old swine understood each other perfectly. We'd been slogging it out for twenty-nine years and were too tired to nurse any resentments.

"Well, Firoze, for the first time in years, you're going to set foot in a mosque. I know you swore never to go back after the Rushdie affair, but times have changed. We have to stick together. Anyway that's where we're going."

The red-carpeted mosque was an ugly duckling. It was down the block on Atlantic Avenue, utilitarian in spirit, located on the second floor of an office building, devoid of holy glamour. It was a service institution. On the stairs was a plaque with white Arabic lettering. Racks of inexpensive grey, brown, and black shoes stood on a rack just beyond the door. On the heel of a shoe rests one's standing in life. These, when I stopped to turn them over, were of cheap local manufacture, Payless and Woolworths brands. The make showed in the leather, the thin heels, and machine sewing. I wanted to think more about the symbolism but Ashraf frowned at the delay. We went in, putting on our caps.

The worshippers, I guessed, were from the practical and technical economy: taxi drivers and dispatchers, electricians, engineers, garment cutters. They must have been Pakistanis, Palestinians, Somalis, Malays, Egyptians, Jordanians. They were fearful, quiet. They were one mishap away from deportation, as we would have been had Ashraf not created our counterfeit green cards.

These worshippers sat shoulder to shoulder with bowed heads, derricks on the worn red carpet, and recited the verses in tandem with the moulana's Asiatic voice. It wasn't often I did anything collective but the effect was multiplied by memories of going to mosque. Those old memories of the Fordsburg mosque were powerful. The soul wants to be a circle, not a line, I guess, and its free ends search unceasingly for each other.

We watched the moulana clear the room in his long white shirt and robes, limping on the one side so as to favour his hip. Moulana Abbas was the guy Atta wanted us to see. Abbas was a massive man in his forties, Cyclopean in demeanour, his damaged eye hidden under a white eye patch. Abbas was Egyptian by birth, a Cairene, possessed of what I regard as Levantine graciousness. He liked to compliment others and would brook no compliment in exchange.

Abbas was polite with Ashraf but it was me he zoned in on. In fact he was supernaturally friendly. He took us down the street to a Pakistani diner. He poured root beer into our mugs. Abbas was good company. His stories were astonishing. He told us how he had lost his eye in a firefight outside Kandahar and talked about the Afghan battles in which he had taken part. Kandahar, Jalalabad, Zaranj, Shinadad, Mazar-i-Sharif were the most musical names I had ever heard. Abbas spoke of them, and of grenades and Stinger missiles, as if he was talking about roses and nightingales. He kept putting his hand up to touch his cheek. I noticed that it was wet with tears. But was he weeping for joy? Eventually he got personal.

"So Mohammad sent you to me? What an odd choice. I appreciate that you are a doubting Thomas, Firoze, my boy. We need more like you, in fact. But the first thing you must learn to doubt are the newspapers and the television stations in this country. Anything they can do to denigrate a Muslim they are sure to do." Abbas smiled. He obviously loved his dialectical brand of logic. "It can corrode your self-respect if you let it. Firoze, I see by your expression you don't agree."

"Well, in my opinion," I said, warming to the subject, "politics is a matter of letting one small part of an idea into your head at once and keeping any real thought at bay with a catchphrase. The two main commandments in politics are the who-are-they-to-say-so principle, and the my-son-of-a-gun principle. Then there's the have-him-pissing-out-of-the-tent-rather-than-pissing-in principle as well."

Abbas was energised by the argument, fingering his long beard furiously and squinting out of his good eye. I didn't mind his mixture of single-mindedness and good humour. I have long suspected that it is easier for a one-eyed man to be charismatic. There's a kind of single-minded intensity about a one-eyed man that is hard to deflect.

"You miss the essential characteristic of Islam, Firoze, which is the desire for justice," he explained, welcoming the waitress with a nod of the head. "You say mercy, pity, charity, love, and I say very good, very good, but the fundamental demand is justice for all. As Muslims we have been stretched beyond the breaking point in Palestine, Iraq, Chechnya, Bosnia, Afghanistan." The moulana smiled through all this and kept pouring root beer. "I am not one to promote violence but trust me on the following point. One side is not going to be doing all the killing. Mohammad, who sent you to me in the first place, feels the same way."

The waitress distributed plates under our arms. She was heavy-set, a coarse blue skirt bound around her large varicose legs, and methodical but very long about her work. Without seeming to listening to our conversation the waitress refilled the pitchers and glasses and gradually stocked our table with salt and pepper shakers, brown bread, and a bowl of pickles.

"It's not Muslims in general who worry me," I told the moulana in confidence. "It's my crazy brother. Ninety-nine out of a hundred Muslims are fatalists. But Ashraf is capable of any atrocity. As my brother's keeper I feel I should say that. I hope you can civilise him. I hope Atta is a good influence . . ."

Abbas cut in. "Yes, I suspected I was familiar with your type, Firoze, but I couldn't be sure until right this minute. Please do not see it as an insult if I say that you are a classic, quite a classic case of the undercutter. A worrywart. There were a number of such people at religious school. Everyone who has tried to reach a deeper truth and feels that he has failed is in danger. You cannot let a statement go by without attempting to knock it down. The good news is that you are really an idealist at heart. And undercutters make the best converts." There our exchange ended. The moulana turned to my brother. "Now, Ashraf, my son, I hear you have some documents for me."

Ashraf replied, "I'll get them to you by the end of the week. Firoze has to help me. If they're going to be convincing we need real social security numbers and addresses to put on them. But I have an idea how to get my hands on them."

The interview was over. A disciple of Abbas's, Sayeed Papindari, called on his cellphone and then came over to the diner with his car. The moulana was loaded into an old blue Mercedes. Sayeed made a point of shaking all our hands. It was a surprise to see green eyes in his tawny, whiskered face. They reached your awareness in the way coins do when they unexpectedly glitter at the bottom of a fountain. I must also mention that there was a trace of his master's smile perpetually floating about Sayeed's dark lips but, in the younger man, who seemed to be on the verge of mocking his listeners, it never settled into a smile proper.

Chemistry is the princess of the sciences and she reigned in our apartment. Piece by piece Ashraf put together a laboratory of his own in the kitchen, buying items from the local pharmacy and hardware stores. We were cleaning money at home. Ashraf had the works assembled on the table: a horseshoe magnet, a packet of blue hair rollers on which to dry paper money, a jar of feathery white iron filings shaken from the inside of an Etch-a-Sketch, a nine-hundred-watt heat lamp, and a supply of rhodamine.

The last, the rhodamine, is a pinkish fluorescent dye dissolved in ethanol, far and away the best way to remove fingerprints from any surface. Dad is strictly old school. He swears by the combination of ninhydrine and ordinary talcum powder, but it's not as foolproof as rhodamine when used properly. I was used to my brother's way of doing things. We had the process down to a ritual. Every few minutes Ashraf handed me an earbud dipped in the ethanol. With it I cleaned a series of bank notes, correcting a detail here and there as if I was doing a drawing. Then Ashraf stretched each note on a hair roller and dried it under the lamp. The element, two loops glowing in the kitchen's gloom like an infinity sign, was bright red. I could see the green paper stiffening under the beam. After two minutes he took the note down and spread a pinch of iron filings across its face. Using the magnet it took no time to check for the whorls of any remaining fingerprints. It was the last of the stash from the Sun City job and represented our only profit on that entire enterprise. Dad was planning to invest it in his life insurance company.

Ashraf was also experimenting with sleeping potions. Inside our apartment hung the persistent strong chalky smell of Largactyl. On the tables were strewn bandoliers of disposable syringes. There was a hoppy tray of piss-saturated sawdust and a string of confused brown mice my brother brought back from a pet store near Brooklyn Botanical Gardens. Largactyl, Mogadon, ordinary

Mandrax were the sleeping drugs he wanted to experiment with. He conveyed his soporific white syrups from a kettle into an empty orange-juice container. He held the light wooden funnel with the care of a man manoeuvring a spirit level, his beady green eyes moving along with the funnel as if they were the horizontal bubble. It took about twenty-five minutes. Then, planning to continue his experiments later, Ashraf packed everything away and collected his textbook and Spanish dictionary.

"It's time for lessons?"

Ashraf nodded. "Felix is coming to collect me. His Spanish is at least twice as good as mine. You wouldn't be bad because you know Latin."

"My Latin's pretty rusty. Knowing Spanish, I guess, is more practical. Try finding a Latin speaker in this part of New York. You're better equipped with your brilliance at pig Latin. I almost wish I didn't have a conflicting class. But we can go down to college together if you don't mind."

As far as the loving tongue is concerned I admit to a certain lunar pang about my new friend and my brother. Felix and Ashraf were going together to evening Spanish classes at Brooklyn College, in Felix's case as a way of getting back to his heritage. Ashraf's reasons I touch on in a moment. Brooklyn College was also where I was doing my first real philosophy course, in metaphysics and epistemology. I didn't necessarily want to learn Spanish because I believed that English is the universal language of reason.

Language classes were held in the basement, six floors below the philosophy department, so I ran into my two fellow students afterwards. We went back to our place which was deserted because Dad was in Gainesville, coincidentally, setting up his insurance company. Felix liked to trot out the more interesting Spanish phrases he had learned in the course of a week, lighting up his conversation with them as if he was striking so many matches in a row. Most of the time though he downright confused me. Sensing this he turned his still cold black eyes in my direction again.

"I can hook you up because I know, Firoze, despite everything which comes out of your mouth, that we're in a situation of mutual respect. As visitors to my country I want to make sure things fall into place for you. Ask me anything. As I say, I want to hook you up."

"You don't by any chance have a library card I can borrow?"

Ashraf, who was usually as patient with me as I was with him, was irritated by my request but Felix didn't flinch. "Talk to my grandmother," he suggested.

113

"She has stacks of books, mysteries, whatever, down in her storage space. If you promise to read them you can have whatever you want. She's dying for a conversational partner. No, I mean, literally. My grandfather, even when he was around, wasn't the type to read a page. Let me spark this up."

"I would be mighty grateful to her," I said.

"Just don't put the moves on her."

Standing up, Felix lit a hollowed-out Philly's Blunt and examined the two of us. It seemed he noticed for the first time we were identical twins. A sceptical grin stole onto his lightly pitted face from somewhere far off-stage. Like Ashraf, Felix's thinking happened deep in the background. It was strange that he held the cigar at so dainty an angle, I reflected, reminding me at that particular moment of a certain maiden with a fan in our high school production of *The Mikado*. Before I got to know *Goldfinger*, by the way, I would have identified my chief literary influence as Gilbert and Sullivan from *The Pirates of Penzance* to *The Mikado*.

"Specifically about a library card, Firoze," Felix continued, his voice slowing to a drawl, expelling a cloud of granulated smoke, and settling into the armchair. "I don't have one handy but next time I am in or around Prospect Park I'll do my best to steal one from a library visitor. When you ask a Latin King, my friends," he explained, his accent perceptibly thickening, "you get the royal treatment. Hence the name. I am going to hook you up with everything you need. Say, is it getting hot in here? Suddenly I can hardly keep my eyes open."

Ashraf said, "Stay calm."

"That's easy for you to say."

Felix's pupils were expanded, I saw, into unsteady whorls of black. On his forehead was a pane of perspiration he wiped with the back of a hand. At the same time he was shivering. In a minute he did calm down and stretched out on the sofa. With his eyes closed he kept talking to us pretty much from his sleep. His zoned-out voice was soon stilled. I had a fairly good idea of what just happened, and of just who might be responsible for this turn of events.

"What did you put in his drink?"

"Two hundred milligrams of Largactyl. Chlorpromazine is the scientific name, but you also hear it called thorazine when administered orally. It's nothing but a fast-acting sedative and, by the way, an anti-psychotic. In case you have any more, ahem, difficult moments in the future, Firoze, I have a bottle in the bathroom."

I asked, "Are you bonkers?"

My brother wasn't repenting. "No, I wouldn't say that I am."

"You have to be raving mad to poison the natives in our first few months in a new country. This is your classmate and my friend." Saying this set off my own feelings. "This is my friend, for God's sake. Have you thought about how you're going to square it with the superintendent having dispatched his nephew to a higher plane? Have you thought about how you're going to square it with me, having murdered my first real friend?"

Ashraf took the blanket from the bunk bed, laying it carefully over Felix. He unlaced my friend's Adidas sneakers, worked them off his feet, placed them side by side beside the couch. To see him do it you would have sworn it was a loving gesture, rather than the flamboyant stage effect of a moral monster.

"Don't worry, Firoze. Felix will be fine, caballero. I'll fill in his hours at 7-11 so you both don't get fired. Meanwhile, watch him. If he wakes up give him orange juice, and don't say a word about the situation. As Felix says, respect him." His thoughts turned to a different danger. "Don't lay a hand on him."

"I resent that implication."

Ashraf has the idea that trading insults is a way of expressing affection. It's his Kojak affectation. A sharper mind than mine could return my brother's mockeries and witticisms, but it's impossible to preserve my dignity around him. Moulana Abbas – I decided while I was watching Felix in his deep-as-a-princess sleep – was wrong. Ashraf is the undercutter and capsizer of everything stable in life. That's why he's a natural in a country which perpetually dissolves its own fixities. Ashraf keeps lowering the tone of the exchange until simply participating in it is enough to make one feel soiled.

I promised an explanation of Ashraf's motivations in taking Spanish class at Brooklyn College. It was the first time my brother had ever chosen to advance the cause of his own education. He enrolled in them of his own accord and was paying the monthly fees out of the till at 7-11 where he visited me after hours. In the back of the store I found my brother memorising lists of vocabulary – colours, Spanish cardinals and ordinals, common names, garments, parts of the body from el ojo, the eye, to the teeth, los dientes, in la cabeza, the head. Spanish, the loving tongue, harmonises with English. At our old school, Sacred Heart Academy, in Johannesburg, Ashraf wouldn't have been caught dead with homework before him unless he was copying it from my notebook.

115

Ashraf's sudden love of learning kindled new love for my brother within my breast until I began to think why he enrolled at Brooklyn College. There was the fact that he wanted to meet girls of an appropriate age and willing disposition, having heard all sorts of stories from Felix about Venezuelans and Colombians. At the back of my brother's mind, I'm convinced, was a certain idea about culture. He wanted to speak Spanish, act Spanish, dress like a kid from San Juan in a padded high-school football jacket, because a new minority imitates a bigger minority. That's my Tocquevillian perspective. But I don't mean to be heavy. To be as light as a swallow is my cosmic ideal.

When imitating the currency didn't exactly work out Ashraf started getting seriously into cards. My brother always liked driver's licences. In Brooklyn he discovered the joys of other cards – credit cards, debit cards, subway fares, sandwich-shop cards, merchandise cards, social-security cards, every manner of card, in fact, except library cards. From a plastic sheet my brother, armed with attitude and a pair of green-lipped garden shears, cut licence-sized portions before wheeling out his tickertape punch. It was his idea of earning a living.

Atta was coming to town, I understood, and there was a big order from Mohammad and his friends. Those Saudi and Egyptian guys, in league with the Pakistanis, were up to something big. They were very concerned that their documents be prepared on time. So one morning I went along with my brother to Long Island Jewish Medical Centre in New Hyde Park. Felix had a cousin who worked as an orderly there who filled us in on the layout and copied his keys for us.

We took the train out to New Hyde Park where my brother attempted the not especially difficult task of persuading the hospital that he was a schizophrenic and had to be admitted. The Jamaican nurse was accommodating, allowing me to sit in on her inpatient examination in order to keep my brother calm. Ashraf rolled his eyes and spoke the few words of Latin he got by osmosis in Standard Five along with many paragraphs of the rolling pig Latin which is the one tongue in which my brother achieves true eloquence. Impressed by this discourse, the nurse advanced us to the attending psychiatrist, a Dr Böhrendorf, who was more than encouraging about my brother's symptoms – the voices he heard, the pig Latin, the alternate identities, Ashraf's fratricidal daydreams. Böhrendorf was particularly interested in Ashraf's relationship with our parents and asked me to assist.

I was pleased to relate my brother's struggles with truth and ladies of the night and the American way. Böhrendorf looked thoughtful as I explained about Fazila and Pakistan and the curse of brigadiers. I was about to talk about Mohammad Atta when Ashraf glared at me and we went on to talk more about what it was like to have an academic as a mother. Although I was in two minds about it at the time, Ashraf's diagnosis of himself as a schizo was maybe not so far off the mark because we are, after all, Geminis.

Dr Böhrendorf was impressed by our joint statement. He wiped his small thin hands on his beard, took copious notes, and mentioned a journal article he was writing that this would be perfect for. I knew that Dr B. wouldn't ever get such a textbook case of schizophrenia since, after all, we had drummed up Ashraf's symptoms from a Barnes and Noble psychiatry textbook. If anyone lives for his textbook cases, I figured, it has to be a Long Island psychiatrist. But that's the worst thing I'll say about Long Island. I won't ever succumb to the prejudices of New Yorkers against certain islands. New York is a city of islands, from Long Island to Staten Island, and Manhattan to Roosevelt Island, and Governor's Island and Ellis Island. A jailbird who believes that every man is an island, and who loves a city of many islands, has no business taking sides in the war of each island against every other.

We were admitted to the inner sanctum of the psychiatric ward. A hair-raising Friday morning ensued in the corridors of Long Island Jewish Medical Centre. We played peek-a-boo with the head nurse and ducked into the billing department. We raced past a security guard before slipping into the operating theatre. Ashraf tried hide-and-seek with an irascible neurosurgeon, a guy who, ironically, had no brains whatsoever.

We couldn't figure out where the patient records were kept. I went one way. Ashraf went the other, and we met by accident in the hospital cafeteria where my brother found a server's apron and a long wooden spoon. Ashraf had a curious chipmunk grin as he lashed portions onto patients' plates. We stayed there until the end of lunch while we compared notes. Neither of us had gotten close to the billing records and their precious data.

Finally we spent hours going from one private room to the next on the psychiatric floor hoping to escape from the same doctor who admitted us in the first place. Dr Böhrendorf wasn't the happy man he had been in the morning. It's sad for any decent psychiatrist when a textbook case fishes your medical degree off the wall of your office, and adds insult to injury by helping

117

himself to your brown-bag lunch. I wouldn't be surprised if that morning was the seed for a ferocious persecution mania on Böhrendorf's part. I waved to him through the window of the elevator as we descended into the basement. Ashraf found a hand truck and carted a file cabinet out of the emergency-room entrance and into the subway. No one followed us onto the train.

It was nice to be out of the city, and then to come back. On our way home from the Island Ashraf and I walked through the evening crowds on their back and forth ant marches. We speculated about people's movements, asked about this one patrolling the corner of Fulton and Clinton, that one opening her bag to retrieve a cheque book, whistled at the beautiful, sharp-nosed girl in a peasant's shawl descending the winding stairway to the C train, hassled the made-up guy who worked at Stingy Lulus on Tompkins Square Park, joked with the rusted, reeling old man in a formal brown buttoned vest and tie who brought jars of brown liquor into the subway in a paper bag. The muscle men, the Circassians, memoirists, sidewalk notables, fry cooks, passing shoppers and shop owners were suddenly our New York brothers and sisters. We were on more intimate terms with our fellow New Yorkers now that we had a random sampling of their social-security numbers.

All in all I was getting to like the city, even getting to be comfortable in Brooklyn. Although I can't honestly say I liked it, I increasingly found Brooklyn to be neighbourly – if by that elastical term you comprehend the neighbourly feeling of the Serbs for the Bosnians and the neighbourly glow that lights the hearts of the Hutus when their thoughts turn to the Tutsis next door. People kept turning to stare at us as my brother tried to keep the file cabinet out of their way.

Our reward was a pile of patient records that yielded many more names, addresses, and social security numbers than were needed. Before five in the afternoon Ashraf produced a wallet's worth of cards, thirteen cards in thirteen different names. Most were blank. Several had a raised thirteen-digit account number that Ashraf ran his fingers up and down like a man who knows how to read Braille. My brother's eyes shone with a cruel green joy. The colour in his eyes resembled the flame off a pellet of sodium. I saw that colour first in chemistry class and never since until this particular moment.

"What do you think?"

I said, "It's a beautiful thing to see, Ashraf. You're finally making something of yourself. You fooled the doctor into thinking you were a schizophrenic, which is a major achievement even if it's also true. Then you make these from scratch. A real day's work."

"You want to take them and go on a spending spree? Go to Barnes and Noble, or the Strand. Get a complete set of, what's his name, Schopenhauer? Chopin-hauer?"

"Thanks but no. I don't want to get arrested like unlucky Felix," I replied. "I have too much to read. Let me see what you're doing for Atta though."

"It's a secret. But now I've finished doing their commission those guys are going to be in town soon to collect. Maybe as soon as next week. You can ask them yourself."

If you define a friend as I do, as someone whose misfortunes are simultaneously sweet and bitter to one, then Moulana Abbas was my friend on Atlantic Avenue. His office in the mosque was right around the corner from our pad and he started calling on me in an inimitably Egyptian manner. Abbas usually had an indefinable cloud about him of attendants, assistants, male secretaries, but he sent them away to talk to me and Felix in confidence. Or he took us out to Damascus pastry shop. I think he saw us both as potential converts.

One afternoon the moulana brought Mohammad Atta by to see my brother and said hardly a word to me. Abbas soon disappeared on the arm of his assistant Sayeed, and left us alone with Atta and his number one friend Ziad. I ended up sitting across the table from them as Ashraf set up his apparatus to show off. Ashraf was concerned to make a good impression because these people, he insisted, could introduce us to Saudi billionaires. Still they weren't easy to get along with. Atta was distant with me, not wanting to talk about our adventures in Pakistan. He seemed to have rolled back all our knowledge of one another. As for Ziad, he was not as much of a scowler as his leader but he was certainly uncomfortable and kept looking at his Timex. Ashraf set up the slide projector and showed them pictures of his new licences.

My brother was professional. "By the way, Mohammad, and Ziad, I hope, if things work out, you mention me to friends and family. To begin with, I've prepared a wallet with everything you wanted. Here's a Florida driver's licence. Here's another driver's licence. It's Swiss. Then there are credit cards, a social security card, everything you need to get a legitimate job. There's a firearms licence, a farmer's explosives certificate so you can pick up nitrates when you need them. If there's anything else I would be delighted to help out. When are you going back to Florida?"

"Tomorrow," Atta replied. "We have a job to do that needs to get done very soon. Say, what do you guys do around here for fun?"

We went to one of Ashraf's favourite places – a Korean massage parlour out in Red Hook where we had separate cubicles separated by paper screens. I was out first, then watched as Atta had his muscular back pounded by one of the maidens. By now you know what she was like, a fierce young lady with a triangular face and linen layers of makeup on her face. She had an expression of terrible concentration as she drummed on his shoulders. The towel was bound around the guy so tight that his face was flushed with blood. He could hardly speak. I sat on the chair next to the bed. There was a curious, very intense look of disgust and pleasure on Atta's big face as his attendant turned him around, lifted up his white towel, and finished him off, as they say in the business.

Atta drank a fair amount of saki. Afterwards he wasn't steady on his feet. Ashraf and I had to support him between us. It was tough being stuck with these two characters. I caught my brother in the cubicle adding Largactyl to Atta's cup and figured we didn't need any more enemies so I stayed close to the both of them. I emptied out the cup when Ashraf wasn't looking. I could hear our visitor talking to himself under his breath but only after a minute did I realise that Atta was cursing the Jews. I paid the bill with one of my brother's cards.

We got the big fellow into a taxi and took him home with us. Ashraf's head was spinning so he went to sleep in Dad's bedroom. I was left to take off our guest's clothing and help him into a pair of my cotton pyjamas. As I had his shirt half open Atta woke up suddenly. He was as strong as an octopus. Atta grabbed me around the neck. His grip was tight and he tried to force his mouth onto mine. I felt his breath dark on me. With unexpected power I pushed him into the bathroom, locked the door, and went to sleep next to Ashraf. He didn't mind sharing a bed with me.

The Farewell Insurance Company was my father's creation which he began working on the very day we signed the lease on the apartment. He had been dreaming about it since I explained the plot of Gogol's *Dead Souls*. Dad's previous idea was to start a restoration house for Fabergé eggs, send imitations back to the owners, and flog the originals. I admit that I pushed Dad towards the insurance company idea in the hope of keeping his thoughts away from the divorce, his no-show brother, and other difficulties. Enterprise, energy, agency were – in my opinion and Tocqueville's – this society's great virtues. I figured it was vital for Dad to assimilate and work is the highest form of assimilation, after marriage.

"You two boys will help me with the business," he assured himself as we strolled down to Montague Street to have a look at the Statue of Liberty for the very first time. The waters were choppy around Governor's Island. "Once I get in touch with Micah's connection Crogan, we will get the ball rolling. I want you two to look out for each other."

"Don't worry about poor Ashraf," I replied. "I'll take care of you, my brother."

"I'll take care of you first."

"You both take care of each other," Dad insisted. "Firoze, you're taking the philosophy classes you always dreamed of. Ashraf, you're learning Spanish at my expense. But please, remember that your primary responsibility is to our financial future."

I said, "Business is business."

The Farewell Insurance Company was registered in a filing with the State of New York on the 4th of January, 2001, for a fee of $1299 plus a 2.5% surcharge. The fee and surcharge consumed the last of our ready cash. One-third of the twelve-ninety-nine was a payment to the state government for accepting our certificate of incorporation, pursuant to section 402 of the Business Corporation Law. The remaining two-thirds went into the coffers of a small-time attorney, C.D. Crogan. The fraction, I saw, was significant. Two out of three joules of American energy goes into protecting oneself and one's property from other Americans . . . and their lawyers. I spent a lot of time with Dad in Crogan's office going over the documentation while Ashraf filled in for me at 7-11.

C.D. Crogan's offices were situated on a nice section of Steinway Street in Astoria, Queens. We spent a good deal of time going back and forth on the subway. Ashraf's absence was a result of his instant antipathy to Crogan. My brother wanted us to find a Pakistan-born attorney, or someone from our general corner of the world. But it's said by people who know that you truly arrive in the United States when you retain the service of an indigenous lawyer.

Crogan had been recommended to my father by Farouk's old connection Micah Tarnofsky, Sol the Rabbi's son, who spent half the year in San Diego, nowadays, and half in semi-retirement in the Cape Atlantic village of Muizenberg. Dad had maintained good relations with Tarnofsky's son, strangely enough, ever since he testified against his own brother at the mental-health hearing before helping to spring Farouk from the Roodepoort asylum.

Crogan himself was a big, ruddy character who seemed to be caged in his law offices, his big elbows pointing out of a battered tartan sports jacket. By heritage he was seven-eighths Irish Catholic and one-eighth Cherokee. The Cherokee part he was proudest of, perhaps because it gave him the authority to scalp people. He was a television Texan with his stature and his crest of red hair that he combed back with his enormous hands when thinking, to reveal stretches of coppery scalp and tiny ears formed in the pattern of a gladiolus. There was a strange perfume about the man that my nose identified as a mixture of fried liver and Aramis cologne.

Crogan, to finish describing him, had the blown out, cellulous cheeks of a cornet player, riding his big belly across a room as if he was mounted on a horse. The guy grew up as a street tough, ninth of nine kids, in one of Philadelphia's Irish and Italian suburbs, and had his law degree from Temple University. He was in his late forties, married to his massage parlours, and a friend of Tarnofsky from some California business they had in common. Since opening his New York office Crogan was fast becoming a luminary of the local Republican party which, in a place like New York, needs all the help it can get.

As is true of many sons of the city of brotherly love, C.D. Crogan was a perky, inquisitive, interfering, and supremely blithe individual. It's just that he presumed to know everything. He asked all sorts of nonsense, made all sorts of pronouncements without belligerence. Bluff, blithe, bullying, call him what you will, I was fascinated by Crogan. He couldn't have been more different from Felix. Amazing I should run into such a stereotype – a blowhard, booster, and a boaster. Crogan put his long, red-furred arms around my shoulders and I imagined I was being embraced by a continent.

"So, Solomon, let me have a look at these papers and then we're going to go out and celebrate." Crogan eased his belly off the desk, and gave the contracts to my father to sign. He pushed his chair back and put his large feet up, showing us the cudgels of two heels. "By the end of the week you're going to be managers of a corporation. It's the American dream to run your own company and it's taken you all of what, three months? Talk about industrious immigrants. Firoze, how are you?"

"Very well."

Crogan fixed me with his bulging eyes. They were big and hard as golfballs, his most prominent feature after that belly. His eyes were suddenly violet and full of menace. He said, "We'll make it even better." He spoke in a deliberate twang as if choosing a guitar chord. I expected him to tell a joke but he didn't. "If we're going to be involved in this together, we have to trust each other. Micah Tarnofsky speaks very highly of your father, Firoze, which is why I am going in on this with you. Just don't expect it to be a picnic. Life insurance, especially from the angle you're going to be approaching it, is a very tricky line of business. People have an ugly habit of dying. You can't trust that only honest, healthy people are going to walk in your door and take out a policy."

To some members of the reading public, it may be unseemly to hear of a company in a work of literature while its operations are the subject of a congressional inquiry and its very name is music to the ears of ambitious prosecutors. To encounter in a literary document the title of the Farewell Insurance Company, whose donations to the Republican Party fell under scrutiny by commissioners of the Federal Election Commission, may strike my readers as a confusion between the sphere of imagination and the domain of legislation.

I hereby state that the material contained here is purely fictional, whatever its resemblance to real corporations and real crimes. I can't resist adding that, in a counterfeit nation, the story of Farewell Insurance may be the very model of American enterprise. It exemplifies the power of pseudo-reality in the United States.

To understand Dad's scheme, you need to know something about how an insurance company operates. It sells policies to individuals but doesn't take any of the associated risks. The reinsurance company is what makes a payout. The reinsurer receives the stream of monthly premiums, minus fees. And in the event of a payout the reinsurer forwards the full amount to the insurance company which disburses it to the victim's family. In sum an insurance company is really a shopfront for a reinsurer. That was the key to my father's scheme.

I was helping Dad set up a variety of imaginary policy holders. We had a bunch of Ashraf's psychiatric patients to use but even then it was a complicated affair. We accumulated a stack of directories, local newspapers, birth and obituary listings that let us set up networks of relatives, printouts of driver's licences and car registrations, arrest sheets, credit card applications, photostats of public records from the town clerk in a dozen jurisdictions from Poughkeepsie to the north down as far south as Wilmington, Delaware. My father had several folders open on the carpet in his bedroom along with pairs of scissors, cardboard, vinyl, file folders, skeletal tubes of glue, string, erasers, and packets of paper clips. The whole thing was conducted in something of the atmosphere of a nursery school project.

I said, "I don't understand how you're going to make all this money from imaginary customers."

"That's the beauty of it, Firoze." Dad took the bait. His masculine love of explanations, I knew, would outweigh the activity, not to say any new thoughts about my mother. "Our reinsurance company pays a considerable bonus to us when we sign up a new account. Then we send them the dues on that account each month out of the bonus money. So far you understand? After some time that customer is going to meet a terrible fiery death. Then we stop paying the imaginary premiums. When the payout on the policy arrives we take that entire sum in addition. After all, there are no widows and children among our customers."

"It would make a nice motto. No widows and children."

Humour started Dad thinking about something else. "All I can think about, during the night, is that it would be infinitely more dignified to be a widower than my current predicament of a divorced older man. Whenever we went shopping, you know, I had no idea that behind my back your mother was robbing the place blind. Perhaps if I had been more domineering, more interested in ruling the roost, things would never have gotten so out of hand."

"Why don't I put some music on, to get you out of the dumps? Sly and the Family Stone?"

We took a break. The Japanese would have called it a tea ceremony but we weren't so formal. Dad was involved in the minutiae of the process. It was all a matter of getting the details right. The rules were elaborate. The kettle must be settled right on the flaming blue stove ring and emptied at the very height of the boil. It sounded like a lullaby. The browning liquid was to be stewed seven and a quarter minutes in an already warmed pot, one Five Roses tea bag for the each of us, one for the gadrooned pot. Hot milk must be stirred in, drop by drop, from a small sterling silver milk jug that was cool on the hands. The right strainer was essential even if we were using tea bags. If the water you were using was hard water, if it was soft water, if it was the colour of tin, or if it was off in this or that way, certain adjustments had to be made in the aforegoing procedures.

There was hardly any other crockery or furniture in the apartment. Acquiring the apparatus for tea-making had been my father's first imperative on moving in. Tea and money were the substances that restored his soul. I gave him the bowl of rock sugar and we sat there on the carpet drinking. Sly and the Family Stone, a minor classic in Dad's canon, played softly in the background. If the Family Stone didn't cheer him up, we'd try the big guns – Aretha, Marvin Gaye, the Marvelettes.

I was still curious. "Are the reinsurers going to catch on?"

"Eventually they are. Then we change our names. Unless we can come up with some sort of accident, some sort of disaster, that would remove a bunch of imaginary customers at once. Ah, Firoze, if we had a catastrophe we could really lose a lot of clients and turn a pretty penny." Dad sipped from his cup. His buggy green eyes were full of green thoughts. "C.D. has some ideas about how to prolong the process. He's eager to start but he suggests we plan on eliminating one-seventh of our clientele each month. Is that in the ballpark?"

"It's dangerous to take out a policy with Farewell Insurance."

"Buying life insurance is like hexing yourself," Dad observed, putting down his cup and bringing our conversation to an end. "Goodness gracious. It's the same as putting a price on your head. You do the numbers."

Whatever reservations I hold about my father he has always been the most interesting personality in the room. Whereas for him, in any room, money is the most interesting presence. Money and myself together are the best combination for my father. Around money Dad can talk to me about matters, like his relationship with my mother, which are impossible for him to address directly. It's as if only the money he's going to make is listening to him.

"I didn't want to talk about it but my sources tell me that Sameera has taken up with a house painter in Australia. Some Chinese customer." Sensing something in my face he added, "You know me well enough to understand that it's not the fact that he's not a Muslim and not an Indian that bothers me, though it's bad enough. But what sort of example does it set for our two boys?"

"It's as if she's trying to sting you to death."

He said, "It's astonishing you understand such things, Firoze, at your age."

"I'm not so young any more. Besides, Dad, I'm familiar with these motivations from Russian novels."

It was the right thing to say. You could see a burden was removed from my father's back. It was the burden of solitary consciousness of which I am all too aware. American readers should know that like most Indian Muslim men, reared in a backwards culture of conversation, the idea of going to a mental-health professional was unintelligible to Dad. My mother's recidivist shoplifting, her dark brew of philosophy and feminist self-help manuals, and his long-range jealousies which hovered first around a mail clerk in Adelaide, then a Turkish butcher who played backgammon with his customers, now this painter who would be breathing in the humid smell of her glossy dark hair, these weren't matters to be discussed with a stranger.

"Firoze, my boy, am I dwelling on this unnecessarily?"

"Not at all, Dad. Quite the opposite," I said. Advice, I feel, should help the other person get in touch with their worse selves. "Dad, to be honest, my view is that you won't have a minute of peace and quiet until you've exacted some kind of revenge."

American proverbs are the most mysterious and the easiest to misuse. In them is condensed the folkish wisdom of the prairies. A drop of honey catches more flies than a gallon of gall. He's like a dog trying to shake his own fleas. That dog won't hunt. I can hook you up. And, of course, you do the numbers.

"You do the numbers" was now Dad's favourite expression in the world. It wasn't clear to me what he meant by it, although it certainly wasn't the original meaning. He probably intended it as an intensifier. Dad had picked up that particular saying from my friend Felix Corvalho Villaverde. Felix was a relentless misuser of proverbs. So they had something in common. My father came to look on the superintendent's nephew as an accomplice, which is really the highest compliment he can pay to a younger man. It's not as if they agreed about what they were saying though. By that proverb Felix meant only to indicate that he wasn't very good at mathematics. *You* do the numbers.

After all, you're better at arithmetic. If Felix said "you can take it to the bank", what he meant was a money order.

Like my mother, Felix's grasp on certain aspects of reality wasn't altogether firm. Felix was a moral amnesiac, quick to forgive a grudge, quick even to forget its reason. Lucky for Ashraf this was so, because Felix didn't look closely into his sudden sleeping fit after Spanish class. Instead Felix thought of it as one of those things that happened in life and turned it into almost a self-deprecating joke. "You remember, caballero, when I just dozed off in the middle of the day? I bet you it was quite a surprise. It must have been that I was listening to your philosophical theories. It's a pity you can't put me to sleep every night. I was as stiff as a board when I woke up."

When he said these things, pursing his long thin dark mouth under his strip of moustache, I liked Felix for his midsummer night's innocence. It was a rare quality to find in a member of the Latin Kings and, in an entirely platonic way, I supposed I even loved the guy for it. And yet I had also begun to fear and mistrust Felix. He frightened me beyond words. It was a great paradox of feeling when it came to my very first friend. Things were topsy-turvy. I thought I was going to be upset by what my brother did to my friend, but instead it was what my friend had so rapidly done to my brother that worried me. The reason? I blamed Felix for being a cotton-picking cultural seducer.

Imagine the feelings of a sensitive soul as the brother with whom he bunks becomes ever more immersed in that immense manufactured cosmos of American names and shows and objects – Taco Bell, Chef Boyardee's (tins of which Felix uncorked in our apartment for his dinner), *Hill Street Blues*, Scottie Pippen, Bruce Willis, Kramer, the Jets, George Steinbrenner. I hardly knew what to make of any of these names and allusions. It was as if Ashraf had begun to live on another planet. He was becoming a real American after so many years of being an American at second hand and the process was happening at the same speed as a photographic plate is stained by exposure to light.

I saw Felix, with his skinny red knuckles, as a kind of cultural Pied Piper. Thanks to his deceiving tune I felt that I was losing contact with my brother. It happened to be Felix but, as I subsequently discovered, just about every American is deputised to act in this missionary capacity. It caused me palpitations to see my brother consenting to be anyone's cultural sidekick. If I didn't mind being a sidekick, well, that had completely different complications.

Felix was the sultan of what he called Drunken Donuts and Ashraf started hanging out there again after class, quite apart from hawking his fake licences there to the Pratt students. It was a place they had independently discovered and it made them better friends. I went along one afternoon to their favourite store on Lexington. Let me offer you the merest impression of the snow-dusted windows of the Dunkin' Donuts store window through which I saw Ashraf leaning his muscular head to one side. Felix and my brother cadged Craven As from the staff, smoked them out the door, and talked big at a corner table. Felix got refreshments, a tray of cups, pastries, sugar, and thimbles of milk. They were distributed in silence. I was on a diet although I hadn't told anyone. I needed to be. So, I told myself, did my brother.

Felix, with the shape of a Bunsen burner beneath his denim jacket, was different. He was, I thought, the Brooklyn equivalent of Sugarboy, that old retainer of the Dawoods. Felix had the kind of metabolism that, in its twenty-ninth year of operation, took in indefinite quantities of Dunkin' sugar, starch, mentholated smoke, raisins, espresso, and marbled coffee rolls without adding an ounce of fat to his frame. He was adapted to an American environment. The great volume of Felix's intake, in my opinion, was burned in the boiler room of his soul and thus created that thick incense of nervousness. On the other hand it was his very nervousness which made him such a good companion. Felix was so far on edge that he couldn't stand for anyone else to be disturbed. It made him a natural host.

"Everyone good? Everyone have what they want, approximately? You know, I envy the Canadians," Felix resumed, raising his eyebrows in an unconscious Groucho Marx imitation. "They have natural relations between the sexes. In this country maybe they are superficially easier but it's only on the surface. The way it's set up in America is that a female gives you grief after she's provided you with a little sugar. That's as opposed to making you pay up front, like in Canada, and then giving you as much as you want afterwards. But look, I don't want to make any big generalisations here. That's just how I see it."

"No, I think you're quite right, Felix," I said.

"As a Latin King I find that this American attitude to men disrespects my dignity." He pulled the tuft of horsey hair on his prow of a chin. "Maybe I would be happier up in Canada."

He and my brother got to talking about Felix's gang of Latin Kings. As it happened I had been doing some research of my own. The Latin Kings Felix kept mentioning were a mainly Chicago outfit. They were low-level operators working out of their clubhouses – streetcorner tax collectors, bagmen for the truly big syndicates, the magpies of city blocks, indefatigable recyclers of stolen hubcaps and car batteries. There wasn't a niche for Latin Kings in the five boroughs, which are a vertical rather than horizontal habitat. Thugs in New York have to use their brains, not their trigger fingers. Yet there was no way to prove Felix wrong on the subject of the New York branch of the Kings. Philosophers believe there's no way to prove something doesn't exist if someone's already given it a name. Plus Felix had the ultimate benefit of his say-so, that very last redoubt of an American, from which no bombardment by contrary evidence will dislodge him.

"Look, what's the point in you two brothers being mad at each other? It's negative energy, man," Felix protested, "and it's getting me down, frankly. You two have to come to an understanding, as brothers. You have to learn to love. What say we go over to my grandmother's place in Stuyvesant Town? It's nearby on the C train. She has a rent-control apartment. You'll like her, Firoze, I promise. Does that sound like an idea?"

Ashraf politely said he would like to meet Felix's grandmother and that was the beginning of half an adventure with my friend. Just when you were about to write the guy off as a talkative gangster along came his grandmother. Gitta insisted on being called by her first name by everyone including her only grandson. She lived in a heavily decorated, heavily furnished, heavily mothballed apartment in Stuyvesant Town, overlooking Peter Cooper and its brown-and-red ziggurats. Gitta's place was curiously preserved from the Budapest of her childhood. She welcomed us into it and set out a round of porcelain cups and saucers.

To go by the fraying net of white hair on her head and chalky complexion Gitta must have been in her eighties though she stayed sharp. She had eyes which were as blue as a March morning but clouded over when she was anxious. Like her grandson she was prone to uneasiness and her thin, silver-bangled wrists, overstuffed with the macaroni of hard veins, were shivering.

Apart from her physical impediments she was frighteningly alert and willing to tangle. She liked to talk, to argue, to debate, to win her point. From watching them interact I saw she had little patience for her grandson. It was a flying guess but I thought she was the kind of tough grandmother who tried to bury Felix under the rubble of her disappointment and then lost interest in him as an intellectual being. It was primarily as intellectual beings that people either engaged, or didn't engage, Gitta's attention. It was clear that she thought of Ashraf as rather a young charmer even if she didn't seem to be charmed herself. I liked Gitta all the more for this although she also intimidated me.

I found out later from Felix that his grandmother had been a chess player, a mathematician, and a tennis star at gymnasium, in Budapest, before ending up here with her father as a refugee. She never really found her feet in this country. Marriage to an American, six decades of radio and newspapers, weekly expeditions to the New York Public Library had left her utterly unscathed and untransformed. With her experiences at the hands of destiny she was a serious gambler . . . but I'll get there.

Thinking about it now, with the luxury of prison-house psychology, Gitta, who preserved the traces of a Hungarian accent somewhere in the region of her mare's nose, must have been the source of Felix's boundless anxieties about life. She might have passed them on through her genes, although more likely, in my opinion, was that she had trained his nerves from a young age. All in all, she was a tough nut, someone who thought nothing of scolding Felix right in front of his friends.

"So what scheme is my grandson talking you into?"

"Nothing that I know of," I said.

"Rubbish. That's absolute rubbish. I won't believe a word you tell me from now on, Ashraf and Firoze. Felix is always up to something, some con job. In junior high he made a pretty penny selling stolen hubcaps back to the Turtle Bay Firestone. I taught Felix to drive, you know, on my late husband's Oldsmobile. Then he used the knowledge to get into all sorts of trouble. You know, Firoze, Felix gets all his ingenuity from my side of the family."

"I can quite believe it."

"And you, young man, shouldn't be keeping company with young men like this. They are sure to land you in trouble. Do you all have enough tea? Ah, if I was twenty years younger I would take the lot of you with me to Atlantic City. I am sure you would be great fun."

In her younger days, as Felix later told us, Gitta had been a regular at the racecourse in Saratoga, New York, at the Bridgeport, Connecticut, dog races, and at Atlantic City. Friday afternoons the buses from Port Authority went up to Saratoga Springs, to Connecticut, to New Jersey, and every Sunday they returned with a cargo of older ladies and gentlemen troubled by the inconsistencies of dogs and horses. Half a lifetime of losing, to say nothing of the influence of historical experience, had left Gitta with an abiding distrust of fate. She was a strongly flavoured woman, I thought, with her accent and her nose, which was positively vulpine. It conferred on her that air of authority towards which, in Gitta as in all other commanding human beings, I am drawn.

In a matter of minutes I developed a soft spot for the woman. Let's say it was even a crush if that word can be interpreted spiritually. It was almost the first time I felt that way about a woman since those fifteen seconds with Tigerlily, and I mean this in the least carnal of senses. Gitta was the most aristocratic person I had met even in the midst of democratic New York. But it was the idea of entitlement that was entirely new to me. It wasn't the aristocratic sentiment common to the Johannesburg Dawoods, which involves the profound love of ease and an ineradicable sense of entitlement.

In Gitta the aristocratic spirit manifested itself as the conviction that she had been created in order to judge the great chain of being and to police its hierarchies. She had such a strong sense of what was right and wrong, good, bad, and better, in culture, politics, morality. I was particularly impressed by her being so unsentimental a creature, as dry as a Chardonnay, when it came to her own family. It showed integrity. All the same, when it came time to leave, she was suddenly downcast. She spread her hands over her grandson's and rubbed them gently, as if she was searching for the bones.

"When Felix was very young I wanted him to be a pianist," she said. "He has such lovely long fingers."

After all her complaining Gitta did take us to Foxwoods the following week in her battered Honda Civic. We lost everything we had and Ashraf blew a lot of money on his fake credit cards to no avail. The drive back to the city compensated a little for our gamblers' sorrows. Everyone in the car was subdued. On the local roads we passed through the towns dotted on Long Island Sound. There were high clapboard houses on the main streets and above the small harbours. There was a good deal of faded, comfortable luxury in these places – Westport, Branford, Stonington. The antique shops with French chairs in the window and the squadrons of yachts at the nearby docks were signs of Connecticut money. It wasn't at all flashy. Even the Bentleys and Rolls-Royces parked at the plummy local restaurants were older models, nicely broken in.

Sheds filled with rigging, bait sold in the grocery, and the schooners on the

mild grey water in the Sound told us that fishing was still alive as an occupation on the Connecticut shore, but it wasn't until we reached Bridgeport that
there was any real industry. Red-brick funnels rising out of the hilltop factories
burned enormous white bales of smoke into the sky. The cranes standing in the
harbour were busy loading pallets on battered freighters. A ferry discharged
cars on to the seafront streets. On the back step of a harbour dive a Chinese
boy was slicing chunks off the large pink body of a fish and queuing them up
in a metal basin between his knees.

The evening we got back from Foxwoods Casino the phone rang in the bedroom while Ashraf was fixing dinner in the kitchen. I picked it up only to
recognise Mohammad Atta's voice by its cracked timbre. His voice sounded
as if it was about to break, especially now that he was agitated. Atta spoke in
Arabic at first which I couldn't understand. Then he switched to unsteady
Urdu of which I knew a few words, and finally to English, when he figured
out I had no idea what was being said.

He was calling from Memorial Hospital in Tampa, Florida. Atta, it turned
out, had been picked up after showing one of Ashraf's driver's licences. The
state trooper checked the name and then took Atta over to Memorial's psychiatric wing because the name he had just looked up was that of an escaped
schizophrenic. The hospital staff planned to move Atta back to New York state
where he was still listed as an inpatient of Long Island Jewish Medical Centre.
Ziad Jarrah, Atta's number-one friend, had been picked up after he used the
licence of a man with dissociative disorder from Suffolk County.

Not only that but the other members of their crew had been in and out
of the nuthouse over the past fortnight thanks to my brother's credit cards
and other proofs of identity. They had been injected, thumped, electrified,
disinfected, zapped, dipped, interrogated, pickled and brined, gagged, and
thumped some more. They had been whopped and paddled. Atta himself had
been let out of his straitjacket long enough to dial our number. I heard the
attendants sewing him back into it even as we talked. The guy was, I suppose
understandably, furious.

"Don't get your knickers in a twist," I said. "Look, Mohammad, I can come
down to Florida and I guess I could even vouch for your sanity. I mean, I
don't know personally if you're crazy or not but I'm willing to believe in you
for argument's sake. Do you want me to come down and tell them you're not

who they think you are? Just for the record, what name are you travelling under?" I looked through Ashraf's book. "Is it Roger Hillensorg? Could it be Frank X. Calluchio?"

"Forget the name. I'll get out of this myself," Atta replied. His voice, which had been bristling with indignation, was suddenly as cold as a soldier's. This sudden coldness may have been the result of the straitjacket pressing on his neck. "Forget my name as well. When I catch up with you ridiculous brothers, you're going to know all about names. We're not the type you can fool around with. Who asked you to give us identities out of a mental hospital? What kind of lunatic would do it?"

"I don't think you're in any position to talk about lunatics. And if this has anything to do with what you tried to pull the other night, please, grow up. Deal with the rejection."

"You watch it, Peer."

لـب

Chapter Six

Sayeed with his detonator and cricket bat . . . upstate New York in burning September when the high grey barns outside Utica disgorge chains of sparrows and redpolls . . . Pearl Bronson naked except for white stockings and pearl earrings . . . a soundless loop of video showing an airplane's cylinder jammed into the side of the second tower while the streets below filled with vaporised concrete and the inaudible music of dragonflies.

That stretch of video, I feel, is as mysterious as the Zapruder tape. Like a spiritual Möbius strip, it will never let us get to the other side of it. Like thinking people everywhere, I have never been one to take sides in a political dispute unless it's against myself. I see no reason to jettison this happy principle, but I woke up every morning after the attacks having suppressed all knowledge of what had happened and, each and every morning, had to undergo a painful suspension of denial. It's hard for a jailhouse memoirist to seize an image from the public's memory and bear it off to his glasshouse. At this contest of imaginations I am bound to fail, so I resign myself to quoting the loop of video and saying that it wasn't the worst thing that happened to us during that week. And it was all my fault.

I didn't mention Atta's threat to Ashraf, I think because I didn't take the guy seriously despite his aroma of sulphur. Besides, we were going on holiday for the first time in years. The three of us would be together and naturally I was taking on Mum's role of making sure that everyone in our small family was in good spirits. Ashraf promised there was going to be a surprise fourth visitor, but I didn't take him seriously either. It's part of my quarrel with stony-eyed fortune that I don't grant her messengers credibility.

That summer was the loveliest season in memory and surely a second coming of August 1914. Dad was in good spirits, having polished off his first generation of policy holders. He was poised to receive the first round of payouts from the reinsurers. Ashraf wasn't even surly. We drove up to the Adirondacks in a healthy frame of mind. Throughout the ride my brother didn't let either of us put a hand on the steering wheel, nor a finger upon the radio dial. He had taken a shine to bluegrass and was happy to inflict his tastes on both of us. We all have different likings. Schubert, of course, is my favourite composer. Under the influence of Lester Flatt Ashraf drove even more quickly. The green exit boards whizzed past the canary-yellow panels of our rented Dodge Caravan and the handful of twenty-four wheel trucks on their way north were as stationary in the afternoon light as cargo ships. Our eventual destination lay outside Tappersville.

In the afternoon, in contrast to the sunlight, the big van was like a shed inside – cool, dark, decayed. Later it was cool outside. Dad opened the window to smoke his Benson & Hedges, left elbow balanced on the ledge. I could still see the bulk of cattle in the darkening fields back a hundred yards from the state highway. There were empty cement dipping tanks, windmills, and trailers with their prominent hitches standing closer to the macadam. Lights strung on telegraph poles came on. Now and again there was a farmhouse lit up across three floors, trucks and tractors parked in front, but there were just as many places which looked to be abandoned. In the car the conversation started and stopped.

"How's Dad doing back there?" Ashraf asked.

"He's fast asleep," I said. "He looks so peaceful under the blanket."

As night was falling we passed a patchwork of horse farms. They were subtended by a six- or seven-hundred-foot ledge that went on for miles in the same direction, and against which we could see the silhouettes of the restless horses. Several turned their heads in our direction as we went by. Others, close to the road, trotted alongside the van for a few minutes before losing interest. A woman wearing a riding helmet was leading a horse towards the stable. There were red numbers and letters on the back of her jacket. Mud came up to the tops of her yellow rubber boots. Holding the reins in one hand, she rinsed the sides of her boots under an outdoor tap before we lost sight of her.

We were now going slowly because of the time of day and had a chance to see a good deal of the land. The silence inside the van and the landscape stimulated odd corners of my soul. We had been pent up in the city forever. There was the temptation to find a horse, grab its reins, and escape over the countryside. The prospect of wild countryside affected my imagination. It was a hope of adventure I associated with Robert Louis Stevenson. But it was an escapist fantasy. I knew my brother and my father couldn't survive without me.

We got to the cabin we'd rented late in the evening yet there was a canopy of blue light amid the mountains. We went to sleep right away and explored early in the morning. The scene was enclosed by stony white slopes that looked down on us like lions. On their flat tops they were crowned with cairns. We hiked up the path and celebrated with a breakfast picnic at the peak. It was my brother's creation – bread, cheese, soft-boiled eggs, and a tin of mustard. To one side below us was the pond, an amber lake, and a clearing in the woods where the cabin's slate chimney could be seen all across this space. On the other side was the beginning of a range of hills that went across to Champlain.

A quarter mile away was a lakeside restaurant with tables arranged on a converted dock. The place was full at eleven in the morning, daylight candles burning in clay lily pads along the side of the water. Music washed up against our mountain with the unsteady motion of the tides. We could hear a passage from Louis Armstrong and Ella Fitzgerald. Scattered notes of the trumpet blew onto our position. It was a dreamy feeling to lie there and wait for the song to reassemble from its separate pieces. Finally we returned to the cabin and went back to sleep for another hour. Then we went out again as if all three of us discovered how desperately we needed nature's spell after being trapped in the labyrinth of Brooklyn.

Ten minutes' walk through the woods from the cabin brought us to a pond and then to the small lake filled with its amber water. The slop of rowing boats could be heard when the boats couldn't be seen. A father and two sons fishing on a bicycle boat came into view. Ashraf cut a dinghy loose from the dock of a house further down and swam it back to shore without oars. He preferred to swim rather than to row and we watched him do freestyle laps of the lake, his sealish head and arms running with brown water. I sat by the edge smoking, my legs crossed, while Dad went inside to finick with his insurance accounts.

"Are you ever going to get out, Ashraf?"

"Go on to town without me if you don't want to wait. I'll catch up. But Firoze, bring my shoes from inside if you're shlepping all the way back here, would you? You might find that Fazila is already here. She was meant to arrive this morning."

"Fazila from Pakistan?"

"Yes, Fazila from Pakistan. Who else?"

The airport limousine was just pulling into the drive when I scrambled back to the cabin. Out spilled Fazila and a hundred bags of different sizes. The last time I had seen her was in the Peshawar airport with Atta, but it seemed like yesterday. The girl was more beautiful than ever, green-eyed and blushing, with as dewy and fresh an expression as an Adirondack daisy even if she was the errant daughter of a Pakistani brigadier. She hugged me, woke up my father from his doze, and unpacked an unending series of presents. There were ties and bowties for my father and me, a scarf for Ashraf, and liqueurs and ointments and leather goods. By the time my brother came back we were opening a series of boxes on the floor.

Fazila brought instant happiness. If it wasn't my crazy family, it would be nice to say that Fazila became a part of the family. A week passed in the mountains, and it was as if we had been in Tappersville forever. Yes, Fazila had a shining, adoring look when she examined my brother, as if she was the flute and his hands were on her stops. Yes, I found Ashraf with his head inside her shirt in the closet one morning, his glazed, guilty expression no match for Fazila's automatic sangfroid.

On the other hand I imagined that my brother might be amenable to sharing Fazila. Why would he keep all the honey to himself? And in any event it was the happiest week we spent together since Ten Percent Farouk's arrest. I thought, if Mom was around, we could get along again as an atomic quartet.

One evening Felix called and told me that one of Mohammad Atta's friends had been hanging around the apartment building, but I thought Felix was exaggerating again. I certainly didn't want to tell my father about it since he had enough on his mind. Anyway, there was no sense in what Felix was saying. I knew Atta was busy with his own scheme, whatever that was, and couldn't believe he was still interested in petty revenge. Revenge is so Jacobean. It's obsolete. Any reasonable person, nowadays, has been wronged by far too many people to revenge himself within a normal lifespan.

We went into Tappersville to have a look around. The main streets of these upstate towns were almost as standardised and interchangeable as strip malls. There would be a petrol station with two morose attendants. One of them, a young chap with a denim jacket and inevitable mullet, would be meditatively smoking beside the single pump. The other would run Ashraf's credit card without looking up. A pot of burned coffee stood on a warmer, beside packaged doughnuts, wiper fluid, and a column of big black car batteries.

Further down was a bar, a video shop, a country bank. The large frame houses were in poor condition, their porches full of junk, from untended sewing machines to doorless refrigerators. The people were big and, in my estimation, suspicious of outsiders. You would have to be fair and say they were no more wrapped up in their own affairs than a typical New Yorker, but they seemed more tenacious, more grudging, protecting their corner of the cosmos. I mention this only to add that horizons are a necessary defence against the inexhaustibility of life but they aren't meant to be a blindfold against other horizons. Who did these upstaters think we were, crooks?

Across the lake behind the restaurant building was an air-conditioner repair shop. One night Ashraf and Fazila and I climbed in through the cellar window and returned with a cornucopia of strange treasures – a repairman's denim uniform with Hernandez embroidered on the front, a voltmeter, and sheetmetal cutters. I have already said that my brother prefers knowledge of a technical to that of a poetic character. In the evening he sat on the stoop and buried his head in a stolen manual while Fazila cradled him in her bony arms. The circuit diagrams showed how to disable an air-conditioner. I knew it was another of Ashraf's bone-headed schemes. Sleeping tablets and credit cards had succumbed to the siren song of the air-conditioner. It was a fiercely hot summer. The streets in Manhattan were Venusian in their poisonous heat. It wasn't the right time to be in the city unless you were in on the business of air-conditioners.

While we were on vacation Ashraf also made small money in the tourist places around Lake George. His meticulous study of Felix paid off. He spoke a fair imitation of Spanish. He was Pablo in the mornings, green-eyed Ramon at the Tappersville Inn in the afternoons, sly César dipping his hand in the till at night time, but to me he was the eternal dolt.

I am serious about this last sentence and, in general, I was rethinking my relationship with the Dawoods and the Peers. For the first time I saw that my family were total losers. Sure they dazzled a yokel like yours truly, but they were never going to rise above the level of needing to make a dishonest living. No self-respecting clan stays in the business a minute longer than necessary to establish itself on a legitimate footing. Even the Sicilians were moving up. In a century's time, I told myself, the Sicilians would be running Princeton while a Dawood or a Peer was still aspiring to some big score in some dusty police station in the Punjab. I was thinking about the fact of our historical futility when Ashraf and Fazila came in from Tappersville. They were in an excitable mood.

"Have you seen what happened, Firoze? Have you heard?"

"How could I hear anything?" I said. "The only thing I can hear is Dad snoring next door. He kept me awake half last night, that, and the summer mosquitoes."

"Turn on the television."

I promised not to wrestle with this loop of video so I won't say a word about it. But I did read the *Post* and the *Enquirer* as we drove downstate. Obviously our vacation had to be cut short. The newspaper pages were alight with rumours and dreadful fears. Invisible armies were poised to strike. There was poison in the mail. When love letters are an impossible luxury can we really say that life goes on? Innocent folks were being clapped into detention centres and bundled off to Syria for interrogation. I should say that I, more than anyone, have nothing against questions. I share a certain sympathy for the torturer because in his zeal to discover the truth he resembles no one so much as a philosopher. My only aversion to all these interrogations was a personal one. I knew that if I happened to be packed into a dungeon no one would believe my answers.

My father kept his thoughts about the attacks to himself, but he can be a bit of a silver-lining plucker, not to say something of a ghoul. Only someone unfamiliar with my family's talent for world historicity – I mean our ability to find our way to the centre of things or to the centre's underbelly – will be surprised to learn that Dad figured out a way to make a profit on every-body's loss. I coaxed it out of him in the van. It turned out the old codger was planning to finish off a quarter of his imaginary clientele at Farewell Insurance and make a killing. It was the perfect occasion for a bunch of his imaginary clients to turn up really dead.

We were jumpy. Driving into Brooklyn there seemed to be eyes in the back of every mailbox and behind every bush. It wasn't the right time to look suspicious. Police Ford Victorias, security guards, off-duty men in brown suits seemed to be on the lookout. Fazila decided to go back to London on the next plane. Even Dad was as retiring as a girl. I once advanced the argument that it is more dignified to be hung for a sheep than a lamb, but it's no sign of wisdom to be hung for somebody else's sheep.

I was suspicious when the outside door to the apartment building was ajar. Fazila and Ash went to return the van to Avis and I brought our backpacks into the house with Dad. The panel in front of the post-boxes had been levered open. Letters stood in the open pigeonholes like slips. Dad looked up the stairway. I went down into the basement and found nothing except the banks of washing machines with their silent red and green lights. Going back up the stairs to pick up the bags I followed my father up to the apartment where we found ourselves staring at a body positioned just inside the front door. It was lying on its back with a note taped to its chest. Dad put his hand on my arm to keep me back. He bent down to read the letter while taking care not to disturb the body. Then he gave me the paper and returned to the victim. It took a moment for my eyes to focus but then I saw, to my horror, what was before me. A black-lipped smile had been carved into its neck. The body laughed at me. After a minute I realised it was Felix.

My brother took charge. He called the police, then Felix's uncle from the basement, then walked through the building with a crowbar to make sure the killer wasn't lurking around. The moulana's dogsbody Sayeed, whom Ashraf and Fazila ran into walking back from the Atlantic Avenue Avis, went along wielding a flashlight. Dad read the note to me while we waited. It was addressed to Ashraf and myself, and purported to be from Mohammad Atta from beyond the grave. All it said was, "Do you take us so lightly now?" I knew that it was a taunt but I was too unhappy to even want to know what we were being taunted about.

It took fifteen minutes before others began to arrive. People's faces – the firemen who came to carry Felix out of the building, the sergeant, my father, my brother, Gitta who was silent and yet seemed to have had all her suspicions about the universe confirmed, Mr Villaverde the superintendent who had lost his nephew and held the body in his arms – were pinched and became as dark to me as if they were in shadow. Fazila was a little different because she was packing her bags and preparing to go to the airport. But I wouldn't say that even she was cheerful, only busy. Somehow Fazila was always on her way to the airport.

The only person at the scene who was in a tolerable mood was Sayeed from Abbas's mosque. The more I looked at him the more I realised his remarkable resemblance to his master. Really it was as if the student's and the master's faces constituted a two-part harmony. In an odd echo of his master, Sayeed's right eye had something of a damaged appearance, as if it was only good for seeing a short distance. He sounded British and had the distracting habit, which I thought rather British, of lifting his pencil-thin eyebrows ever so slightly at the end of each supercilious sentence. But he was helpful with the police and seemed to have some legal training, so we were grateful for his presence.

Abbas telephoned me his condolences through Sayeed but the master was in Buffalo, upstate, and couldn't be in New York City for a few weeks. Instead of thinking about what happened to Felix, and whether it was my fault after all, I calmed myself by studying our new acquaintance. When Sayeed hung up his coat and duffel bag in our apartment I noticed a square detonator and blasting cord tucked into the far end of his bag.

I mentioned Sayeed's smile, which floated in the neighbourhood of his mobile black lips. There was something beautiful about the dude which couldn't be gainsaid. The vibration I caught from him was familiar to me, oddly enough, from Peshawar and its veterans of Soviet days and their Thermopylaean lover's war. It's a famous observation in Pakistan that men who served in Afghanistan look at each other with bright eyes. I felt that Sayeed Papindari fell in that tradition but not because he showed any interest in the author of these pages. If anything he was bored with me. He probably needed a racier companion. In the middle of our conversation about who attacked Felix he seemed to be yawning off to sleep in the British fashion. The explanation of his manner, as I discovered, was that he might well be a high-school dropout but the school he dropped out of was Eton. He was the eldest son of a well-off Pakistani businessman, once the bearer of his family's highest hopes.

Days of subsequent research at Brooklyn Public Library informed me that the Papindaris are a former feudal family, but very different from the Zafirullahs and the Khans. Brigadiers and landlords are, of course, the principal beneficiaries of the post-colonial ruin of Pakistan. I don't know why I became so interested in Sayeed. Perhaps I wanted a chance to take my mind off Felix.

The Papindaris were great manoeuverers in the field of tariffs. They circumvented the prohibitive import duties on certain goods while knocking off imitations of foreign products. They were relentless diversifiers and monopolisers. As much as possible was done by hand because machines were far pricier than people. They manufactured pylons for the telephone company, gauges and tubing in their Lahore ironworks, white rubber tyres and cans of sealant in conjunction with a Hong Kong investor, ceramic tiles in their Karachi kiln. In Sayeed the Papindaris imagined that they had manufactured the fondest hope of every family in the land – that is, a cricketer. A spin bowler on Pakistan's first eleven was the equal of any title below Commander of the British Empire.

But family wishes are unreliable ways to manufacture anything. Instead of creating a cricketer, the Papindaris ended up providing Moulana Abbas with a sort of substitute son. In shifting proportions Sayeed was also enforcer, validator, forger, lieutenant, persuader, messenger boy, gofer, bodyguard, secretary, accountant, and chauffeur. In short, he was all that a one-eyed man could want in an asthmatic young follower. Sayeed said that for several years he had lounged around in Lahore and Karachi before meeting Abbas in Leeds and shipping out to Brooklyn. Abbas was his North Pole.

But things were changing for the moulana and his spiritual child. No one felt secure in their daily lives in New York. Someone called in to the mosque and warned of an arrest warrant being issued for Abbas. That's why Abbas was in Buffalo, and then possibly moving off to Canada. Others brought reports of an ongoing grand jury. Beyond this it was known that no legal process was really required if they decided to take you in. It was an atmosphere reminiscent of South Africa. Talking about it to me got Sayeed impassioned.

"Save your breath to blow your porridge, Firoze. It doesn't matter whether you're a believer or not. Once an outside force dictates who you are, it's no longer a question of free will. Admit it, and you can avoid a lot of heartbreak pretending to believe in this country's so-called idealism. Look at what happened to Felix and you have every reason to fear the future. Religion, I can promise, will cure you of that ill among many, many others." He placed his hand on my shoulder. "It brings peace of heart."

"I've never been much of a joiner," I said. I counted out the negative reasons to myself. "Of course no one's wanted me to be part of their group before. Felix was the one exception. He was a true friend. So, since we're talking, why the detonator?"

Sayeed asked, smiling, "You saw that?"

"It's hard to miss."

"Don't worry, Firoze. We're not reckless individuals. It's there in case we have to send a message," he replied.

"You could write something."

"That I'll leave to you, my friend. Until I met Moulana Abbas I was completely tongue-tied," Sayeed admitted. "At least now I can speak and people will listen . . . and so on and so forth. When it comes to putting things on paper, from school time to today, the most terrifying object in the world, for me, is a blank sheet of paper."

I said, "Actually, you sound just like a writer."

"Now, Firoze, you're flattering me."

As a thinking person I should have turned the whole bunch of these people in to the authorities – beginning with Abbas and Sayeed and ending with my father, brother, and mother. Sayeed was the worst of them. It's a universal truth that message senders are the most dangerous people in existence, because they don't grasp the value of understatement. And Abbas's ideas about the world would have been viewed as regressive during the Dark Ages. Yet my feelings towards both of them were paradoxically warm and engaged. I was curious to see what, if anything, Sayeed planned to do with his detonator and I was hopeful he would help me figure out whether Abbas had been complicit in Felix's murder. In retrospect I neglected the rule that intellectuals who associate with more interesting people go to jail in place of their interesting friends.

The oddest thing was to watch my brother developing a connection to the mosque out on Atlantic Avenue. Sayeed was the intermediary but my brother's sudden interest in the mosque puzzled me. In my experience he wasn't notably religious. Nor was he specifically anti-religious. I thought maybe it was a reaction formation. There's nothing like people thinking you're guilty to make you take pride in whatever they're singling you out for.

Or maybe it was simply that my brother saw a business opportunity. There were all sorts of ways to make money out of the situation. Flocks of Pakistanis on imaginary visas, schools of Egyptians who had overstayed their welcome, herds of other Muslims who yearned for a milder spiritual life in Toronto and Ontario, were breaking up their houses and heading for the Canadian border. Ashraf told me he was sympathetic to their plight. Not everyone had a fake green card like ourselves, and he wanted to do something reasonable to help (in exchange for a reasonable fee).

When Sayeed asked us to drive him north to Buffalo to hook up with Abbas, Ashraf jumped at the invitation and invited me along. He wanted to try out his air-conditioner scheme somewhere outside the city, where the heat, in more than ways than one, was less intense. Dad was going down to Florida for the month to escape an audit. It seemed like the right moment to get out of New York. Besides, all true New Yorkers leave the city in August. And I didn't want to be around for Felix's funeral. I didn't think I could look Gitta in the eye.

And doubly besides, there was someone out there doing the posthumous business of Mohammad Atta. It might be a good idea to stay out of the way of whoever that was. I did go over to the precinct office to talk to the police and my decided impression was that the authorities weren't treating the case with the necessary urgency. They had other things to worry about. Even if the supervillain has absented himself from my narrative his posthumous effect upon our lives was even greater than anyone humous. It's a defining trait of great villains, I think, to flourish in death. Ashraf and I went so far as to pack up the apartment and store our possessions in the basement, with the super's permission. Once we had dropped Sayeed off at a Mobil gas station where Abbas would find him, it seemed as if we were arriving in the New World for the first time – in Buffalo, of all places.

Stories in nutshells are plausible only to nutshell believers, the beautiful souls of the cosmos. There, anyway, is the explanation of how we ended up in Buffalo, New York, for two weeks in October, totally out of touch with everybody. Ashraf had some mad scheme as usual, the same scheme he had been cultivating since the summer. He moonlighted as an air-conditioner repairman while we set up in a motel room.

And that's how we met La Gioconda, the love-crazed Mona Lisa of upstate New York. Gioconda was the stage name of an actress called Pearl Bronson.

Yes, it's a ridiculous name but we're also ridiculous, none more so than my brother in his new duds. All the world's a stage for a repairman. The stage is a world for a love-starved actress. In Buffalo, of all places, world-stage and stage-world touched. After our two weeks in Buffalo I knew that my brother would never be a sincere lover and that I had more of a right to Fazila Parker Khan than he did. But I get ahead of myself.

Ashraf's new job left me a lot of time to look around. There's no need to be disparaging about Buffalo, its brown brick buildings, half-deserted offices, and run-down suburbs, its universal air of 1970s seediness that settled upon it from a *Starsky and Hutch* episode. Buffalo, New York, is one of the numerous cities of the north-east blessed with little beauty – Worcester, Hartford, Lowell, Newark, Rochester, and Buffalo. In this cold and charmless provincial city my brother decided to launch his new career and ended up, oddly enough, falling in love and, for the first time in his life, acquiring the rudiments of an artistic education.

Gainful employment was good for Ashraf. He dressed well, in his short-sleeved blue shirt, dark blue nylon trousers, and rectangular brown loafers. If you were to unfold the overalls he held in his arms you would find a navy blue badge above the heart with the name Hernandez picked out in white cotton. I felt the uniform suited him. Uniforms build discipline. That, in turn, bolstered his sense of self-respect. He got his hair cut around the corner to above the ears. After this he could even be said to be handsome after a fashion, a sort of Muslim Brando in repairman's plumage.

It struck me again, in looking at him every morning before he went out to distribute his business cards and disable as many built in air-conditioning units as possible, that if my brother really wanted to, with his chameleonic temperament, he could fit into this country far better than I ever would. I wanted to tell him as much, but he wouldn't have taken it as a compliment at all. He would have interpreted it as condescension. It's condescension, what Ashraf imagines as twenty-nine years of my condescension, that drives my brother's feelings about me. Sometimes I think if Ashraf didn't have my condescension to blame he would be at a loss to account for five-sixths of his actions in life.

Our fortnight in Buffalo reminded me of Robinson Crusoe scavenging the bays of his island for equipment. There were things we salvaged from the apartment in Brooklyn – lock picks, a can of polyurethane, an infrared lens,

V.O.M. meter, and Ashraf's diamond-cutting blade. Crogan, a friend in need if ever there was such a creature, sent up the rest of the equipment by parcel post, including an oxygen regulator, manuals, burlap bags, and a heavy burning bar that contained an electrical ignition snaked around five cutting rods. It was everything a burglar's heart could dream of if his green eyes brooded on Whitehall Diamond Jewellery and Precious Metal Brokers in the arcade of the Statler Towers situated on charmed Delaware Avenue in Buffalo.

The main thing missing was a van to transport this inventory. Ashraf was reduced to taking a bus to the nearby railway station and storing his stuff there. One morning I accompanied him, consumed by sheer hatred of the Starsky in the Sky Motel, and motel life in general. The laundry room with its unplugged drinks machine, the sheeted swimming pool, the green oblong of television sets behind each horizontal blind churning every brain into cheese, the sparse suburban boulevard, were horrible.

That's to say nothing of the evenings when, from the dugout of his bunk, Ashraf poled from channel to cable channel with the remote control. It was my one experience to date of true domestic life, of American life, with my brother, and it was excruciating. Ashraf's shows were indiscriminately chosen, from *Wheel of Fortune* to the Weather Channel. They made me want never to spend another minute indoors even when the green radiation of the television set was stilled. So it was with a sense of relief that I followed my brother downtown and cased him as he cased Whitehall Brokers.

Whitehall was a reduced version of the Diamond Dealer's Club in Manhattan. There were resolute groups of Buffalonians in threadbare three-piece suits ambushing one another in the entrance. They argued, joked, swapped numbers and orders. But there wasn't the kind of whirlwind activity one saw in Manhattan. It surprised me to find I missed it.

One man stood apart from them, leaning against the door, and sorting small stones with a tweezer, the double-sheeted package of white wax paper opened out in one hand to show a lining of luxurious blue tissue. It was odd to see anyone handling gems outdoors. He was quick about it, an expert with the tweezer, who rubbed his eyes after he finished separating the stones. He placed his buyings in an inside pocket. You could see by his expression he was doing calculations in his head. He frowned afterwards and went back into the building.

With a black shawl it was easy for me to scout out the exchange and report

147

back to Ashraf. It was just the one side of the one floor of the Statler Arcade, nothing fancy to look at. The entrance was low. Tall men stooped as they entered and studied the many notices in tiny script, often in foreign languages, Hebrew, Russian, Hindi, which were pinned to both walls. Eleven large clocks showed the time in time zones from Byelorussia to Melbourne, Australia. Alongside them was a framed painting of Ramat Gan in Tel Aviv, the twin diamond skyscrapers.

A thin orange carpet covered the floor of the atrium, from which extended several hallways. No one stopped me exploring. There were cubicles in the back, where face-to-face business was transacted. Each cubicle was equipped with a desk, a low-hanging lamp on a flexible arm, seven or eight magnifying glasses, and an array of loupes. These were the easels and brushes of the jeweller's art. I was familiar with them because we had all of them in the Fordsburg house. A notice advertised the presence of a laser saw and a Polariscope in an adjoining chamber. There were several small air-conditioning units stacked in the windows, but it was too busy to disable them in plain view.

It seemed as if the back room at the brokerage must be the only flourishing place in Buffalo. No time was wasted on pleasantries. Time, even when we forget, is always the essence of life. Buyers and sellers were arguing, agreeing, disagreeing, promising delivery, counting out sums of money, examining particular diamonds, ranging them in and out under the tabular eyes of magnifying glasses. Sleeves of diamonds were exchanged for chits. Information was recorded in looseleaf notebooks. It was an old Johannesburg trick I learned from my uncle. You could tear out the pages to hide them from the taxman.

I felt a sense of spiritual connection to the diamond folk who have been so close to my family, wittingly and unwittingly, for so long. They were, like us, lunar people. They preserved something that went back untold thousands of years. For me the unthinking act of preservation was far more valuable than the diamonds themselves.

By the time I got out of the diamond exchange, my brother, in a spirit of making do with what's available, had commandeered a window-washer's platform. From the other side of Delaware Avenue I watched him paying out the rope as he descended to the street. The buckets, mops, and poles, grouped in one corner against the rope sides, shivered. It was odd to see my brother settling on the street from above. It gave him the theatrical feeling of a returning angel, a special-effects angel. In certain religious sects, of course, like the Manicheans and Yazidis, the angels are no better than my brother.

The plan was working. As my brother returned to earth the apartments in the Statler's right wing lost their air-conditioning. Ashraf had disconnected the tubing that connected their unit's motors to the outside. The idea was to take over an apartment and drill through the roof into the diamond store. We needed money to get back to the city. Besides that, I wanted enough to hire a detective to find Felix's killer. The building was immediately hot as a furnace. And La Gioconda, to use Pearl Bronson's stage name, was already on the other end of Ashraf's rented cellphone. We were just about to meet Ashraf's second great love, or was it his third? She had found the card he'd pinned up in the laundry room.

"No worries. We'll be right over, Madame Gioconda. You found my card, huh? Second floor? That sounds ideal. I can see your place from where I am standing right now," Ashraf promised. He closed the lid of the cellphone. "My brother, let's get our stuff from the railway station. La Gioconda was what she called herself. Does that sound familiar to you? Any reason to think it's an assumed name?"

"I don't see why, Ashraf. I'm sure she was born with that name. It does happen to be the name of a Ponchielli opera, which was itself named after the generally accepted Italian name of Leonardo da Vinci's most famous painting. You know, the Mona Lisa?"

"No, I don't. But is there something you're trying to say?"

I shook my head. We were soon inside La Gioconda's establishment. It was paved to the very door with red carpet. The red, in case you didn't guess, was the colour of Valentine's hearts. There were a number of imposing pieces of furniture in the spacious corridors – an oak dresser, a music box with a slender brass key in its side, a vanity chest on top of which stood the hemisphere of a mirror studded along the arch with the sea shells of a dozen dim yellow light bulbs. The bedroom that contained the air-conditioner was equally hideous. It had gold wallpaper from ceiling to floor and a gold-finish four-poster bed, and a sofa heaped with strawberry pincushions and heart-shaped pillows, along with a cage of nervous lovebirds.

There was a mock Japanese theme to Pearl's crib: plates filed along a backlit bookshelf, an open chest displaying a selection of blindfolds and kimonos, and with the frayed ivory strap of a brassiere hung on the front, partitions arranged around the bed underneath several rows of framed pen-and-ink representations of women in various states of passion. Stools of different heights, without backs, were scattered about the room.

The most imposing piece of furniture was the Gioconda herself who greeted us in high-heeled sandals and a robe decorated with oriental motifs. It was as if she had intuited the nature of the man on the other end of the telephone. Her imitation Shalimar perfume, paint stripper, was enough to give me a headache. To Ashraf it was a nose-borne elixir. There's no need to rehash his garish fixation on cathouses, massage parlours, women of pleasure, girls of easy virtue, geishas, and ladies of the night. La Gioconda was definitely my brother's type. These two romantic phonies were made for each other.

La Gioconda wasn't that much older than us but, I thought, the years had been as cruel to her as her many men. There were many fine distortions around her eyes visible beneath her pancake make-up, as if a painting had been unsuccessfully restored. In her lair on Delaware Avenue she had been waiting for love all these years. Her long, thin wrists came snaking from under the tassels of her silk robe. There was some flash in her henny-brown eyes that I noticed when she studied my brother in his denim uniform.

"You're sure I can't get you anything? I insist on treating you and your workman decently, Mr Hernandez. Or is it your brother? Benny and Leonard Hernandez. While you're fixing the motor, Benny and Lenny, I am going to go into my kitchen and rustle something up." She touched Ashraf lightly on the cheek, showing polished red nails. I saw the gloss of lipstick on her mouth and heard the sound of a television in another room. The flowers on her gown, I noticed, were orchids. She said, "It's the least I can do. I don't believe in the class system. Besides, I have free time on my hands. I am not going on stage until half past eight this evening. We have everything in the building. Would you like, maybe, to take a sauna? Would you like to take a bath?"

"Mrs Gioconda?"

"Actually, it's La Gioconda. It's a stage name. It's a long story but I've always loved that particular painting. I do a lot of shows here upstate. I'm Medea, Lady Macbeth, Maria in *West Side Story*. Right now, Leonard, I'm starring in *Cat on a Hot Tin Roof* at the Shea Centre right around the corner on Main Street. My given name, though, is Pearl, so you know – Pearl Bronson."

"Well, Pearl, I have bad news for you and I have good news for you." With what I thought was a nice sense of dramatic effect my brother produced a revolver from his overalls. It wasn't pointed at anyone. He weighed the thing in his hands, a perfectly friendly assailant. "My dear, we're going to have detain you for the evening. Benny and myself won't lay a finger on you just so long as you occupy yourself and allow us to drill through your ceiling." He spun the chamber around a few times. "I only wish there was some other way we could do this."

"But it's only my second week in the role," La Gioconda protested. "That understudy, who's a perfect sneak, has been waiting for an opportunity to shine. Leonard, my dear, I'll get fired in favour of that Alice if I don't have a good excuse."

"You're being held at gunpoint. What better excuse is there? Don't worry, my dear Miss Gioconda. To me it's obvious you have a great gift. I could see it the instant we walked in here. It shows in every little thing you do and say. You were born to be an actress just as I was born to be a gangster."

This did the trick. "I'll cooperate. I'll cooperate willingly," she said. Her lips were parted. "Besides, I have the strangest, most mysterious feeling, Leonard. I feel giddy, funny, wonderful. But I can see you want to get started with whatever it is."

As the witness of so many of my brother's amours, I confess that he has a way with the right lines. La Gioconda considered the matter settled and retired to the bed where she sat reading an issue of *Cosmopolitan*. Ashraf locked the door and stripped out of his overalls. He was my father's son in as much as he liked the right clothes for the job. He had a new black turtleneck and sweatpants, thick black socks, black underwear, and black sneakers that he took out of the toolbox. For a moment I relented and saw the side of my brother that women find attractive. His thick brown-black hair, a bear's brown, was combed, slicked back, and parted, its ripples set like icing. He had brought along hairnets, from Gold's Salon on Atlantic Avenue, to catch any stray evidence. They could trace you by the splinter of a fingernail nowadays. Finally Ashraf pressed his gold earring into his right ear. It was for luck, the hoop shining like the new moon.

"Meryl Streep is my idol," La Gioconda observed once we had set up the drill in the middle of her bedroom. Chips of screeching particleboard flew in every direction. "Look, Leonard, if you want to be absolutely sure that I won't be going anywhere, you can tie me up. There are handcuffs and blinds in that chest. It's no trouble for me. Men tie me up all the time. They like doing it."

151

"Well, if you insist, Pearl. I was going to take you down into the vault with us."
She said, "I think it's better if I stay up here."

Tying up La Gioconda, for Ashraf, was a joy, not a duty. There was something going on between those two that made me reluctant to turn my back on them. I was getting to be an expert on love at first sight. Ashraf's pleasure in his undertaking was obvious from his manner – that loving, voluptuous manner so familiar to me – with which he dropped the blindfold around La Gioconda's head. As he did so his hands rested on the short, very white back of her neck that contrasted with her straight, glossy hair.

La Gioconda kept talking as he bound her. She was a mile-a-minute lady, a full-blown instance of the American tendency to confide the deepest currents of your soul to absolute strangers. Was Lenny his real name? Was Benny his real brother? She asked after Ashraf's parents. Her own father, La Gioconda explained, was a jeweller, owned half of the Bronson & Boulder gem store in Bayridge. Jewels, she said, were the closest that nature came to penning a love letter. Her father's occupation was the reason she felt at home living on top of Buffalo's small diamond district. Now, ironically enough or fittingly, depending on how you looked at the facts, it was the reason that their two souls encountered each other. She had long-ago dreams about this very day.

The amazing thing was that my brother, with all the education I tried to provide him, should agree with any of this New Age nonsense. "It was inevitable that we should meet, La Gioconda," he said, finishing with her wrists. "Kahlil Gibran, the philosopher, says, trust in dreams, for only in them do we find the hidden gate to eternity. My brother can never comprehend that truth because he's the prisoner of his own mind. Well, that's not true of you, of me, of Gibran himself."

"Do you believe that?"

"Another saying of Gibran's is applicable to you, La Gioconda. He would have said that your beauty, your beauty, Gioconda, is like eternity gazing at itself in a mirror."

If it wasn't for the fact I know my brother to be a complete and total ham I would have been impressed. But he's too much of an adapter. Around La Gioconda he switched his manner, instinctively, to something gravelly, poignant, and sinuous, what I can only describe as comic-book Egyptian, like Omar Sharif in *Marco the Magnificent*. Eavesdropping on them was excruciating for anyone as finely tuned as myself to my brother's fraudulence.

But I waited to confront him until he returned. Even then I whispered so as not to disturb our hostess.

"How's it going with the drill?"

"The drill is fine," I replied, "but I have something else on my mind, if you will allow. Do you have to be such a poser, Ashraf? Do you have to speak in such lofty terms?"

"You're the one who uses the lofty terms, chum."

There was something about the speedy way in which Ashraf was sure to dismiss me that infuriated me all over again. It wasn't until we were down in the darkened store that I could think again. Around Ashraf I was used to having my heart beat at this secret tempo – now slow, now filled with covert intensity over my brother. There was a column of light that ran through the opening in the ceiling and the long yellow beam dense with a myriad dust particles was in some way comforting. It reminded me of going to sleep in our bedroom while our parents were awake and about in the Fordsburg house.

Then my feelings turned inside out. Seeing Ashraf operate the safe, the pianistic fineness of his movements as he caught, lost, and recaught the alignment of the bolt, his monkish green gaze appearing in the beam of the flashlight like cat's eyes on a highway, his fine, corded brown hands, his strict-as-a-schoolmaster's bearing, I was immensely proud of my brother. Even as I wondered when this Judas brother was going to betray me, when his old sarcasm would strike up again like a spark, I saw that he was forever my moon, my sun, my true and magnetic north, my how-beloved adversary. And that, by a roundabout route in the heart, made me angry again.

"So what, you really like La Gioconda?"

He didn't look up. "She's a spectacular lady, don't you think? So full of life, so full-figured, such a fighter. I want to go and see her perform. What an amazing coincidence it is, the two of us meeting. The chances must be, what would you say, a million to one that you could meet someone like this."

"On the contrary, Ashraf. A house invasion is a very romantic situation. It brings out a certain lovely side of people's personalities."

"Hand me the goggles, would you? Doesn't La Gioconda remind you of Mom when she was young? Am I crazy to think that? You think she liked me?"

"Yes."

"You really think so?"

"Yes, I do. It's obvious from the way she looked at you. Now, for heaven's sake, get on with the job."

Three drill bits were destroyed before Ashraf switched to the blowtorch. I stood in the far corner of the room and watched the blue sparks stream past his face. The pencil-thin gas cylinder was quickly exhausted. Ashraf took the torch from me and played the beam across the front of the safe. Next to it were storage lockers. Ashraf got a wrench and searched around against the wall for the brackets. He found the iron plugs with his hand. Using the wrench he tried to twist them out of shape. Eventually he managed to stove in the back of one of the lockers and fished around inside with the wrench. Some stones came out one by one. He handed them to me to examine. I liked rubbing the cold sides against the top of my hand. But I was still provoked on La Gioconda's behalf.

"So a repairman has the cheek to quote from *The Prophet* to a lonely lady while he's roping her to the bed. Although the closest this fellow has ever come to Kahlil Gibran are the proverbs on the Pirelli calendar. Don't you stop to consider the emotional impact on that woman before you say these things? That woman up there has been waiting all her life for love. By the way, since when do you know the first thing about Kahlil Gibran?"

"You gave me a copy of *The Prophet* for my sixteenth birthday. Mum had to pay a fine for me at the Magistrate's Court when I got caught stealing with her. And remember how terrified she was Dad would find out? For once you behaved like a brother to me. I am pretty sure Gibran was the author of that volume. Now do you remember?"

We had just heard two men in the outside room, turned the torch off, and stood there in silence. It gave me a moment to reflect about my brother. Ashraf is like the next villain when it comes to claiming influences that reek of a disorganised mind – Nietzsche, apparently, the I Ching, the *Far Side* calendar, *Siddhartha* by Herman Hesse, the *Kama Sutra*. Meeker minds like Pearl Bronson's on the third floor were impressed by the dimestore philosophy, which includes his sense of the beast dwelling inside the breast of modern man, his appreciation of the Oriental attitude towards fate the I Ching exemplifies, his identification with Gibran, his love of landscape, his desire to explore the *Sutra*'s contortionist splendours, which he considered his heritage as a son of the dusky subcontinent.

Nothing in the list would trouble the pond of a sophomore mind, but not one of these aforementioned works, excepting Gibran, have I observed in my brother's possession. Reviewing my memories adds only my mother's copy of *Atlas Shrugged*, which Ashraf scanned for any passages concerning sex. There was an immensely big-breasted blonde in a cream blouse on the cover, her pinked lips slightly parted like Pearl's. That image in its hill country of décolletage (a word as lovely to a twelve-year-old boy as its smiling francophone cousin lingerie) shaped our fantasy life in a South Africa that banned girly magazines and relaxed its Calvinism only for works of high literature which boggled the Dutch Reformed morals of the government censor.

Calvinists, censors, churchmen, we Johannesburgers owe them so much in the imaginative sense. I trace my literary bent back to those unexpurgated classics such as Ian Fleming and D.H. Lawrence, which stung our hands with their sexual amperage. To the covers of the paperback editions I trace my brother's sexual interests. But did Ashraf pay a morsel of attention to Rand's emphasis on individual creativity? Did Ashraf, as a schoolboy, look beyond the characters' pornographic sighs, their interpenetrating glances, the caressing of a silk knee on the way to a silken entrepot, the bedroom theatre of master and slave, to a deeper truth of existence? I think not.

Back in Buffalo we heard the hoarse voice of a dealer in the hallway outside the back room. The man wasn't upset. He did sound as if he was one of those people who are always crowing over something or the other. "You won't get a cent from them for those. As for the others, if I get I buy. I don't hesitate."

"That's the general idea," the second man said. He had a soft, thoughtful, foreign accent, I thought, as if there were a glove over his voice. "I can't criticise."

They engaged in a complicated negotiation for a few minutes. The light went on in the next room. The on-and-off hiss of the depleted blowtorch, the very light clank of the wrench, told me that my brother was at the storage lockers again with the tenacity of an army ant. I waved at him to keep quiet but he didn't listen. Ashraf wasn't in a cautious frame of mind. Meanwhile the conversation continued outside.

"You get any good white ones, big ones, hold for me," the first man was saying. "Not long, anyway. For a few hours. A day. I'm not asking for favours."

"If I get some I'll try. I am not going to promise you the moon," the foreigner answered. "What do you mean, big?"

"Seven and up. Remember."

"Don't worry. I'll remember. Say, do you hear anything in there? Let's check. No, wait. My friend, you go stand by the alarm in case you have to pull it. Let's give these ruffians the fright of their lives."

We were in such a hurry we never made it back to the motel in Buffalo. The stepladder was pulled up behind us. For humanity's sake La Gioconda had to be scissored out of her bindings, and a bus that paused on Delaware Avenue had to be boarded with our toolbox in our hands. At two in the morning we found ourselves in a suburban train station west of the city. It wouldn't have been safe to catch the train back to New York from downtown Buffalo. My brother took advantage of the late hour and the desolate station building to check through his slender takings from the Whitehall safety-deposit boxes. He rubbed the stones on his tooth and decided, with a faltering heart, that they were only costume jewellery. If I haven't yet mentioned it, Ashraf, though he never forgives, is also not the type to forget an argument.

"Firoze, if you meant half the things you said to me! You're too fond of how something sounds to imagine how it feels to the other person. Plus, you know, I am your only friend." He poured the worthless paste gems and a pair of fake pearl earrings into my hands. Between my nails I felt the glass core of each false pearl. My brother seemed happier that it had all been for naught. It fitted in better with his scheme of life. He continued talking, with a curiously blank yet savouring face that pointed at the train yard outside, "I gave one of these to Gioconda as we were leaving. I told her it was something to remember me by. Perhaps it makes sense that it's a fake. Ah, and I know a lot more from Gibran. How about this, because it seems appropriate? Paradise is there, behind that door, in the next room, Gibran says, but I have lost the key. Perhaps I have only mislaid it."

"What did you say to La Gioconda as we were racing out the door?"

"I told her that I knew, in my heart of hearts, that her acting career was about to take off. I told her to persevere. Faith, Firoze," he said, reciting another of his useless proverbs from Gibran, "Faith is an oasis in the heart which will never be reached by the caravan of thinking."

"It's not enough that I have to succeed," I replied. "My brother has to fail."

"That doesn't sound like Kahlil Gibran. It sounds like you, Firoze. Actually it sounds like what you think I think."

In the morning Ashraf tried to raise some money on the strength of the costume jewellery. The pawnshop owner, whose livelihood depended on having a suspicious nature, wasn't having any of it. He worked from a hole-in-the-wall beside the Greyhound bus terminal and had, as a result, seen the worst that mobile human nature had to offer.

"You won't get a cent for them. They're made out of paste. It will cost you fifteen dollars to get the same lot brand-new. They'll have a laugh at your expense if you try to unload them anywhere else. Maybe they'll also put a word in with the Buffalo police department. Might as well leave the set with me. Look, I'll give you what's in my wallet. Three dollars and fifty-five cents, and it's a steal on your side."

Ashraf was at his menacing best. "We'll take a risk on the stones. You keep the money."

"Well, don't say I didn't warn you. Where are you fellows from?"

Ashraf said, "Puerto Rico. But we live in New York."

"Well, you look Jewish, buddy. Godspeed on your trip home."

Three months later, by the way, we saw Pearl Bronson once again. I had been merciless with Ashraf on the subject of his thespian love yet he couldn't forget the mysterious charm that lady had placed upon him. A playbill distributed by the Aurora Players out of Albany, New York, announced the casting of La Gioconda as Katisha in their new production of *The Mikado*. Albany, reachable by an afternoon train, seemed like a good place to fan the embers of whatever transpired between them. I was dubious about these embers and about embers in general. On the other hand, the advantages of marrying my brother off were no trivial thing. If he found true love, I could stop looking after him.

Security in a theatre, where the rewards are as low as an evening's pleasure or displeasure, is rarely tight. It was child's play to join the cleaning detail at Park Playhouse and arrive at the dressing rooms for actresses. Backstage was a fancy place, and otherworldly. Lamps were built into the ceilings. Bonsai trees were presented in alcoves. Stern Japanese gentlemen in white leather riding trousers and multicoloured tunics filed past us and down the stairs. One buckled the crescent of a sword to his hips. A bare-chested, bare-stomached man with a sumo wrestler's physique bore a kettledrum along with the group. In the rafters a workman paid out electrical cable from a pail filled to the brim with insulated wire. An older man with a track of brown beard was consoling a

157

much younger girl in a bodice and leaning over, whenever no one was looking, to sample a powdery kiss from her powdered mouth.

Around us was the haphazard condition that seizes a playhouse five minutes before the curtains rise. With mops and buckets we stood five feet away from La Gioconda and watched her busily powdering her cheeks in a dressing-table mirror. She wasn't fooling. She was professional, applying a violinist's intensity of purpose to the task at hand. She closed one eye and then the other as she worked around them, the heavy apricot blush breathing out of the foxtailed make-up brush at every stroke with the consistency of chalk. Her eyelashes were encased in mascara.

La Gioconda was obviously fussy about her looks, not unlike my mother, who had always been repairing and refreshing her face, though from the time she was fifty my mother gave up entirely and lived in a track suit. But I was ridding myself of my brother's habit of comparing every woman to our mother. By that standard, what woman would stand a chance?

To look at La Gioconda in front of the big mirror was to see an old-time Paris opera singer, or at least my reflected idea of a Parisian prima donna. Hung in the sectioned glass, moreover, was a half-unsmiling woman who had been waiting for true love all her life, from the cradle to her pink-sided coffin on Delaware Avenue. There was nothing inexplicable about my brother's liking her in return. The depth of La Gioconda's need would seduce almost anyone exposed to it. The cookbooks in her Buffalo apartment, the Valentine's Day décor, that four-poster bed and the pairs of high-heeled shoes arranged by colour inside the glass cabinet were the objective correlatives of half a soul in perpetual expectation of its other half. In terms of romantic ecology La Gioconda was an ant lioness and here I was, with my brother in tow, providing her with ants. That's how I figured it. So La Gioconda's cool response to our appearance in her dressing room rather startled me.

"So you're here. What are you here to steal, Leonard? Just so you know, the precious stone you gave me turned out to be paste," La Gioconda told my brother immediately. She produced the gem in question from a drawer and pinched it dismissively between her fingers. "Oh, it's symbolic. You left me with a hole in my floor, a lot of explaining to do to the local cops, and a whole lot of false promises. Love doesn't mean you come in and out of someone's life like a drunken sailor. Love doesn't mean chaos and three months of silence. Love means beauty and tenderness and responsibility for someone's feelings.

For your information, Leonard or whatever you're calling yourself today, I have an amazing amount of love to bestow on a lucky someone. That lucky someone is not going to be a creep who ties me up once in a blue moon, and then afterwards pretends the whole thing never happened. That lucky someone, for your information, is going to be a gentleman."

"Pearl, let me make it up to you."

"Well, I suppose it's a good sign you came to see my performance. It shows commitment. It shows you're thinking about somebody other than yourself and that half-wit brother. To be honest I think it is my greatest piece of artistry to date. In many ways, Leonard, I was born to play Katisha." La Gioconda turned bad-temperedly back to her lotions. "Curtain call in five minutes, I'm afraid. Come back and see me after the show, Leonard. I'll leave instructions with security."

"Break a leg, La Gioconda," I said.

"Thanks."

For the author of these pages, Fleming's *Goldfinger*, Nusrat Fateh Ali Khan's earliest songs, which were never recorded, and the first tuneful act of *The Mikado* constitute the Himalayas of culture. And there's an argument to be made that, of the trio, the first act of *The Mikado* is the very greatest. Ko Ko has been sentenced to death for flirting and simultaneously promoted to the exalted rank of Lord High Executioner. The first person he has to behead is himself. Pish Tush brings an instruction from the emperor that heads must begin to roll. The minstrel Nanki Pooh agrees to be the very first head, on the condition he can be married to Yum Yum for a month.

The Mikado is musical theatre unconquerable by the greatest dolts, the very definition of a classic – yet the Aurora Players gave it a go. At first the Aurora's pack of brayers and snappers could do no damage to the Sullivanian melodies. The three maids did their introductory number as if they were caterwauling and the play sailed through their vocal broadside with nary a scratch on its superb construction. It glided past the whirlpool of a rattish Pish Tush and scabrous Nanki Pooh, skirted the Scylla of a laryngitical Pooh Bah and the far side of the Charybdis of a noneuphonious chorus, drowsed on the Sargasso Sea of an unpractised Pitti Sing without taking water aboard, and was only definitively hulled by the appearance of a Katisha who showed no distress at fumbling every note. Yet it was pure pleasure from beginning to end.

To offer a few helpful words of dramatic criticism to the Aurora Players in their future performances, La Gioconda, with her bone-white eyelids and a black, strictly parted and pigtailed wig, was remarkably still and undemonstrative on stage. In the aria in which she vows to see the emperor and reverse her beloved minstrel's engagement, La Gioconda didn't emote. She appeared to believe it was the audience's duty to make the first move before she would unload her cargo of love upon them. An actress, a thief, a philosopher, anyone who chooses to importune the world, has to be ready to do the hard business of introductions, in my view.

In truth I didn't pay enough attention to the subtleties of La Gioconda's thespianism because by then several state policemen were browsing the aisles of the playhouse with flashlights, respectfully demanding the tickets of the more exotic looking men in the audience and checking identification. Three or four of the men they questioned were forwarded to the entrance for further investigation. The curtain came down prematurely before the end of the second act.

Ashraf may have imagined he was in love, but my brother was still as shrewd as they come when the subject was the potential vagaries of the human heart. About such things he's as much of a seer as any playwright. He took the precaution of putting on a short green raincoat. We sat to the side where the footlights prevented us being seen from the stage. We slipped through the fire doors at the front of the theatre without anyone noticing.

Out on Main Street, from across the way, we studied the playhouse for a moment and its pattern of long light-and-dark windows, which resembled white and black piano keys. On the upper floor we saw a torch beam dipping, broadening, and then sweeping across the inside of each chamber. In its unsteady yellow trace I saw or thought I saw reflected the sludge of green tears in my brother's eyes. But I couldn't be sure and the next time I checked, on the midnight bus from Albany to Port Authority, his gaze was rinsed clean. Inside that big empty missile of a bus Ashraf held his green expression up to my query as if it were a revolver.

لـ

Chapter Seven

Charles Crogan, bare-kneed, Sammy-Gigante-crazy, shod in ventilated slippers, wrapped to the gills in a pashmina above which one saw the green of his eyes . . . the portico of the White House on which stood, in their untidy robotic ranks, the sodium lamps guarding a corps of armoured cameras . . . the scarab keys to a Mercedes . . . the archipelago of emerald tennis courts running the length and breadth of Princeton, New Jersey . . . the fruity Princeton expert on Muslim civilisation with sparkling old man's eyes, a chuckler who enjoyed a joke at anyone's expense but his own, who rubbed his stomach with a Buddha's soft presumption, the same man who tried smilingly to push the recorder of these papers onto his four-poster bed . . . the firm hand of the president and his smile thrown across the abyss of his mind like a rope bridge.

But let me begin with an evening of spring cleaning. Spring cleaning is a cheering ritual of life which is improved by a bonfire. Our last evening in Brooklyn was spent at a midnight auto-da-fé. Out on the fire escape the records and archives of Farewell Insurance turned into bales of smoke that went up into the black space between our building and the one adjoining. Big yellow telephone directories, utility bills, photocopies of car registrations curled up and burned. I doused them with lighter fluid, and set them alight with an electric spark. Ashraf helped me, the sodium green of his eyes burning against the unlit brick wall. My brother took a particular delight in setting things on fire.

Putting books to the match wasn't something I realised could be so satisfying. It was all per Dad's instructions. We had to move, and soon. In the confusion following the attacks, my father was cashing out a grand total of seventy life-insurance policies, but there were some signs of suspicion on the part of the reinsurers. Dad was summering in Fort Lauderdale to escape the heat. The federales were rounding up associates of Mohammad Atta. Eventually they would get around to checking out my brother. Finally, there was the little matter of Atta's accomplice in the neighbourhood. It was improbable that he would retire. Felix's murder had ruined Brooklyn for me, so I was happy to leave. We were moving in with Crogan in Astoria. Queens was a new galaxy in the cosmos of New York city. But first we had to get rid of the evidence in our old apartment.

Crogan himself was getting nervous about the heat. Since he couldn't communicate directly with my father he talked to me, to dispense pin money in case we were running short, and to alert me to the sayings of a little bird about the investigation into the Farewell Insurance Company.

"We have to wait it out, until the reinsurance guys decide to pay up. They don't want the publicity. If necessary, I have a contact at the *Wall Street Journal* when we need to embarrass them," he explained. "I hope it doesn't come to that. At the same time the Justice Department thing is worrying."

People like Crogan, people who know about such things, will tell you that a Justice investigation is the equivalent of a wildfire. It's advisable to move as much as possible out of its projected path. Non-existent law, as in South Africa, and omnipresent law, in the United States, work out to much the same thing; everyone has something to hide. With his legal training Crogan was good at hiding things. Luckily he had planned for this eventuality beforehand. He seemed to like the thoroughness of the work, making sure of every detail – moving money around, changing forwarding addresses, notifying clients, creating deniability. The two of us spent the afternoon pestering our accounts from the local Chase and putting them in Crogan's name. Dad could take out money at the Florida end.

Afterwards we moved our suitcases to the spare room in Crogan's office and he took us both to his favourite spot to unwind in his cruise liner of a Chrysler. The Lotus Leaf was up on St Mark's Place in Manhattan. It was, predictably, a massage parlour. Outside, a plot of garden ran in between the lanes of traffic. On that block was a mixture of establishments from a pottery studio to a leather boutique.

To get to the Lotus you went down two turns of stairs and stood inside a black marble portico that bore on the entrance. A spyglass gave us a positive review and by dint of this and Crogan's credit card we were soon wrapped in fresh green towels. Crogan arranged his belly comfortably inside his towel and submitted to his shirt's removal. The private room we found ourselves inside was a minor masterpiece of chinoiserie, as if Pearl Bronson's tastes had been turned into brothel form. The thick black ceiling paint complemented the tiled black floor and the onyx urns of jacuzzi and bathtub side by side. A low bed stood against the wall. Its black metal frame supported a wafer of a mattress covered in dark satin sheets.

The attending priestess of this bed went by the unusual professional name of Chrysanthemum. She had the commanding air of a karate teacher. To put it another way, she was more a sadist than a masochist, ordering my companion onto the bed and flushing him out of his towel. Chrysanthemum pummelled his back. Then she turned him around and dealt with his chest, large legs, and roseate belly, using descending chops. Crogan's belly reddened even further under Chrysanthemum's ministrations. Her black eyes were narrowly focused on the activities of her hands. Her name, I discovered, had no relationship to any floral personal qualities. It was just that the Lotus Leaf called its staff members after various types of flower.

With her brooding sense of dominion Chrysanthemum ruled our evening. A flurry of blows was unleashed, scented cream was applied to the offending region, then more blows. It went on for about twenty minutes, the tenderising of this gigantic man Crogan, and it gave me time to reflect about my upcoming ordeal. I saw that my brother was uncomfortable. Finally Crogan's ordeal was finished, and it was Ashraf's and then my turn. Crogan took out a cigar and sat there, watching us suffering. His thighs, pressed upon one another beneath the towel, were as full as tree trunks. Smoke in brown volumes came pouring off his cigar. I was resentful for one second and thought that he reminded me of Jabba the Hutt. But Chrysanthemum rapidly pounded any thought out of my mind. Meanwhile Crogan and Ashraf went on speaking.

"I've been thinking a little about your brother," Crogan announced, "and it strikes me that Firoze has a golden opportunity. As I see it, this country wants definitions." He addressed me. "Someone like you, someone who has a real way with words, is just the person to give it the right definition of a Muslim. Some kind of apology on behalf of the religion would be very much appreciated. It would have a calming effect. People have been asked to keep an eye out for a suitable editorialist. Firoze fits the bill. Remember that we, Republicans I mean, created our own cosmos of newspapers and television. We have sympathisers everywhere. If you make the right noises." Crogan tipped his cigar at me. Ashraf went off to pee. "Who knows, we might even come out ahead? It might come to the attention of certain people who can take the pressure off Farewell Insurance. This could go to the very top of the party."

"Why would what I write matter to the Republicans?"

"They figure if they can have a Muslim intellectual to refer to in their speeches it makes justifying what they want to do that much easier," Crogan explained. He studied our masseuse. Chrysanthemum was finished with me and was busy in the corner with a pair of tongs, refilling a bucket with hot coals for the sauna. "Time for a steam bath. But look, Firoze, you don't have to decide right away. Sleep on it. Now you guys are going to be living with me you have all the time in the world to think. Incidentally, how do you like Chrysanthemum?"

"She's very energetic."

"I've always found her so."

All this is a roundabout way of saying that the germ of my famous article in the *Wall Street Journal* is to be found in the seedy circumstances of the Lotus Leaf right off St Mark's. The phoenix of the imagination is born in impurity and burns off its contexts in flight. Let's therefore delete any mention of the three flexible ladies who oiled and paddled my companion and later retired with Crogan behind a burgundy curtain woven with a tapestry of trompe-l'oeil dragons and merciless orange eyes, which stared me into submission. Let's say nothing of Geranium's glossy pigtail and the bobbing silken collar of her tight red blouse, nothing of Daisy and her cruel mouth, nothing of Cherry Blossom's sinuous somersaults. Let's in fact make no further ado about the accidental brothels, as full of fluttering breasts and thighs as a chicken coop, which play so unfortunate a role in my literary efforts.

However delicious, these are details which can only lower the tone of my prose. Not that I give myself false hopes. No one's paging through my manuscript because of the minor key melodies of its Cherry Blossom sentences. Literature is the apprentice of publicity. My audience expects the inside scoop on a parabolic man who went from obscurity to the nation's editorial pages and the green drawing room at the White House, before descending in the manner of an Icarus to a holding pen in the Metropolitan Correctional Centre. It's the briefest quarter of an hour in the history of fifteen-minuters.

It was around this time my brother began to arrest various residents of New York state.

He dreamed, I think, of having authority. With my father in Florida there was no force to restrain him. I suppose Ashraf, who parted company with his superego in utero, reacted to the lack of a guiding presence poetically by becoming his own authority figure.

Most of the time I was too busy writing my article, hanging around with Crogan, and avoiding being served papers as a party to various lawsuits involving Farewell Insurance to keep a proper eye on my brother's activities. I do know that he was talking to my mother in Australia. In general there was no money, no schedule, nothing steady, and yet I had more hope than ever before. In many ways those short months were the most thrilling period of my life. As far as Ashraf is concerned, a student of scripture knows that our moral history as a species only begins with one brave soul refusing to be his brother's keeper. It's also true that the two of us had never been so distant until then, but I ascribe whatever alienation of affections occurred to the reality that I was acting independently for the first time.

Ashraf was struggling. He didn't make any real dough from the week he spent at the headquarters of Philip Morris unless you count the leased Mercedes-Benz C 220 he adopted from the company garage. It was powder-blue and loaded, moon roof, white leather seats, and a dashboard that would make a pimp proud. He kept the Mercedes a secret from me until I saw him parking it in a sidestreet lot. I waited to ask him about it the next day. He led me to believe it was a loaner car and was going back to the dealer in a week. It should have given me pause. About little things at least, it wasn't like the old Ashraf to lie to me.

Should I have been my brother's keeper? Ashraf's new way of talking to me in a warm whisper, all the time he was spending with Miss Lee and Madam Lee, they were warning signals I didn't compute. A New Age psychologist, a Long Islander like Dr Böhrendorf, might call these symptoms a cry for help, but the language would be unfortunate because my brother was helping himself to pretty much everything he could lay his hands on. But what good did it do him?

You would have thought Ashraf was the type to prosper in a country of pure simulation and pseudo-occurrences but the truth is quite the reverse. That

165

sense of falseness which clings to an intellectual's mind makes him beautifully adapted to American society. It seemed to me that my brother and I were ever so gradually changing places with one another. In this country I was ever more the junkyard cynic and he, Ashraf, was the idealist, purist, transcendentalist, and mystical dreamer, with moon in his pie, pie in the moon in the sky, and moonpie on his mind. With the help of the aforementioned Mrs, Miss, and Madam Lee, he could be as strange a creation as he could wish.

Since I am trying to arrive in the vicinity of 1600 Pennsylvania Avenue by plausible stages I will relate the memorable adventures my brother experienced in the supposed employ of the U.S. Fish and Wildlife Service. During our first month in Brooklyn Ashraf did some preliminary research on the various government agents who had the power to detain their fellow citizens. That kind of technical information Ashraf liked to know. City, county, state, and federal jurisdictions overlapped and underlapped in a Venn diagram. A resident of New York City and thereabouts could be arrested by the representatives of any of 67 different agencies ranging from the municipal tobacco revenue unit to the Secret Service.

He paraded around Crogan's office in a series of strange uniforms. "Firoze, what do you think of this outfit? It's Mrs Lee's doing."

I asked, "What on earth is it?"

"It's Adelaide's interpretation of the Onondaga Park Police get-up." He touched his shoulders. "You see the stripes? That indicates the rank of sergeant major."

I said, "You'll be the most senior officer in Onondaga Park, Ashraf. Can you handle the responsibility? As for the costume, in sartorial terms, I like it. It's slimming."

"That's all I wanted to know."

Of all these the Fish and Wildlife Service was, in my judgement, the best imaginary employer my brother ever had. It got him out of doors. It was harmless to others. It enlarged the range of his interests. It took him into nature, and she is the acknowledged source of all our wisdom by direct or indirect means. She broods on us when we are in her bosom.

Ashraf is a city slicker, so he started close to home. There were all manner of regulations that could be enforced upon the strollers and urban fishermen of Jones Beach, Rockaway, Coney Island, Wolfe's Pond. He caught the bus on Atlantic Avenue. The fishermen were loiterers, middle-aged men of recent

South American and Russian origins who took advantage of their afternoons of unemployment to drop an idle line into the Atlantic and watch as the gunmetal water parted around the tackle.

There was no real market for the catch. People fished almost without purpose, hardly even for the pot. They were not acclimatised to English and uncertain of their right to stand up to a policeman. It was among these semi-foreigners that Ashraf became a true fisher of fishermen. He waited until he found a man on his own and swooped down on the guy. The first thing he held up was a pentagonal badge obtained from a costume store in Alphabet City. Badge, credit card, and revolver were soon tucked back into a wide brown leather belt. In his tan trousers and a shirt decorated on the sleeve with a law-enforcement patch, my brother looked authoritative. There weren't many questions about his standing. If there were any questions it was probably a native New Yorker, no easy target, and the scene would be brought to an end with gruff words of advice from my brother.

Two-thirds of power and its mystique involve imposing documents on other people. Ashraf had drawn up and photostatted his own series of forms at Kinko's. They were made out for Title 16 Chapter 9 violations, which punished users of improper bait for any failure to throw protected species back into the water, for fishing on a protected beach, and for the inability to produce a necessary licence. Ashraf got a signature from the fisherman and then picked through the catch, sharply removing the packing ice from his hands as he turned over each fish. He squatted over the box, checked the types, gazed into their ricy green eyes, and measured every fish with a tape measure. Some of them he weighed on a portable scale. Ashraf told me that he liked the sensation of the cold silver scales sliding through his hands. They were like cold feathers on his palms. I thought it was an oddly delicate perception on my brother's part.

In order to impress his knowledge on the fishermen Ashraf became something of an expert on marine life. On the Atlantic beaches the common finds were smelt, bluefish, dogfish, flounder, whiting, and hake. From the Hudson under the G.W. Bridge came bass, bonita, false albacore. Bass with its red and black diagonals had the deadly beauty of a mamba. To my mind there was something ineradicably snakish about such a large volume and multiplicity of fish. Ashraf came home with whole piles of smelt, catfish, his beloved walleyes stored in padded, ice-stuffed mailers, and from inside the damp brown paper came the overpowering odour of snake. I wanted to faint.

"Can I fix you something?"

"I'm fine, Ashraf."

"I'm going to fry something up for myself, and maybe for Crogan." He was on good terms with our lawyer nowadays. "So it's no trouble. Besides, Firoze, since Dad went to Florida we see each other once in a blue moon." He tied his apron on his hips. "I worry we're falling to pieces as a family. The only other person is our mother and she's at the other end of the earth. As for you, Firoze, either you're conspiring with Crogan or you claim to be writing some article. Sit down, for a change, and I'll tell you how I got this batch from a bunch of Russian guys at Brighton Beach. It's just the kind of thing you like to hear."

"Maybe you could tell me the story and spare me the fish."

There were other locations my brother patrolled besides Rockaway and Jones Beach. The lighthouse on Roosevelt Island, Orchard Beach in the Bronx, and Battery Park City on the south shore of Manhattan were some of his other hangouts but there were more professionals and nosy parkers in these parts and along the dams of Central Park than was to the taste of a fictional inspector. There was no shortage of places for him to move on to. Beneath New York's endless landfill of battlements and ramparts is the original chain of islands which bears its endless shorelines. My brother dispensed enough twenty-five-dollar tickets to keep us in pocket money while we were hoping for our Farewell policies to mature. He chose the amount so that people paid on the spot. Otherwise he wrote them a ticket for double and rented several anonymous post office boxes around town to which he directed their payments.

There were times he had to run for dear life after provoking the wrong man. Once I had to bail Ashraf out of a holding tank in Brighton Beach on a charge of making false statements to a police officer. That was when he tried to give an off-duty cop a fishing ticket. But every occupation has drawbacks. Otherwise it was really the perfect occupation for Ashraf. Meaningful labour is, of course, the greatest medicine. He looked healthier than ever. It brought out the sardine green in his eyes. With a tan and his new gear and his wisecracking soul Ashraf reminded me of nobody so much as Huck Finn.

Even if we weren't getting along I took a new shine to my brother. It's a paradox that you can have a better feeling about someone when he isn't so close to you. For the first time I almost admired my brother on the ethical plane. The outdoors, the exercise and whatever sunshine he could get in this hemisphere, the kick of collecting on a ticket, the sheer love of selling fishing licences on the spot, the moral discipline inherent in taking pride in a uniform and needing to farm his mailboxes once a week before he got busted, the sheer pluck it took to talk his way into and out of these situations were (in my Tocquevillian view) American virtues.

Ashraf got to be an enthusiastic angler. He went alone rather than with any friends. We had a lot of equipment stacked in the closets. When he couldn't collect a fine from his fishermen Ashraf took away their bait, their rods, and their fish. Basically he wasn't doing it for economic reasons. It was the wild joy he took in the whole process that drove his expeditions and the pleasure he took in telling me and Crogan about it afterwards. Those two old battlehorses began to get along. I would get back to Astoria from the Public Library, and find Sayeed and Crogan and Ashraf five sheets to the wind, shooting pistols in the office, and terrifying the angling fish in the big tank in the front of the office. Sayeed's smile was radioactive in the fluorescent atmosphere of the law office.

Like most thoughtful people I write at glacial speed but things were coming together. My essay was printed almost without alteration except for a change from British to American spelling. It appeared in five long columns in the 21 February *Wall Street Journal*, where the curious reader may consult the full text and compare a charcoal portrait of the author with the living reality.

Charcoal as a medium makes for a flattering portrait. It confers a relaxed dignity on the lines of one's face and a sense of bearing and composure upon one's posture. In my view the different media have completely different spiritual charges. Charcoal drawing is to be recommended to those engaged in public life, luscious black-and-white photographs to poetasters and versifiers, colour Polaroid to mothers and fathers, a roll of black film to a thief.

Looking my opinion piece over I fear that it fails to persuade on account of its nouveau riche sentimentality and, above all, its unjust sense of elevation. Just who do I think I am? The editorial reads like something composed by a man who, late in life, has discovered the power of simple feelings, if I may offer a pre-emptive judgement. My essay was stitched together in a mood of true grief for a lost form of life. It's an elegy (but of course words like grief, sorrow, loss, and mourning are useful only if they awaken a reader's heart to the sorrow of his own funerals). My

169

theme was as follows. After that one September morning, the thousand unsleeping eyes of the United States would be fixed on us Muslims forever. Invisibility, something the Dawoods and Peers crave, is a prize that you can only pine after when it's gone forever. We would never be anonymous again, never again invisible to the thousand and one peacock eyes of the American Argus.

"We Muslims are history's brokenhearted," I wrote, "but even if our nearest brothers and sisters have been altered beyond moral recognition by their pangs there are many of us who choose to abide by the laws of humanity. We melancholy, musical Muslims may welcome these scenes of ruin and destruction with open arms, but many of us are good enough to wish for our own destruction . . . and for the confusion of our brothers and sisters. We as Muslims feel our complicity, and ask only that we be the first to blame ourselves. Permit us only to abuse and berate ourselves on your behalf. In this way our complicity will be undiluted with a drop of cultural defensiveness. It's been said that nightingales and roses fill one chamber of our hearts and that the music of the bullet rings in the adjoining chamber. It's been noticed that the pursuit of happiness is too rosy a slogan for ears that hear only a seashell's terror and its thousand tragedies. It's been seen that we pore over our almanac of forlorn battles but if so much is true, then conquer us and place our brothers in chains."

Uninterested readers may skip to the top of the following page, but, as a matter of record keeping, I here offer a précis of the argument as a whole. My essay alternately trudges and flies through twenty-six succeeding paragraphs, citing under the letter 'M' Michel de Montaigne on the variability of men's fortunes, Montesquieu's *Persian Letters* on the character of men's minds under a despotism, Michelangelo on the significance of the human form, Midori, Robert Michener, and the example of Mozart on the dissolving power of beauty when it acts on a received system of ideas.

My quotations from A to Z, by the way, were taken from the third (1974) edition of the World Book encyclopaedia, which my mother lifted from a travelling salesman and which had been carted by this author from its Johannesburg home all the way down the Maine coast to Atlantic Avenue in Brooklyn, and now to Astoria. My mother still wondered where her encyclopaedia had vanished to and complained about having to use the library at Monash University whenever she needed to look something up. That was my mother all over again. It was just like the solipsist she was to believe she was the only person in the universe.

My principal contention in the *Journal* piece was the existence of two distinct strands of Muslim consciousness. By this I did not mean the obvious outward split between the Tao of the Shi'a and the way of the Sunni. I referred to the inward bisection between the violent, the impetuous, the capitalistic, and the revengeful, on the one hand, and on the other, the mystical and the worldly, the rational and the scientific, the socialistic and the philosophical, everything peaceable and progressive. The one was dominant, the other recessive, in every Muslim heart. In all of this you might think I was simply putting a gloss on my own family life and rationalising my own existence, but if you did you would be wrong for the indisputable reason that a family is the molecule of a civilisation.

Crogan was the first to see the draft of my essay. Like any new author I was worried about my first reader's response. My heart thumped in my ears as he studied the pages on his belly. I shouldn't have been so fearful. Crogan was delighted with the ideas I presented and thought they would be exactly what the times required. The honest grin couldn't be extinguished on his face. There weren't any thinking Republicans in New York that Crogan knew of, so he faxed it from his office to all manner of people on the Potomac.

That fax machine was one nerve in a national network of faxes. It was strange to me that an unexceptional man like Crogan should be a gifted propagandist but he had an ear for it. By the next morning I had the contract with the *Journal*. During the following week I attracted the attention of a conservative publisher, another publisher, a consortium of rightwing publishers, a local television station, the New York *Daily News*, and a lecture agent. By six o'clock in the evening I had a standing invitation to go down to Princeton, and an interview set up for a researcher's position at the Middle East Institute in Washington where a friend of Crogan's was on the board.

Unlike Ashraf I am not one for boasting. I won't repeat any of the kind words I heard from these sundry rightwing nuts, but it's obvious that the worldly forms of discourse are the real literature of the United States. We, in the United States, tend towards the practical, the how to, and whodunit. Novels, poems, philosophical flights of fancy may not sell like hot cakes, but polemics, confessions, memoirs, flagellations, sociological treatises, celebrity verse, any kind of self-help and connect-the-dots psychology, New Age textbooks, market analysis, and enquiries into business charisma do very well.

And culturally speaking, I mean, it's not like anyone else in the world has a better idea. For me the real revelation in the reception of my article was that I had found my true calling as a writer. This kind of writing, my kind of writing, helps people to believe what they already know. Plus, there are no readers so beneficent as Republicans.

A few words about Republicans are in order. If I say that they strike me as a local version of the Khmer Rouge, don't mistake my attitude for ingratitude. They practised the kind of political belligerence a South African appreciates. I owed them a good deal. Crogan was a Republican. There was a religious dimension to my affiliation. The Democrats, with their liking for energy, had long been the Jewish party and so, by the logic of Middle Eastern religions, the Grand Old Party, the party of stability, was more attached to Muslim interests. The party operatives who contacted me must remain nameless, but they were easy friends to me, good at connecting and forging connections. They organised an informal think tank in Princeton that specialised in Muslim and Arab mentalities. They also set up an appointment with their Princeton guys.

Dean Sets Khardozian and his Lebanese-born sidekick Ahmed Herazi were the nation's leading Republican experts on the Orient. They were familiar faces. Sets, a dodderer and nonagenarian with a soupy Oxford manner, had been wheeled onto the news shows frequently in recent months to denounce the culture of the Muslim Middle East.

Ahmed Herazi was universally known as Joe Herazi. I read his column in the New York Post with some fascination. Joe regretted the days his Shi'a brothers and sisters were born, and was happy to explain to the public anything that needed to be said by a self-critical Arab. He was a proponent of strong remedies and nothing but strong remedies – assassination, large scale detention, occupation, and blockades of the various Muslim nations. Herazi was a pithy speaker, a man who had the strength to be a television pessimist, and who was generally admired for this reason. He was fond of saying that the language of force was the most eloquent of tongues. He lingered over his inventory of maxims. Force, he would tell his interviewers, was the universal language that succeeded the destruction of the Tower of Babel.

Herazi and the dean were rumoured to be lovers by the more refined mosque-goers on Atlantic Avenue, but it may simply be that the Muslim world tends to think of its determined opponents as homosexual while being blind to the friendliness of men on the Peshawar frontier. Before long I had a chance to decide for myself. My life at this time was a whirlwind in the hands of drivers, radio hosts, promoters, newspaper stringers, the corps of public relations, and all the supporting troops of the army of publicity. The United States perpetually dissolves its own certainties and the hijackers had mysteriously intensified this accelerating process. A century's worth of progress, a thousand years of Dark Age regression, could happen in the space of a month under these new circumstances. Individual history was similarly accelerated. My parabolic life certainly was . . .

I found myself settling on a divan on Dean Khardozian's balcony, noticing that the tennis court on his lawn was a puzzlingly beautiful composition in emerald and turpentine, almost a Mondrian and, from this angle, a parallelogram. The court was a shade of green I had seen before only in my brother's eyes, and then only at moments of great intensity. It was almost painful to see the Princeton undergraduates striding across the turf in their white outfits. They were very young, smooth in the face, and if anything, almost featureless.

It wasn't until later in the evening my host told me that it was a distinguishing mark of Princetonians to be fresh. The dean brought out a tray and served our party with his own hands. His crabbed hands shook as he poured mint-leaf tea into china cups and handed them around. Then came slices of eggplant, pickled onions, rounds of bread, and red-bean pâté. He liked having people around.

Khardozian, a disciple of Tacitus, referred to the Princeton boys as his minnows. He was known to molest them in the friendliest possible way. It was a very Ivy League arrangement. They came over to his ranch on Witherspoon Lane for seminars. They drank Armenian cognac, browsed his pickled onions, admired his collection of first editions, and allowed the dean to seat one or two of them on his lap. It was a cheerful exercise, as close to above-board as such things can be. At table, beneath the board, the long legs of the boys wriggled over the thin legs of the old man as they tried to find a comfortable position. The dean would smile over their shoulders at the other people in the room. Really, no one gave the matter a second thought.

Everything Khardozian did, in fact, was accomplished in an extremely British and friendly manner. He put his hands on your leg when sitting beside you, measured the life lines on your palm and told you that he had learned the art of

173

palm reading from a gypsy man in Yerevan. He raised his dandelion eyebrows so high on his forehead every time you said anything that you felt they would never come down again, and, in general, petted his friends and visitors.

If the author of these papers admits to being the object of these attentions for an evening and affirms that he relies strictly on the testimony of his own green eyes he's not claiming the mantle of a victim. The greatest thing about Khardozian and his accomplice Herazi was that they didn't make you feel like a victim. Nor did they mind you deflecting their advances. If you were lunching at the round table on his balcony, two floors above the green block of the tennis court, and the dean put his hand on your knee, you returned it to his lap and it went scurrying off in the other direction. I could see the discoloration on his neck as he stretched it in the direction of his other neighbour.

From the balcony we surveyed the doubles matches on the lawn. Each side was made up of two blond men. The arcs of the orange balls, as the serves rang out, bent in the high wind. Around the court was a black wire cage into which a door and a ball basket had been built. The cage was as tall as the house. The dean and I noticed each other looking down at the players.

Khardozian continued prattling on about the Arabs without skipping a beat. The dean was the rarest of things, a glittering conversationalist who didn't tamp down his guests. There was something unexpected in almost everything he said to us. He told obscene jokes. He ribbed Herazi. He talked about the steps involved in distilling Armenian brandy. His mother, an actress in Paris, and his father, an émigré businessman who invested the remnants of his Armenian fortune in a Sussex Rolls-Royce dealership, were the subjects of many of his stories. I had never met someone who had so perfectly organised a stream of material at his disposal. Pranks at Brasenose College in Oxford, the deficiencies of the Democratic Party, the sexual proclivities of politicians, St Augustine, Bing Crosby, and the mechanical virtues of the four cylinders in an MG engine, all marched across Khardozian's tongue. Eventually he turned serious and told us about his dealings with presidents from John F. Kennedy to the current occupant of the White House.

"We must say that Joe and I were very impressed with Firoze here's article. My many years of research on the Ottomans have taught me that overwhelming force is the one value that Muslims have always respected throughout history. That's a message our current president can't hear enough. His resolve is the nation's vital asset. Joe and I want you to help deliver that message. I will be honest, young man, we wanted to get someone like you, from each Islamic region, to speak to the president. We tried to find a Syrian willing to speak out, an Iranian, a Pakistani, an Egyptian, a Saudi, but these people are brainwashed. They won't say what we want them to say."

"Maybe a Palestinian," I said. "Surely that would be the most convincing voice considering the situation they're in."

"A what?" Khardozian asked. His tongue slid around the inside of his mouth. I could tell that he was genuinely puzzled, as if I had used a word he wasn't familiar with. "A what-did-you-say?"

"A Palestinian would be a good person to validate your ideas."

The dean looked across the table. "Joe, do you understand him?"

"Palestinian, Sets. He said Palestinian. It was an honest mistake on Mr Peer's behalf, I believe." Herazi was a lively, excitable man with the ready-to-boil temperament of a true Middle Easterner. He threw his small hands into the air. "Firoze, you're probably not aware that, for many years now, Dean Khardozian's scholarship has been devoted to proving beyond the shadow of a doubt that there are no such things as Palestinians. After all, what are Palestinians? Do you know what you mean when you use that term? Because I don't even know what you mean. Like unicorns and Santa Claus, these Palestinians are figments of imagination. As an Arab myself, it disappoints me that the Arabs invest so much time and worry in imaginary constructs. Moreover, they take joy in our sorrow."

Herazi stopped for a moment and then seeing something in Khardozian's face he went on. "That's not an opinion about the non-existence of the Palestinians, by the way. It's the upshot of thousands of hours of Khardozian's research. Having proved the non-existence of the Palestinians, he has done the logical thing and forgotten the name itself. Khardozian won't tell you this, but his intellectual integrity, in this sense, is unrivalled. He's an Orwell to the president's Churchill. Like Orwell, Khardozian doesn't hold any truck with the use of language to befuddle others. We don't claim any special distinction in this nation of a million Orwells and Churchills. The misuse of language is the hallmark of tyranny, and of the Arabs."

"Look, Joe," I said, "you can't begin to understand how Muslims feel about the rest of the world until you realise that the Palestinians are our cherished people. It's the mirror image of this country and Israel."

"Well, I don't know about that. Frankly, Firoze, we do better to watch our words rather than fuelling ancient hatreds," Herazi replied. "The dean's point is that an entire religion has been bewitched by something that doesn't exist. The only cure involves the application of unbearable quantities of military force. Believe me. I should know because my own brother is himself a terrorist."

At this Khardozian came back to life. "Ahmed here, Firoze, is very courageous. He's been my right-hand man since 1982. He won't tell you, but he comes from a very distinguished Shi'a family in Lebanon. A long line of Herazi scholars and administrators dates back to the Persian empire. He's a true Arab, as well as being an ancestral Persian, and a stalwart friend of this country, not to say a real lover of a superb cognac. Since the day I met him he has been warning us of an attack on the homeland. Of course the Jordanian government, in their hatred of Arabs who speak out, had to fabricate a bank scandal to discredit Joe. That's when he came to this country. It's a fascinating story. One Herazi brother went down the road of scholarship while the other one, Amin Herazi, is a senior Hezbollah commander. He's supposedly fighting against the Israelis, but of course, as the Arabs learn every day, the Israelis are anything but fictional. Ah, they're masters of warfare. Absolute masters."

"That's very interesting, what you say about Joe's brother."

"Yes." Khardozian chuckled. "But for me the greatest thing about Joe is that he was really born a Muslim. That's what's so unusual amongst our crowd."

"I didn't know there were so many converts," I said. "How strange."

It was even stranger that I saw parallels between Sayeed's smile and Khardozian's. A smile, I said before, is like a flash from the lining of a man's soul. And yes, I know the differences between a madman and a bomber, but a parallel like that is a cosmic indication. Sayeed's smile, of course, was that of a young man with a detonator and a message to send that remained thankfully unsent. Meanwhile the dean was at the very extreme of old age, smiling and revealing the very thin, heavily peppered jelly of his gums and the uncertain moorings of his worn-down teeth. But more than anything I had been noticing Khardozian's tongue. It was pythonic in repose.

One organ is most physically prominent in each person and this sluggish tongue was dominant in Khardozian. Purple, muscular, and nodulated, it uncoiled to wet his mouth in conversation and then settled back down. It was the nerve at the centre of his being and it took on mythical proportions as I watched. From nowhere came the stray thought of stabbing its life out, then escaping as the blood sizzled in the dean's mouth. But this was an idea worthy of Ashraf, not me. Khardozian was more than polite over lunch. He was positively gracious. His hands didn't come near me again for three-quarters of an hour. He took me seriously as a human being and he was perhaps the first person in my life to do so. He may have been a perpetual smiler but there was also a deadly serious element to his character, something as slow-moving and muscular as that devouring tongue.

The dean wasn't the type to leave a question unanswered. After a minute he picked up the conversation where I had left it. "You ask about the converts. I call them Washington Muslims to compare them with Washington blacks, Washington homosexuals, Washington Hispanics. The Washington Muslims are people who have recently converted to Islam in order to criticise it more effectively. Now you understand what a godsend you could be to us, my boy. Come with us to the White House next week. Now . . . can I introduce you to one of my minnows?"

The quartet of minnows, in their nicely pressed white shorts and polo shirts, had a curious lightness of being. Although these angular-bodied students towered over me they seemed as if they were about to levitate. They hailed from here and there on the east coast – Maine, Massachusetts, the mainline suburbs of Philadelphia – but from what I overheard they had been going to the same debutante balls, charity auctions, and the same New England islands for most of their overlapping lives. They had in common a certain caramel complexion, invisibly freckled, and a direct blue or grey stare that seemed to be cultivated. Wavy blond hair descended into tanned curls and the fuzz on the sharp spine of their necks had never known a razor's kiss.

Perhaps they were so similar because they were the archetype to which the dean's taste ran. The minnows were the true delight of Khardozian's existence, apart from tormenting Muslims. I suspected they were the only flavour that would never go stale on that empurpled tongue. For students they were on rather casual terms with their old professor. It was obvious how fond they were of the old man to see them surround him, methodically finger his dewlap, and fold their fingers into his cronish hands. I was jealous of their ésprit de corps, their gregarious insults, and their readiness to burst into a capella song.

I tell you so much about the minnows because I got to know them pretty well during our weekend decampment to D.C. They accompanied the dean, Herazi, and myself down to Washington, and slept two abed in Khardozian's suite at the

Omni Shoreham. The minnows were hard not to like. I had a smaller room to myself in the other wing. I was nervous about meeting the president. He was, after all, the beating heart of a heartless country. I came in during the evenings to find the minnows sunk in the tub, playing charades as Khardozian dozed in his chair, cadging shampoo from the maid service, cartwheeling along the corridors, and now and again bringing the dean up to a crescendo of fruity laughter in order to justify their keep.

Legitimate society accepted the satellite status of the minnows to the degree that the White House extended invitations to the four of them, as well as to Herazi, myself, and Khardozian. On the evening of our visit they were dressed in light blue tuxedoes with matching powder-blue cummerbunds. Lucky for me they were there to distract me from my premonitions. Their glow-worm faces in the rearmost seat of the limousine were soft and luminous. I identified a girlish quality to the minnows as they huddled beside each other on the car's long black leather bench. They giggled, gossiped, stroked Khardozian's small head, and felt each other up. I had more reason than ever to be grateful for their presence. They chose a tie for me, reassured me, and ushered me into the limousine before going back to get Joe and the dean.

As to their determination to protect their master there could be no doubt in the mind of an observer who saw them deployed around him at the appointment gate on West Executive Avenue where the limousine dropped us. The seven of us proceeded through the security check with the precision of a convoy. The outside of the White House is too familiar to describe and familiarity, as I previously pointed out, is an enemy of the memoirist. Inside, the White House was lit up like a ballroom.

In the rooms we passed chandeliers hung from the decorated ceilings. Men and women in black evening clothes swept grandly along the corridors and through the small palace en route to some event. Stationed at various points on the way were Secret Service men and women, impassive watchers who without looking away spoke into their microphoned lapels. They frightened me, but at the very same time their severity promised that we were approaching the centre of the world. It's that sense of centrality, I reflected, which goes a long way to explaining, and excusing, the American disease of self-righteousness. It was a disorder easily forgiven by a generous man of foreign birth.

The president wasn't yet in attendance. An aide brought us upstairs to the green drawing-room. It was a receiving area of modest size done up in the plush style of the eighteenth century. On a square glass table stood an ornate bowl of red punch and an assortment of tumblers of unequal heights. There was a cake to celebrate Khardozian's recent birthday. When I cut myself a slice I couldn't help imagining that its dark, moist, molasses consistency released a faint but inexpungible odour of tongue.

No one else tried the cake. It was a small crowd, not markedly hungry, and by standing next to the dean I became aware of their stature. There were personages like congressmen and journalists who had proved their devotion to Khardozian's Middle Eastern projects, but otherwise the minnows screened their man from any buttonholer below the status of senator, appeals court judge, bureau chief, ambassador to a significant land, or captain of industry. They were not unfriendly to me and Joe, but it was clear that Khardozian was the only person they were interested in listening to.

The Princeton dean, his chromatic eyes twinkling, leaned against the minnows and laid out his course for the future. He wanted us to be tough on these Muslims (except for the Jordanians and, in a pinch, the Turks). He saw totalitarianism everywhere, including in the left wing of the Democratic Party and wanted us to vanquish it. Either we level our adversaries, as he put it, or Islam levels us. In retrospect I wish I had listened closely to Khardozian's speech. It was hard, of course, knowing one was about to be introduced to the president of the United States.

Even in the green room Khardozian was a great host to his audience, part of that Near Eastern talent for endlessly celebrating one's friends and visitors. He floated these ideas in a slow-as-custard voice. The harsher his prescriptions became, the larger the population to which they were applied, the slower and sweeter and more British became his voice. His strong, probing tongue flickered into existence and then vanished as he progressed. Joe Herazi stood at his elbow and, as an Arab, made the occasional remark in agreement with the dean's arguments. For these senators and congressmen, I realised, Khardozian was a Svengali figure. The anglophone accent helped. I resolved to work on my elocution. It created the sort of unearned confidence that paved a way for one in this country.

The United States, by the way, is the only land in which colleges and towns develop their own foreign policy. To hear Khardozian tell it, Princeton foreign policy was from Mars. It called for the invasion of a string of enemy states from Iran and Syria to Lebanon, Saudi Arabia, Yemen, and Qatar. It was the people of Qatar, to be sure, and not their government that was hostile, but the only way to put the people down was to replace the government. Let them see what happened to people who let the wrong kind of tyrant rule them. Then there were differences with Papua New Guinea, Venezuela, and Turkmenistan over which no responsible individual would gloss. When the decks had been cleared, there would be time to prepare for a much longer and more nebulous conflict against France that had to be waged at the level of culture and ideas.

Dr K's explanation of this last point succumbed to a great hush settling over the green room. It was the president, who entered and made in our direction. He breasted the minnows and shook my hand with laudable and even, I will say, Churchillian firmness. The leader of the Free World, I can say, has hands which are notable for their stringy toughness. They are hands to hold the reins of a headstrong Arabian mare.

Allow me to make the single observation of the man's remarkable resemblance to the muse of *Mad* magazine, Alfred E. Neumann. A president is impossible to dissolve into a piece of imaginative prose. The president of the United States is the only being who is surrounded by a simultaneously positive and negative cult of personality, stirring the hearts of a hundred million admirers and despisers on a daily basis.

This president, who was wholly fictional to begin with, is even more elusive a target of the pen. To be a president is already to possess a face that invites comparisons, so I claim no originality for my Neumann simile. If anyone has been reading my manuscript solely for a sketch of the president, I worry they may be gravely disappointed by the meagreness of the insights provided. We exchanged few words in five minutes, the president and I, but those very few were in a spirit of good humour and I will relate them in the finer mode of indirect discourse. The president saw that I was a good fellow on the evidence of my green eyes and green soul and chucked Ahmed Herazi under the chin. He wished me well in my endeavours. He furrowed his brow and, in his capacity as a marathoner, advised me on physical fitness. In all his utterances he was as innocent of the sin of grammar as a child of three. Across an abyss of incomprehension was plastered the banner of his smile.

With the president's unmeaning smile before me, Dean Khardozian's grin, and Ahmed Herazi's sarcastic laughter slurring in my ears, the green drawing-room was full of comparisons on the subject of laughter which fascinated me. The loop of my parabolic career, however, was set by something other than my thoughts – the perfect separation of one's thoughts and one's fate is a metaphysical fact. As for my fate, it was fixed at the very instant the official White House photographer snapped the famous portrait of myself, Herazi, Khardozian, and the president of the United States against a backdrop of rococo wallpaper and a Steinway piano. It was of course the picture that the president's critics seized on because it showed him associating with a known enemy of these United States.

In that picture, which was rapidly translated into another charcoal drawing by the artists of the *Wall Street Journal*, one sees the big man's big hand resting on my shoulder and Khardozian's small rib of a hand brushing against my hip. The president, in a bomber jacket, is a man who is used to being photographed and knows to jut his jaw after the manner of Gary Cooper in *High Noon*. Sets Khardozian is above the medium of photographs and maintains a stern expression. My poor appearance scarcely needs words to be spent on it. As for Ahmed Herazi, it's invisible in the drawing but his small black eyes are filled with tears. Joe is weeping for the Arabs, whose sin is existence.

The article on Khardozian's birthday party at the White House ran the next day in the *Journal*'s A section. When I got back to Astoria and brought a copy home to catch up on the news I found, on the very same page, a report on a local conman who had been victimising corporations like Philip Morris and R.J.R. Nabisco and who had been linked to the hijackers. The sketch of Ashraf showed him with a fishing rod over his arm and an imperturbable grin. I was furious with my brother but at the same time I thought that a book written from his warped point of view would really be a bestseller and a sure-fire television movie. Of the two of us he had always been the likable one. But by then it was too late to solve any of the mysteries of my brother. Johnny Law read the *Journal* just as religiously as I did and noticed the coincidence of the photographs.

The state police were setting up a perimeter around Crogan's office when I found myself on the rooftops of Steinway Street with the keys to the Mercedes-Benz Ashraf pretended not to have stolen. I looked down at the keys so as not to see the line of Crown Victorias with their flashing red and blue lights. There were hieroglyphics on the scabbard. In my hands the cool metal keys were as heavy and reassuring as a revolver. I always resented my brother's imperial presumptions about cars. There was no reason I couldn't drive the Mercedes if I put my mind to it.

Being on the road, I told myself, was the birthright of an American. I could

181

maybe drop in on a Tappersville girl I met at a gun show upstate. I could get to the airport and fly into Fazila's arms in Golders Green. These happy thoughts possessed me as I passed through the washing lines on top of the buildings on Steinway Street. I thought nobody had spotted me although I could see Crogan arguing with the cops in front of his office. But when I slid into the Mercedes I barely managed to put my seat belt on before a gag was fastened around my mouth. The cloth gag smelled of hospital anaesthetic. It made me dizzy. I tried not to breathe. In the mirror I saw Sayeed Papindari half standing up in the backseat, throttling me with all the strength in those fat white public-schoolboy hands. Then I couldn't see any more. There were stars and bars in front of my eyes. I slumped back in the seat and Sayeed released his hold on the garrotte. He was grinning. Suddenly everything was obvious.

"So you killed Felix?"

He said, "It wasn't my choice. It was your choice all along. You insulted Mohammad Atta. You insulted our entire way of life. People have to learn that you can't insult our way of life with impunity. Now, Firoze, I have to slaughter you the way I did your friend. Don't worry. I'm not going to use a knife. This is quite sufficient. Then I'm going to get started on your brother. But you're the real adversary. You're the one we have to finish off. Mohammad always thought as much."

"Does Abbas know what you're doing?"

Sayeed shook his head. His eyes glinted like a tiger's heart. "Abbas is too gentle to understand. Never mind. There's room in the movement for more than one kind of soldier."

It was then that I pushed the accelerator down and crashed the Mercedes into the front wall. This wasn't what I meant to do. There was a great bang. I knocked my head on the windshield. Sayeed laughed. At that everything spun around and settled into the right place. I put the car in reverse and slammed it against the back wall. Sayeed came flying into the front seat and I pushed him out the door. I left him in the garage. Ten minutes later my erratic driving got me pulled over on the West Side Highway. The rest, as they say, is history, but, considered cosmologically, as a vehicle for the soul, history, as that great driver Henry Ford liked to say, is bunk.

ل

Chapter Eight

Let me reverse the direction of imaginative current and ask the reader a light-hearted question. How is it possible that any manuscript has been completed without someone's first imprisoning the author? After 5.50 p.m. the penitentiary sleeps like a princess within her endless bed of forest. Blackjack oaks and squares of pitchpine intrude on the prison yard. Mount Holly bears five hundred square miles of wood upon her shoulders, and nets of weed – hog huckleberry, lowbush blueberry, and broomsedge, beard grass, which catches in the ankles of the trees. Coming to Fort Dix in August I dreamed in the sunshine I was on my way to nursery school with my mother. Along Route 68 were vast summery banks of purple and yellow flowers, common marigolds and flurries of Queen Anne's Lace, growing in the margins of untilled agricultural land. Pollen-dusted pintails and terns, the pollen thick as saffron, flew up at the progress of the bus.

The red cement ziggurat of Fort Dix could hardly be more conducive to a writer's self-imposed sense of mission. The gym is the centre of common existence. A bank of six mounted televisions is useful for a student of the culture, showing college basketball, Channel Six local news, a pixilated image of the prison's television studio, and that show beloved of convicts, *Days of Our Lives*. It reminds me of Jo'burg where everyone is a fan.

Only the malcontents don't look up from their games of chess and Chinese checkers when the three-note fanfare plays. They hunch all the more over chess sets manufactured with toothpaste caps and squares of black-and-white wrapping paper. Among the malcontents and discontents, I make my temporary home.

My little platoon includes Yaponchik, a muscular slab of a Murmansk Russian by way of Brighton Beach, with damaged Asiatic features and a knifer's reputation. He's the official chess champion of the state prison system, named for the smoothness of his countenance. His big body smells of Vicks Vaporub. For all his size Yaponchik has a hairdresser's manners. He's super-finicky about his boards and his pieces, polishing them on setting them out and then again on returning them to the box. He presides over five, six, seven games at once, playing black, taking his moves with a flautist's fine propensities. Between turns Yaponchik alternately picks at his salmonish gums and exercises his upper arms with small weights. On the other side of the board I watch his well-oiled biceps and triceps thudding out in sequence. They switch with chess-clock precision.

Yaponchik is a great one for moods. They stand out on his hairless but imperfect face. An endgame finds him as solemn as the grave. When he matches an opening he's as flighty as a bird, strict and Confucian when he calls check, and at all other times as gay as Liberace. Do I read him correctly when I observe his affectionate treatment of the younger players? Did I interpret his rubbing my neck during one abandoned game with too much asperity? Does Yaponchik harbour feelings for me beneath his solid pectorals? His manner certainly reminds me of the curiously friendly men we encountered on the Peshawar frontier.

When I went down to the gym to see about a rematch, Yaponchik repudiated his proffer of friendship. He was leathering the inside of a shoe with a Dr Scholl's tongue and didn't have time for small courtesies. It was beneath his dignity to acknowledge my presence beyond the narrowing of one fierce plum-coloured eye. Yet I felt more than ever that we have a great deal in common, Yaponchik and I. As a victim of Stockholm Syndrome, of course, I imagine bonds of commonality with the strangest characters. Yaponchik's reserve reminds me to append Jean-Paul Sartre's opposite-to-mine opinion that hell is other people. Need I add to this my own observation that human beings are the only thing that stands in the way of my loving humanity?

I looked over his shoulder and asked, "How are you doing with the shoe, Yaponchik?"

"How does it look like I'm doing? It's okay. It's okay. Don't worry about it. And don't look over my shoulder."

"Feel like a game?"

"Not really. You can ask me again tomorrow."

I said, "Well, maybe I'll do that."

"And maybe you will," he returned.

Yaponchik, so you know, is a former associate of the once-upon-a-time mob boss Joseph Kobzon, singer of old Russian ballads by appointment to Brezhnev, and a big wheel in the organised-crime circles of the Soviet era. Music, theatre, crime, and make-believe go together everywhere. Kobzon, in turn, was mixed up with characters hailing from Soviet Central Asia, including Gennady Kharkov. Kharkov went by the name of the Mongol and was among the first to make the break from Moscow to Brooklyn and Brighton Beach. He it was who brought along my chess-playing friend. Russian friendships last forever except when they don't, and Kharkov's bond with Yaponchik came to some dreadful end on the Drax rollercoaster on Coney Island.

I mention Yaponchik because his presence suggests the theme of the globalisation of crime. It confirms the *Scarface* idea that the United States is a constitutional fraud. The place has been a beacon for scam artists since the 1979 Mariel boat lift. But I'm not one to judge. Let me just say, en passant, that the affinity to Yaponchik I sense may be a mutual love of riddles, puzzles, and paradoxes. If I am a bishop at this cosmic game, then my brother is a knight. My brother's style of chess, by the way, involves recycling his captured pawns back on to the board. It's a hyper hyper modern style of play.

On Yaponchik's right in the gymnasium, to complete my still life, are the martial arts experts who practise on a number of blue rubber mats. Behind them is Marian's corner. A double mirror stands on a desk along with basin, ashtray, towels, fixing spray, and curling irons with metallic jumpers that give off the half-sizzled odour of an oven. The proprietor sits behind the desk, eating curds and whey, with her strong dark legs folded into a short skirt that rides up on prehensile thighs. The skirt is not more than a handkerchief's worth of brushed brown cloth, alarming to watch, tossed here and there as its owner changes her sitting position.

As for Marian, her loaded eyelashes are thick with mascara. When she focuses on a client they vibrate as rapidly as a hummingbird. She may not be a biological woman, given the black velvet muscled shoulders revealed at the back of her shirt. Still, her hair is subject to the severest discipline – braided, knotted, beaded, tightly curled, and the resulting clayish rope highlighted and rinsed. I see that every morning her devout energies are put into controlling this mass of hair before getting started on her customers. They pay her in the currency of Newports. Prisons, of course, are smokers' last stockades in this country.

Marian lives with a Newport permanently burning in her mouth. The long silver filter slouches past an oval of religiously refreshed maroon lipstick. The vicinity of her desk is saturated in menthol from the Newports, and piercing deodorant, and soldered hair. Even Newports, deodorant, and vaporised hair attach themselves to memories. The Motown songs Marian warbles, while smouldering her cigarettes, remind me of my father. Smokey and the Miracles, the Commodores, and anything by Aretha are on high rotation. She's good too, sings louder when I tell her about the association with Dad. As a thank-you I trade her whatever happens to be in my pockets. To a prisoner pockets are meaningful in a way they aren't on the outside.

Marian improves her condition by barter. She braids men's hair in exchange for her Newports or anything she can swap for Newports. She performs the functions of a trading post. On her desk items of various description materialise for a couple of days until they can be traded away. With the battered desk as its rotary, a caterpillar track carries these next-to-useless articles from one inmate to the next. Shoelaces, rubber bands, the corded tape mechanism from inside a Walkman, a video cassette with parting brown loops of tape showing inside the cartridge are some of the recent arrivals on Marian's desk. You're invited to make a bid and feel a glow of satisfaction when Marian agrees even if it's not something you can use.

I notice there's not an item which doesn't find a taker sooner rather than later. It follows from an inherent principle of psychology I can't exactly formulate. Prisoners, I find, are inveterate swappers, bargainers, and borrowers. They dedicate endless mental energy trading one item for the next, that for the subsequent thing, hoping to end up with one object that matches a wish. It confirms my impression that a prisoner's spiritual condition is a Persian miniature of the free individual's. Such metaphysical conclusions are ductile, however, and I leave them to the public to draw as it chooses.

Marian spends much time explaining about her plans, her brothers and sisters in Albany, the strengths and weaknesses of her appeal. All the while her big rectangular mouth and the sunken apparatus of her Adam's apple work hard to produce that submarine voice which, in its thrilling energistic cost, reminds me of Lauren Bacall. In a friendly, housewifish mood Marian speaks with the physical intensity of someone handling a stubborn stick of chewing gum.

She catches my hand. "You're going to see your lawyer, darling?"

"I have three-quarters of an hour to burn, since Yaponchik turned me down. At least I now have a lawyer, Marian. I believe it's the most significant relationship you can have in this country, between a man and his lawyer."

"Be sure and ask him about my case, will you? Seven years for accidentally robbing a Rochester bank, and they expect me to believe there's justice in America. Why, they give seven years to people who deliberately rob banks." Her shellacked hands go back to her hair. "The guards harass me in here. I just got a 118 21 this morning. Would you believe it?"

"Is a 118 21 for cleanliness and orderliness?" I ask.

"That's a 118 30, Felix." My question irritates her. "You should know that. In answer to your implied question I never received a 118 30. A 118 21 is for creating a so-called fire hazard. They caught me using my hairdryer in my cell."

"It doesn't seem right."

"They wouldn't treat a white woman the same way," Marian concludes, now in a thoroughly bad temper, so I don't ask which of these two categories she's emphasising. "Tell that to your fancy lawyer and see what he has to say about it."

Murray Sternhill waits for me in the middle booth of the visiting room, studying documents. We're separated by plexiglass, beneath which one exchanges papers. I'm careful about what I say. The prison believes that our conversations are recorded. In any event I count myself unique among memoirists in doubting the therapeutic value of speaking openly. And besides there's no time for pleasantries with Sternhill. My new lawyer is a dedicated toiler, and looks the part. There, again, is that bald battering ram of a head on account of which I hired him, those hedgerow eyebrows, that syncopated neck which bows and straightens in time with his eyebrows. The whole ensemble operates at steamship capacity the moment you engage the man in a discussion, as if his gobbling, squinting, and eyebrow raising are a side effect of mental processes. It suggests faces I know from television – Sam Donaldson the news reader, Dan Hedaya the actor. For all this motion Sternhill's manner is dry, even abrasive, and he gets right down to brass tacks. One sign is that he goes by last names only.

"You've lost some weight, Peer. Good for you. Here are the precedents I plan to present to the Court of Appeals. The Second Circuit is our venue because you were arrested in New York. The way I see it they're not going to make new law in a case like this. The country's not in a progressive frame of mind. So we rely on precedent." He passes a folder to me. "Have a look through and send me any comments. I believe you will find it remarkably clear. The footnotes, ah, the footnotes are a thing of beauty."

"Isn't it unreasonable that I was seized instead of my brother? Isn't that enough for reasonable doubt?"

"Reasonable doubt, I told you during our first conversation, begins with the payment of a reasonable fee. Even if I wanted to argue that line the court remains very sceptical concerning the existence of your brother because there are no immigration records, no social security number, no eyewitnesses." Sternhill hooks bifocals upon his ears. His blue diver's eyes swim up beneath the flat lenses as if searching for oxygen. "Whatever South African documents exist aren't admissible. They don't prove your brother's presence in this country. They still haven't found the body you claim you left in the parking garage. And what kind of defendant owns up to an attempted murder that no one's thought of pinning on him? Frankly, Peer, why shouldn't every nutburger hive off his crimes to an imaginary friend? I believe you but other people, you know, aren't paid to believe you."

"We're not perfectly identical, my brother and I," I say. "Variation is so much a cosmic law that no two things can be truly the same. Underneath his right ear Ashraf has a vanishingly small mole. There's a Popeye and Olive tattoo on his right arm which, if you touch it, feels like a bag of iron shot. If you absolutely have to tell us apart, ask him a non-trivial question about philosophy, Schopenhauer, classical music, Persian poetry. As my brother I love him but a few quotations from Gibran is his limit. It's not that Ashraf doesn't learn. He actively repels knowledge. It's why he likes this country. Can it be in his genes? Can it be a matter of culture? And anyway, forget Ashraf. You only have to ask my dear father to confirm the details of my account to the court."

"I was getting to that. We sent a detective to Toronto. Last week he interviewed the man at the residence of the guy you claim is your father. You can find the specifics of the interview in the folder. Your presumptive father is fighting deportation charges brought by the U.S. attorney in Manhattan who wants him to answer for the collapse of Farewell Insurance. In Canada, you know, they can't tell a madman from an absolute lunatic. The guy denies all knowledge of your existence. On the other hand he did pay my fee on your

188

behalf. He says he always dreamed of having a son. He says he can't bear to say goodbye to the insurance business. Even if this guy stages a miraculous recovery his credibility is low."

"It's Dad's sense of humour. I'm confident he'll come around. And I have one additional question. By any chance do you think I could hire your firm's detective? I want someone to keep an eye on a girl."

"You want our guy to spy on a girl you're sweet on?" Sternhill puts his spectacles away. He lowers his battering ram of a head and touches his salt and pepper eyebrows, smoothing them into place. "Peer, I salute you. I really do salute you. Crogan is right to love you. More people in this world should have their loved ones watched. More work for me, inevitably." Sternhill is growling which, I know, means he's happy. "As for the detective, you can't afford him."

Who's the girl? I'll tell you in a second. First let me acknowledge that an under-sexed Mohammedan narrator, an epicurean of the *Pink Panther* trilogy, a child of divorce, can expect little credibility with the general public. Studio audiences won't trust a recovering sex addict even if he suffers less from straightforward sex addiction than a jailhouse addiction to thinking about sex, musing about it, and building his weird daydreams upon its rock. Perhaps a note on influences will help. I have mentioned the name of Schopenhauer as a formative influence on these pages, along with the condensed *Reader's Digest* editions to which my mother subscribed in Johannesburg, and the Saint, Scarlet Pimpernel, Ibn Khaldun. If constellations were books, then Pascal is my north star and *Goldfinger*, by Ian Fleming, my Cygnus the Swan.

With that small preface, back to the girl. I received an interesting postcard from Fazila, who's come to New York to be with Ashraf during this difficult period. The picture on the postcard is, predictably, the Statue of Liberty. Lady Liberty's a favourite of my brother on account of her enormous green bosom. Ashraf calls her statuesque.

Fazila writes in cursive. It snakes from top to bottom in green ink. I noticed at my trial she has one of those fat, spring-loaded ballpoints with four different colours. I would like to say a few words about her breathless, schoolgirl's style. To zigzag, double back, double cross, and circle around is a writer's mode of manoeuvre, whereas Fazila lurches ahead. It's an appealing feminine quality to one who hesitates a thousand times before committing his thoughts to their vehicles.

189

Dear Firoze, or do you go by another name in America?

Thanks for your letter which I just got forwarded from Pakistan today. It's marvellous but what do you mean, top of p.2, talking about Ash, when you say that a recidivist is only a man who wants to be true to himself? Just checking. Firoze, I have news and I wanted to be the one to tell you because of my admiration for your intellect. I'm pregnant, Firoze. Ashraf is the father although in his retiring way he says he doesn't like to take the credit. Once you're released we hope you will come into your own as an uncle.

Yours, Fazila.

An interlude. If Hollywood is willing to listen to so dark a suggester may I just slip in a word to agents looking for an authentically grizzled corrections officer with an ample helping of stage experience. Cast your eyes no further than Angel B. Ramirez, Esq., High School Equivalency, and a graduate of the Utica Academy of Dramatic Arts. Write Sgt. A.B. Ramirez, c/o Dame Gloria Ramirez, 29 Sunflower Boulevard, Apt. 5, "Azatlan," Buffalo NY 14051. Private security companies in search of a reliable employee, a master of the Stanislavski technique, and an overall good sport, would be well advised to correspond with the same address, Angel's mom's pad.

Gloria, can I add, is a lovely, buxom, buxom woman who's done everything for her son in the absence of a certain foolish Ecuadorian man who doesn't deserve the appellation of marido. Gloria takes pride in herself, basting her fingernails with red nail polish on the bus to New Jersey and getting the highlights in her dyed red hair fixed once a week at Tony's Salon. On a personal note I observe that Angel has offered me the use of a typewriter in exchange for this short advertisement. Angel has a touching reverence for memoirists. With his fabulously fine manners for a twenty-three-year-old Utican, the style of a bullfighter or a courtier, I suspect that Gloria trimmed his gestures with the care usually lavished on a bonsai tree. So he may be gracious, clean-shaven, and crisp about physical details, but he's also a tough guy. And as we South Africans like to say, Angel has advice for Africa.

"Please, don't sit scrunched while you work," he tells me, adjusting the gold cross which sits half inside his shirt. "Take care of your skeleton, my mother always says, or one day those bones are going to take care of you." He continues over my shoulder, still suspicious. "You're not blowing smoke? This manuscript could make it to the big screen?"

"Son of Sam permitting. Some big shot will discover that the only name in it that hasn't been changed is yours, Angel. It'll make you famous."

"What are you going to call it?"

"*A Brother Betrayed*," I say. "Alternatively, *A Metaphysical Muslim Reflects*."

Angel shakes his head. "That's way too heavy. Way-Too-Heavy. A title is the most important thing to get right. It's the one thing I read. Most of my education in high school was the titles of my school books."

"*An Idyll in Dunkin' Donuts? Manhattan on $400 a Day of Other People's Money? The Pages of Sin?*" I look at my critic. "You don't like anything? Maybe I don't want an audience, Angel. Maybe a few well-chosen souls is best. In my view a book is a means for finding affinities between people. It's like a spirit level for souls. Angel, I just don't imagine there are a million people out there who have an affinity for me. For goodness sake, I wouldn't want to live in such a world."

"Now you're thinking of reasons to fail, cabrón," Angel replies in a way that suggests he's quoting Gloria. From nothing I write, by the way, should it be inferred that Angel Bianca Ramirez is a mother's boy. He doesn't display a mother's boy's optimism. Instead he has rather sour good looks, like Al Pacino, thin-eyebrowed brown eyes, and Pacino's lean face. His movements, I suspect, are borrowed from Pacino in *Scarface*.

Angel is permanently disgruntled. For this very reason he may be a great actor waiting in the wings because creative forms require a certain rejection of the universe as it stands. There's also a curious disgruntled blackmailer's smile Angel has, which reminds me of my brother. Of course everything reminds me of my brother. A romantic intellect perpetually discovers resemblances: a nightingale in the velvet countenance of the sky.

Angel and I have found a connection. He's Felix in Brooklyn's second cousin and the two of them used to meet up once a month in the city, to drink jungle juice and visit a few clubs. Angel, like my beloved and forever absent Felix, enjoys cynical sayings. He comes up with something new each time we talk, repeating it as if swilling a cherished brandy in his mouth. You have to kiss a lot of toads to find one prince. You never know the length of a snake until he's dead. And so forth. I never get anywhere with Ashraf's favourite maxim, you get more with a smile and a gun than with just a smile. Angel just shrugs. He has developed a poisonous enmity to Ashraf.

"You don't take me seriously because I speak Spanish," Angel complains. "Why do you take that brother of yours so seriously when he's a . . . don't know how to be polite about it. He got Felix killed."

"You're overestimating him. He doesn't have the ability to pull off something truly evil. Ashraf, Ashraf, Angel, how do I explain? Ashraf is my cult leader," I reply. "In the negative as well as the positive sense. How do I know where I stand unless he's around to disagree with? Ask me how convincing Ashraf can be."

"Not every brother is a hoodlum who skips out and leaves you to be the fall guy. And let me tell you something else you don't know. Someone I don't want to mention sent his photograph to a reporter on condition it ran the same day you were in the White House. And someone enticed you into a Mercedes, although he knows you can't be trusted behind the wheel of a tractor. Once a brother shows you that lack of respect he's got to go all the way and annihilate you, or you annihilate him," Angel explains as if he's figuring it out for the first time.

"And he's not just any brother. He's not just a brother from the streets. He's actually my brother."

"That's what I'm saying. Now I have to lock up."

I ask, "How can you be sure of all this?"

"Some guesswork, cabrón. But let me tell you, my cousin kept his eyes open when he was alive, and my uncle who was the superintendent still sees your brother everywhere in Brooklyn even if he's living with your pal Crogan. Ashraf's gloating really gets my uncle's goat. Gitta says the same thing about your brother, and that lady is definitely the sharpest knife in the drawer. Apparently it never fails to bring a smile to that worthless guy's face that he keeps you on the inside with worthless promises while on the outside he's doing some confidential entertaining. And let me tell you that your brother knew about Sayeed all along and gave him permission to murder Felix. That's the word on the street. It's certainly Gitta's theory. Let me have the IBM please."

Angel's duty in the evening is to lock the corridor doors and check the cells to make sure everyone is present and accounted for. He packs the typewriter in a box. Since I have no cellmate he often stops for a few minutes. The bunch of keys you hear clanging up and down the stairs when he leaves. After he puts off the hallway light there's only a red bulb singing above the fire extinguisher's cabinet. This evening I don't want Angel to leave. I also don't want to go back to the topic of Sayeed because I fear my own response.

We Geminis, after all, Jekylls, horoscopological jackals, mosquito-fast talkers with our changeable chalk-and-cheese natures, don't like to be left alone with our sorrows. Gemini is the sign of the storyteller, which is logical because a story is a form of mourning the past. Plus, a Gemini can harmonise with everybody because he's out of tune with himself. So, yes, we Geminis are superficial, never sure whether to judge a book by the front cover or the back cover, so yes, we know too much about the perils of fraternity, and, yes, we dislike any denial of the basic solitude of consciousness, but as my brother's victim, as a Gemini's Gemini, I detest being alone when I am glum.

"Wait a bit, Angel. I have a question I want you to answer. What's the most frightening single sentence you heard someone say?"

Angel hesitates beside the red cylindrical bulk of the fire extinguisher wrapped in the brown arms of its own hose. Across the hall we hear the witchy cries of an inmate who had been sewn into a restraining corset. Finally Angel says, "'I'm a man underneath this bikini.'"

"No, be serious."

"I am being serious," he returns. "What's it for you?"

"'All men are brothers.'"

The impression of easygoing charm perhaps produced by the author of these pages will be dispelled by the confession that during my nights in prison I dreamed over and again of murdering that small, devilish brown brother of mine, especially when I found out about his association with Sayeed Papindari. All I wanted was to laugh in Ashraf's dark face as he had been laughing in my face all my life. I would say more on the topic except for the fear of prison censorship. It's the rare warden who doesn't keep a watch on his literate prisoners in the hope of confiscating their royalties under the Son of Sam laws, according to which convicts can't cash in on their crimes by writing books.

An idea that had been dawning on me ever so slowly since birth was undeniable in the light of Angel's revelation. I always knew Ashraf was a traitor to me but now I couldn't refuse to know that I knew. Circumstance x, after all, destroys a man's peace of mind when he finally can't deny it. Another way of putting it is that denial is the source of all my peace of mind. The place I turned for relief was the *Meditations* of Marcus Aurelius. It was a 1960s edition discovered in the prison laundry with print that smudged on my fingers, a cosmic message in a bottle. It was a mysterious indication that some thinking person preceded me at Fort Dix.

Does it remain to be said that Aurelius teaches us that suffering is the very brother of happiness, that resemblances repel and opposites attract, that the soul is the only substance which can be in three minds at the same time? Does it remain to be said that revenge is a dish best served suddenly? That a green-eyed monster mocks the meat it feeds on?

Of all people, my mother arrived on the scene. She had ridden out the trial at Monash, figuring it to be another of my father's escapades, but the prospect of being a grandmother brought her to the dreaded United States for the first time in her life. Mum's never finer in my opinion than when she descends on a situation and takes complete charge. She had Fazila in tow. The two of them had taken an apartment with Ashraf in Park Slope, right off Seventh Avenue, where they were setting up a nursery in one of the rooms. But my mother was still my mother, the liver of a life ruined by ideas, and thus armed with her usual flotilla of ridiculousnesses.

She was, though, unusually soft-spoken. "You know, Firoze, it was very difficult for me to come here. You know of my longstanding horror for this so-called country, the so-called freedom you have here to be anybody and his brother. But I'm here and I am going to take charge of everything. First of all, your court case. We'll have you out of here in a jiffy. I will also be here to help Fazila with the pregnancy, to prepare Ashraf to be a father for the first time, and, frankly, to prepare you to be an uncle. You've never had that kind of responsibility in your life before. I was talking about it to Farouk in Bombay when I was visiting."

I was incredulous. "After all these years you saw my uncle?"

"Yes, there's been a rapprochement. In these difficult times we have to stick together as a religion and also as a family," Mum said with a distracted smile. "He doesn't boast of being Ashraf's father anymore. Do you know, Farouk had the oddest character living in his apartment? I believe you know him, a Sayeed Papindari."

"My God. Sayeed tried to kill me. He murdered Felix."

"Don't level these wild accusations, dear," my mother said mildly. "But, my dear, there's something else I came here to say. Every cloud has a silver lining. There are huge emotional opportunities for us as mother and son. That's the suggestion of my therapist, Sheila Gordenfus, in Melbourne. With all your reading around and rootling around you haven't heard of her?" She stopped for my answer. "I'm disappointed. I've been seeing her since your father and I split up. Oh, if you could only keep an open mind about the value of analysis. It runs on the male side, this hatred of introspection. If only you and your brother had agreed to hold a joint session with Dr Gordenfus earlier we could have solved our problems as a family before they deteriorated. I brought you the bottle of Largactyl you wanted, by the way. It's from your crazy uncle who, incidentally, offered to pay for your entire defence."

I took the vial. "In our family we never got to the stage of admitting we had problems."

Mum was suddenly indignant. "That's a low blow. And let me tell you something for a change, buster. You look like a crazy person." She folded those milkmaid arms in her lap, and said, "It's true that I care for you and your brother at the same time. Is it suddenly a bad thing to have too much love?"

"It probably is. But you know, I have difficulty arguing from first principles. So what kind of an apology is this? Are you going to say sorry for my child-hood? Do you have any regrets about how you set my brother against me? Plus, Mum, in case you didn't notice, Ashraf has this ceaseless masculine desire to dominate me, to displace me. He's a castrator and throughout my childhood you handed him a knife."

"Dr Gordenfus said to tell you the following about your brother. You don't remind me of him. He doesn't remind me of you. The funny thing is that I admire totally opposite qualities in each of you. You, Firoze, are thoughtful even if you're not so bright. You're strange, self-involved, with your unique brand of tortured integrity, whereas Ash is funny, daring, outgoing, hand-some. Sheila said that should put your mind at rest. You're not somehow in competition with each other."

"We're identical twins. If he's handsome, I'm handsome."

"Yes in theory, in theory, but can an ordinary woman spend her life with you? I was talking to Fazila here." She pointed at Fazila, who touched the wooden coins of her earrings. "This, here, is a lovely girl for you. If you haven't found out already I should have told you. Look at how thin she still is. Fazila and I have realised that we agree completely on this issue. Most women need to be with a man with a touch of badness about him."

"I'm getting a lot worse," I said.

"You'll never be bad enough."

The scene was typically perverse, an enactment of the same Stockholm Syndrome which has afflicted my life. Ah, through its unhappy history how my heart has leapt out to whoever tortures me . . . Am I the only sufferer of the Swedish malady and its negative Valentines? Right then, to my Stockholmed eyes, my mother had never seemed so commanding and Fazila never so beautiful.

I said, "Mum, compared to me Ashraf is a total piker. What he does in reality I do a thousand times in my imagination. If you had to see the terrible thoughts I record on the page, you would see." I turned to the woman on the other side of the plexiglass, the one whom I loved unendurably. "Fazila, choose me over him, when I get out of here, and you'll never have to believe you ended up with the better man."

"Fazila doesn't want to choose and neither do I." Mum got up from the cubicle and took a turn around the room. She came back prepared to say what she wanted to at the outset. "Maybe everything doesn't need to be so cut and dried. That's Shirley's, Dr Gordenfus's, opinion."

"Some people don't even believe my brother exists."

"That's crazy," Mum replied. "I never met someone so alive as your brother. From a very early age Ash hummed with life. He's brimming with life, death, madness, what he says is poetry. He's a beautiful boy. Look, Firoze. I'm going to ask Ashraf to come and see you himself when it's safe. I have one last suggestion from Dr Gordenfus and Fazila agrees. Shirley Gordenfus asks, why don't you send Ashraf a letter? You have a real gift as a letter writer. Here's paper and a stamped envelope. Tell him all your feelings. Be open with him. What do you have to lose?"

"Bother Dr Gordenfus." I took the envelope anyway. "Since you're here, Fazila, can you tell me one thing about Ashraf? Clear something up."

"Ask anything you like."

"Be straight with me. Mum, let Fazila answer this question. Does he know some secret about feminine physiology? Is there some trick? In short, is my brother some kind of sack artist?"

To my relief Fazila shook her head. It was just as I hoped. Fazila's organism was every bit as complicated as one expects of a female member of the jet set. Like her mind her body wished to be the locus of endless forms of priestly activity emanating from her companion. That was a central tenet of Gordenfusian doctrine. I couldn't imagine my self-gratifying brother altering his sporadic way of interesting himself in a girl's organism. Dr Gordenfus might prefer a chaotically pure incarnation of the id to someone more mixed in the matter of mental government, who had checks and balances in the executive branch of his brain. But I was sure that I was the better companion for Fazila, even from a Gordenfusian perspective. Oh, and by the way, Fazila wasn't even showing.

The letter I wrote to my brother on Dr Gordenfus's relayed suggestion was the most complicated exercise of my writing career. Admittedly I am no professional, limited in my achievements to a series of teenage haikus, an essay on the philosophy of history, the above-mentioned editorial in the *Journal*, and postcards to my mother in Australia. People define genius as the ability to take infinite pains or perhaps to be in infinite pain. If so, my only regret was that the greatness of the audience should fall so far below the level of the letter . . .

My one and only brother, Ashraf, east to my west, south to my north, my vinegar and my ketchup, my Cain and my Abel, I am going to confirm Dad's sanity to the prosecutors and do my best to turn you in unless you follow my instructions. I have always been your hostage and now you're mine. It occurs to me that, unlike me, you're the perfect immigrant, devoid of shame, caste, internal borders.

Ashraf, I salute your ingenuity. You ceaselessly undermine me. It's the one department where you show a touch of Mom's intelligence. Tricking me into jail, sending your photo to the Journal, *using my love letter as your note of introduction to assorted floozies, quoting to Pearl Bronson from a pocket edition of Kahlil Gibran, taking Fazila away although she clearly was beginning to like me, it's your cosmic jujitsu. O you enemy! How you laugh at me! But beware of jealousy, O my brother. Its green eyes smoulder in your countenance like priests.*

Are you a symbol, a black magic pentagram? Our natures, like straight lines, touch at one point before diverging to infinity. The list of items

to bring, by the way – a beard, a hat, a decal mole, a suitcase, pliers,
an extra tie, an ultraviolet stamp, and a copy of Constitutional Law *by*
Erwin Chemerinsky. The new edition would be a nice gesture.

Yours in fraternity, Firoze.

I wrote at the outset that the heart of an inmate sings through his tender appeals and also that the prisoner has one decisive advantage over the man at his own devices, which is that his condition can be appealed. Being of the conviction that in a nation of laws every memoir should begin and end with a court case, let me hasten the day of my appeals hearing before the Second Circuit of the Appeals Court. To my foreign readers, if any, I remark that every institution in the United States has a distinct moral and metaphysical character, from dogcatcher to the Smithsonian, and that the Second Circuit has a reputation for merciless dispatch, for Reaganism, and for elevating parsimony to an eleventh commandment.

Twenty-four senior judges comprised the bench. Individual cases were heard by three judges chosen by lottery. My doubts were intensified by the fact that Parker Khardozian, brother of the Princeton professor, was selected as head of my panel. The brothers were close in political spirit. Parker even attached a witty rider to the Patriot Act praising the legal island of Guantánamo Bay as a Cuban paradise. He was a friend of the White House, a vociferous moralist, member of the church, and worst of all a red-haired man, presumably with a full dose of the perversity that accompanies these characteristics.

Logically I was prepared for the worst in the guy, and yet not one of my readers will be surprised to find that, as a result of my metaphysical masochism, that I found myself liking his manner and adopting it myself. The Khardozians, I reflected, possessed considerable interest as a clan. Parker was rapid, rampant, devoid of sententiousness and pomp, neat in his dress, a perpetual-motion man with a disciplined Egyptian wedge of a head resembling his brother's. His Hibernian flow of jokes, asides, chestnuts and old saws was, like his brother's, never going to run dry.

Parker, like Sets, spoke at high pitch and with a flourish of Republican courtesy that followed immediately on our opening statement. "I congratulate you, sir, on retaining a lawyer for this portion of your legal travails. Counsellor Sternhill is a favourite of this court. You couldn't find a more energetic representative. Now, Murray, would you care to refresh our memories about certain aspects of your client's case?"

I praise Sternhill's vigour, his idiom, and above all his infinite stock of bowties. They were his one formal touch. I had prevailed on him to lend me one for my day in court. It was a remarkable green-and-salmon dotted silk. Its green-and-pink pressure at my throat reminded me of the proceedings in which my role was a humble one. Dear Sternhill, court-mopey, muttering Sternhill, how you paused to shape each stegosauran sentence, how you knotted my bowtie without caring to smile, how you provided this foreigner with the best defence that could be purchased on a forged credit card (since I wasn't taking Farouk's money). I could never have dreamed that the steamship of a man would sound this way before the Second Circuit. Sagacious Sternhill, you maintained an old-fashioned disdain for typewriters rather than being progressively old fashioned and rejecting word processors in favour of typewriters. You read the body of your argument from a yellow legal pad.

"Your honours, if I may address the bench within this hallowed, ahem, palace of justice. This hall of compassion, these honourable pillars, eavesdrop in due sympathy on a defendant who raises the bar on all future cases of mistaken identity. A brother's crimes, and they are proved to belong to a brother by new evidence, can never be imputed to an innocent defendant. Indeed, the sins of the brother are precisely what we leave behind in our legal identity as Americans." After a hesitation he went on. "When I consider the lost liberties of a man of foreign birth, when I reminisce about every man who shed his blood serving the cause of freedom, when, in addition, I consider these tumultuous times when our continuance as a nation may turn on questions of true and false identity, then, ahem, I am chastened, your honours. I am duly chastened."

Despite my fears during this speech the three judges, mounted on their platform like hunter's trophies, were moved and softened by Sternhill's language. Judge Sorenson, on the left, wiped his rheumy eyes. Judge Khardozian, normally too funny to be sentimental, was impressed. Words of praise for America, this fortunate land, can never be unwelcome to Americans. Even I was impressed in my capacity as a semi-hemi-demi-American and slavish americophile.

Encouraged to proceed by Khardozian, Sternhill launched into the second part of his peroration. "Your honours, you recall that Mr Peer was apprehended on the West Side Highway in Manhattan. Let us look at that highway as a stage where rest the eyes of a hundred nations, and vindicate to them the quality of our justice. There is no dispute that Peer has no business being at the wheel of an automobile. Anyone who's driven with him will testify to that. But the subsequent charges of impersonation and abuse of assumed authority are the result of a mix-up between my client and his brother. In my appendix, before you, we include photographs of the offending brother, letters from him, and testimony by several friendly parties proving that my client, as I must insist, is the victim here."

Such was the condition of Judge Sorenson's tuberous eyes that he seemed to be weeping inside his black robe as he adjusted them with a handkerchief. His crafty, unsteady lawyer's lips muttered beneath his nose even before he started to ask a question. "Counsellor, from my review of the documents it's clear that the existence of this Ashraf Dawood has not been established as a legal determination. Thus his existence, valid or otherwise, has no bearing on this appeals process."

Sternhill had anticipated this line of questioning. "I grant your point. As a real person I cannot vouch for the existence of an Ashraf Dawood. But Ashraf's psychological significance, indeed his centrality where the accused's state of mind is concerned, cannot be doubted. Under undue pressures of interrogation, my client did indeed produce his brother's wallet and produce a social security card with yet another name on it. It purported to belong to a Dr Jonas Radinski, I believe. Firoze assures me he would not have taken such a drastic step had it not been that the fear of his brother, his fear of being apprehended in place of his brother, weighed prominently on his mind. Any connection between the defendant and Mohammad Atta is, I argue, purely circumstantial. I believe the court should delete from its purview my client's actions after apprehension and set him free to answer the civil complaint about his driving."

A lengthy legal discussion ensued. It astonished this particular scribe that so many wise heads participated in deciding his fate. So it's true that the intellectual power of a group stands in inverse proportion to its size, but nonetheless there was an uncanny look to the assembly of judges. They would weigh everything up and render a final judgement on my life. Such was my theory, but when I looked to Sternhill at intermission his expression was forbidding. If his expression is clouded he expects an immediate response from the observer.

"Is something wrong?"

Now that we were on recess Sternhill returned to his pugnacious mode of conversation. "Perhaps you can tell me. Did you know you have a visitor from the South African embassy? A guard will escort you to the conference room if you wish to speak privately. I wish you had informed me. We don't want the appearance of a foreign power interfering in our judicial process." Sternhill sighed. "Go with my blessing. Perhaps he has some useful information. Perhaps he'll offer to pay my fee now that the credit-card company has cancelled your account. I had a short conversation with him over the telephone before I got here. He's a most unexpected fellow." Sternhill's pale grey eyes sparkled. "Who would think the South African embassy would hire a guy from Puerto Rico?"

"Puerto Ricans are a versatile culture, Sternhill."

"To say the least."

Two dozen cubicles with chairs and desks occupied the conference room. From the coffee pot at the entrance I poured a cup. A window was set into each cubicle so the guards could monitor what happened inside. They could see but not hear anything. My guard was a stocky black man who didn't believe me when I told him I had been put behind bars by mistake.

"Sure you were. You say your real name is Ashraf? The court has you down as Firoze, but I suppose I can call you whatever name you like. It's a free country. The embassy guy is keen to see you. You have until after lunch."

I asked, "Can I watch him from out here a minute?"

"As I say, it's a free country."

Through perspex I studied my brother and his outrageous appearance – the bouffant haircut which rose each morning at the point of a blower, the lipless mouth along which hunts his tongue whenever he's unsettled, the deer-skin complexion in which are suspended two globular eyes, enormous green cameras obscuras holding the impressions of every act of violence, every paid woman, every precious stone he's ever encountered. This brother who took me hostage from the instant of my birth wore brogues and a forest-green shirt with matching white-and-emerald bands on his tie. The triangle of a green handkerchief and tie pin displaying the new South African flag were nice finishing touches, I thought, as was the weedy moustache beneath his crooked little nose.

Was I happy to see him? Do I look crazy? There's a better question to ask me about my feelings where Ashraf is concerned. Do I acknowledge this thing of darkness to be my own? But that's too simple. Ah, where this dark thing is concerned, this dark thing I wish would acknowledge me. Ashraf's face was more familiar to me than my own. It seemed my brother and I would always be inseparable, that I would speak inside of him and he inside me all our divided lives. This feeling, this incurably deep sensation of heartbreak, rippled through me. Then, in a New York minute, I was furious with Ashraf all over again. I went inside and closed the door the better to confront him.

"How can you show your face?" I exclaimed. "You ran off with my girl and my precious love letter. You're a negative Cyrano. I bet you forgot Mom's birthday last week. That's to say nothing about your friendship with Atta and now Sayeed, which is ongoing after he killed Felix and tried to polish me off into the bargain. I should punch you in the nose."

Ashraf wasn't giving any ground. "Golly, it's nothing you wouldn't do if the positions were reversed. I know you, Firoze, better than I know myself. With all your self-pity you're far worse than me. Your envy, your secret rage, your brooding, old woman's temperament is enough evidence for me. I see how you look at my girls. Fazila noticed it when they visited you. You can't believe a non-intellectual has the rights to anything of his own. The irony is you're lucky to have a brother like me. With me to kick around you never have to ask yourself if you're maybe in the wrong. But look, relax, sit down, and let's not quarrel about ancient tragedies. I brought you what you asked me to." He pushed a bag over to me. "I picked you up a sandwich as well."

"Did you know about Sayeed?"

"Maybe I did and maybe I didn't."

"Did you set me up after the gig in the White House?"

He arched his back against the chair. "Well, let's see. Maybe I lent you my wallet accidentally on purpose. Maybe I knew the Mercedes was hot. Maybe I dropped a dime on you. Maybe I sent my photograph to the papers. What is that, seven maybes? I have been working jolly hard to get you out, to help Dad, to hold Mum together. On top of it all I have to learn what it means to be a father. When it was a choice between you being in here and me I had to think of fatherhood first. Meanwhile you had the luxury of reading and writing whatever you wanted. Correct me if I'm wrong, but this penitentiary sounds like the perfect place for an intellectual." Ashraf pulled at the knot of his tie. "Once in your life, Firoze, look at all the good things you've gotten."

"Have some coffee, Mr Ambassador."

"I don't mind if I do." He was relaxed again. "You put sugar in?"

Until Fort Dix, by the way, my brother and I were never separated for more than a few days. Like the two dials on a chess clock we were connected and antithetical, the one clicking into movement as the other froze. In a manuscript presuming to offer insights into the condition of man unrivalled since Part II of *The Godfather*, certain straightforward propositions about human nature are to be expected. My dark brother is my beloved subject. Let's while away the time until his long eyelashes fall like the hands of a clock. Beneath the veneer of Ashrafian familiarity, I realised, was the strangest entity in the universe. Closeness, more than distance, creates a spiritual gulf. In my view it's only possible to feel close to something to which intimacy doesn't apply. Thus people feel close to a religion, a nation state, a celebrity, a child, a work of art.

After our months apart I noticed the crow's feet beneath my brother's eyes which resembled the cratered surface of my mother's cake of blush. I saw the relaxation of the pelt around his neck and chin. Things which previously slipped my attention now blared out. Ashraf's screechy, vulgar slang, his slyness, his crude grin and his piggish South African brand of truculence, all the streetworthy qualities by which he conned me as much as his rented girls were excruciating. They seemed to rise up on his green-eyed face. If there was to be a new start for the Dawoods and Peers over here – in these great United States the principal recommendation of which was that rational humanity opposed it – then this peculiar fellow had to be marginalised. I saw that in future, like other people, I would have to be my own worst enemy and harbour my own worst impulses.

I turned to Ashraf. "Ashraf, you look exhausted. You look worse than Atta and Sayeed. Let me help you off with that lovely green jacket. It's more my colour than yours, don't you agree? One more thing. *You're* the nutball."

My brother's pupils were dilated under the influence of 25 milligrams of Largactyl. It produces the symptoms of paralysis but leaves the mind alert for five minutes after paralysis has set in. Ashraf wouldn't have noticed it in his coffee. From this moment, not twenty hours ago as I write according to my new Seiko wristwatch, I concluded that in life every spiritual conundrum has a pharmaceutical solution. It worked, at any rate, in curing myself of the disease of my brother. Meanwhile his mummied lips, like Justice Sorenson's, kept muttering independently of his will. Frankly, Ashraf made more sense in his sleep.

The beard, moustache, green jacket, South African flag pin, and silk tie fitted me to perfection. It's an advantage having a twin, you know, because it's easy for them to get the right size for you in everything. The ultraviolet stamp I asked Ashraf to bring was a standby in case I got checked. Visiting minimum security prisons, people used to wear two sets of clothes, strip, and give one to the prisoner who could simply walk out. The ultraviolet stamp was something the guards used to make sure you were a visitor and not an inmate. But it turned out not to be necessary. Even today, late as it is in spiritual terms, people honour the diplomat's profession.

On my way out I made sure to consult with the guards at the entrance. The man posted to the desk not twenty yards from my transfixed brother paternally touched his gun, his truncheon, and his radio. He wore his blue uniform with soldier's pride. I think it's my mother's talent for sociability that gives me a liking for striking up a conversation with a stranger. It feels like striking a spark off a flint. It was especially pleasurable to be chatting with Mr Carlucci. My heart sang as we spoke.

Carlucci, to offer you a last portrait of a mobile nation, was what they used to call the salt of the earth before they got to be afraid of such perfectly service-able expressions. His pudding nose was irregular and perforated in a thousand places. There were boarish red hairs curled aristocratically about his nostrils. He was unaffected by the courthouse atmosphere and remained a profound admirer of his wife's egg-salad sandwiches. He offered me a bite of one. It was impolite to refuse even if I was in a hurry.

Carlucci had been consuming his sandwiches when I came up. They were on the thinnest white bread conceivable, diagonally cut, laden with mayonnaise and the broken grey caviar of the yokes, smelling of salt, pepper, vinegar, and almost, though here my nose must have gotten confused, of the black Saxon syrup of Vegemite. I mention this encounter only because in those heavily salted egg sandwiches, it seemed to me, Carlucci perceived the divinity of his wife. On those milled white strips of bread he counted his blessings each and every courthouse afternoon. Doubtless I will be accused of over-romanticising the man but only by the same people who accuse others of over-romanticising a veal chop.

All in all Carlucci was straight out of a much earlier decade. He was one of those curious Long Islanders, those most provincial of islanders, who seem to have absolutely no connection to the perpetually mobile and radiating character of the metropolis. His presence was crammed for me with the aroma of junkyards, diners, television dinners, cruise ships, and Knights of Columbus clubhouses. But don't take anything I say on this topic seriously. My imagination was strangely active at the time. The seeming affection with which Carlucci talked about the ruses of escaping prisoners touched me again.

"They are always trying to get out of here, Mr Ambassador. I don't know what it's like in your country but our criminals take a back seat to nobody in terms of ingenuity." He explained as we sat there and shared his sandwiches and a bottle of roseate iced tea. "They try every trick under the sun. With the help of an outsider they dress up as lawyers, firemen, Arab women in their robes, judges, and they expect to saunter past me without being nabbed. Well, it doesn't work. Some people take pride in their work, even though if it was up to me I would empty all the prisons. You say Mr Peer, asleep in there, is convinced that he's the honorary consul instead of you?"

"He suffers from delusions. He's also thinks he's a novelist and a kind of cosmic philosopher although he's as shallow as two bits of wood."

"Obviously, if you don't mind my saying so, he has no idea of your graciousness, and how difficult it is to duplicate that if you're not a born ambassador. It's my opinion, take it for what it's worth, but there are only a very few souls in this world who are suited to the task of representing their culture in another country. There's no more difficult task. I can say that on account of my own heritage."

"That's very kind of you to say, Mr Carlucci, and let me thank you again for the sandwiches. Right now I feel almost as if I dreamed that horrible man up from start to finish. Do me a favour. Give it a while before you wake him up and take him back to his hearing. He's out like a light." I handed him an envelope. "Give that miscreant a few dollars on behalf of me and the South African embassy. That way, at least, I've done my good deed for the day. You know that they say all men are brothers."

"It's a lovely expression. Unfortunately, the way I see it, the way this world is going it's just an expression."

"I couldn't agree more, Mr Carlucci."

The courthouse adjoined Federal Plaza and Police Plaza. Above me was the turnstile of Brooklyn Bridge with her cabled rafters and her four chains of traffic. The seagull horn on a tugboat, the armoured clank of bulldozers at a building site on Fulton Street, and the untuned engines of the sanitation vehicles, mechanical melodies, were music to my ears. I decided to walk across Brooklyn Bridge, Whitman's bridge, before taking the train to Astoria to pick up my things from Crogan. The whipping wind made me feel very high up. There were unending brown fortresses stretching to the land horizon on Long Island. On the nearby sea, as if mounted on a transparency, was perched a huge orange moon, friend through all the years to the Dawoods and Peers.

Bridges bring cosmic thoughts. I wondered about the endless generations of bridge crossers, jail breakers, bail jumpers, brothers in arms, who were to follow. These Ecuadorians, Hungarians, Pathans, Han Chinese, would they pursue the cycle of three generations from hard scrabble to professional to ethereal and back again? Will they love the music of the bullet? Would they have any cause to remember me by? It was improbable. America's kaleidoscopic thoughts, like mine, are perpetually on the future. Ah, this leopardine, leopardistical America which constantly changes its spots! Brother America! The powerful tugboat horn sounded like a trump of doom over the water and I wondered, did any of this ever happen? Am I lying with two bullets in my chest in an Atlantic Avenue apartment with my brother's green-eyed smile gliding through the outside door?

Six hours later I am with Fazila in our new Park Slope apartment, wondering about that curious odour of her body, unforgettably like pickled mushrooms, and what she thought about my letters, my poems, my songs. Not that she knows they were my productions. Fazila, to make it clear, is more than happy to see me. She thinks I'm my brother and thus her baby's father. And she's not the kind of girl to hold back. Mum's in Connecticut for the weekend so we have the living room to ourselves. Is this first base? Is it second base? Does it count as heavy petting? These are American questions, of course, formulated in a country which leads the world in popular sexology.

Fazila's not a dreamer but at times her mind congeals and is as slow-moving as gravy. She's a Pakistani, after all. It's so dark that her hair in my hands is the same as my mother's, glossy like a Chinawoman's. Through the blinds glows the pumpkin light of the moon. Those eternal sounds of New York traffic grumble far below the window and yet it's as still in our pad as the night before Christmas. She rolls over on one side, smoking with one hand and moving the other arm across the neat silver stitching on her bra. With humanity and the cosmos I am briefly at peace. This may be a strange moral for a love story but